Praise for the
Maxine O'Callaghan

"O'Callaghan has . . . a cinematic touch that sears images into the reader's mind, and a breathless pace that will leave you weak in the knees."
—*Reno Gazette Journal*

"Solid pacing and detection."
—*The Washington Post Book World*

"A tidy, tight plot . . . The characters are sharp and definite."
—*Ft. Lauderdale Sun-Sentinel*

"O'Callaghan's polish and her eye for detail amply entertain."
—*Publishers Weekly*

"Fast-paced, well-plotted . . . a must-read."
—*Booklist*

"Compelling characters, gripping suspense."
—Judith Kelman, author of *One Last Kiss*

Jove Titles by Maxine O'Callaghan

SHADOW OF THE CHILD
ONLY IN THE ASHES

Only in the Ashes

Maxine O'Callaghan

JOVE BOOKS, NEW YORK

If you purchased this book without a cover, you should be aware that this book is stolen property. It was reported as "unsold and destroyed" to the publisher, and neither the author nor the publisher has received any payment for this "stripped book."

ONLY IN THE ASHES

A Jove Book / published by arrangement with the author

PRINTING HISTORY
Jove edition / June 1997

All rights reserved.
Copyright © 1997 by Maxine O'Callaghan.
This book may not be reproduced in whole or in part, by mimeograph or any other means, without permission. For information address: The Berkley Publishing Group, 200 Madison Avenue, New York, New York 10016.

The Putnam Berkley World Wide Web site address is
http://www.berkley.com

ISBN: 0-515-12077-4

A JOVE BOOK®
Jove Books are published by The Berkley Publishing Group,
200 Madison Avenue, New York, New York 10016.
JOVE and the "J" design are trademarks
belonging to Jove Publications, Inc.

PRINTED IN THE UNITED STATES OF AMERICA

10 9 8 7 6 5 4 3 2 1

For Laura, as always

My thanks to firefighter Robert Borchert for brainstorming sessions;

To Ben Nixon, Battalion Chief, Phoenix Fire Department, for sharing information about the PFD;

To Sylvia Moreno for correcting my Spanish and for making my life a little easier;

And, again, to the Fictionaires, especially Gary Bale.

Only in the Ashes

Ring around the rosy
Pocket full of posies
Ashes, ashes
We all fall down.

—CHILDREN'S SONG

Earth to earth; ashes to ashes;
dust to dust . . .

—BOOK OF COMMON PRAYER

one

ANNE MENLO RECOGNIZED THE SMELL SECONDS BEFORE she turned the corner. The powerful, pervasive stench made her hit the power switch to close the car window as she coasted slowly, checking addresses.

No desert landscaping here. In this older, middle-class Phoenix neighborhood, the brick houses had green front lawns and neatly clipped shrubs. Amid this order, the charred rubble looked shockingly out of place, a grim reminder of how quickly something solid and long-rooted can be destroyed.

Thinking perhaps she had the right address but the wrong street, she kept driving, going on down to the corner to check the sign.

No, there was no mistake.

She turned around and drove back, once again looking at the numbers painted on the curb. The address was unreadable because the paint had blistered and peeled, but she could tell by the sequencing that this was the right house.

Or had been.

There were several vehicles parked along the curb. Anne pulled into a slot on the opposite side of the street and looked out the window at the burned remains, struck

by a vague sense of alarm, reflecting that there was something about a house fire that touches us at the deepest
level.

Anne wasn't the only one attracted by the rubble. Two
other people stood, staring, in front of the house next door:
a woman in her seventies hugging a sweater around her
shoulders and a younger man dressed in a paint-splattered
T-shirt and old camouflage army pants.

A yellow plastic ribbon encircled the lot where the
house had sat, which meant an investigation was ongoing.
Maybe the cause of the fire was still unknown, but judging
from the amount of damage, the blaze must have been
swift, hot, and all-consuming. Even so, there was still a
suggestion of walls, furniture, and a chimney, the melted,
grotesque forms limned in ash and black soot.

Somehow the devastation seemed worse by contrast to
the brilliant blue skies and glorious sunshine. This was one
of those perfect February days that guarantee the yearly
migration of snowbirds, people who flock to Arizona to
escape harsh northern winters.

As Anne debated whether she'd transposed a number and
written down an incorrect address, an old Toyota Celica
approached slowly and parked in front of the burned building. A woman got out. Her shoulder-length strawberry-
blond hair glinted red in the sunlight, and she wore
oversized sunglasses.

Anne couldn't have guessed the woman's height and
weight, but she had an impression of youthful sturdiness;
what she did see, even at this distance, was the way the
woman moved with weary reluctance as she exited the car,
how she sagged back against the Toyota for support as she
stood looking at the house.

"Her name is Kathleen Graley," Rosemary Beiderman
had said earlier today over the phone. "I doubt you'll
thank me for this, Anne, but I'm sure you're the one person who can help her. Her situation is . . . unusual, and
complicated."

Unusual. Well, so far that certainly described things all right. Kathleen had called shortly after Rosemary hung up, sounding distant and distracted, saying that she wanted to speak to Anne about her six-year-old daughter and that it would be easier to explain if they met at this address.

During her career as a child psychologist, Anne had instituted few rules that were hard and fast. She felt strongly, however, that the whole therapy process from first interview to subsequent sessions worked best if it took place in her office. She agreed to change her normal routine only because Kathleen Graley was Rosemary's referral.

And a mysterious one, to boot. Rosemary had declined to supply any details except that the woman was a friend of a friend, adding, "You really ought to hear the story from Kathleen first. Then we'll talk. Just keep an open mind."

Anne had to admit she had been intrigued. Now, as she got out of her car, that little tingle of anticipation was replaced by a growing unease as she was assailed by the pungent, metallic odor that spoke of more than just burned wood and plastic.

With the smell strong enough to burn her nose, Anne came around the back of the Toyota. The small car's metallic green paint was dull and faded. She saw a Bruins bumper sticker next to the California plates and noted that there was no child inside, no car seat.

She said, "Ms. Graley?"

The woman kept staring at the charred house. She was a good six inches taller than Anne's petite five feet and wore rumpled beige cotton slacks and a dark green knit top. Tousled curls escaped from a couple of bobby pins that were meant to keep the hair off her face where the fair skin looked leached of color beneath a dusting of cinnamon freckles.

"I talked to one of the firemen who was here that night." Although the sunglasses hid most of her emotions, there was no hiding the raw pain in Kathleen Graley's voice. "He said they weren't sure what happened, but the fire was hot—and—and quick." She paused, her gaze still fixed on the house. "I was in a car crash when I was ten. It was all noise—confusion—like a dream. Dr. Menlo, do you think—would it be like that—if you—if you were—" She couldn't verbalize the rest of the horrible scene she must be picturing.

"I think so, yes," Anne said gently. "Usually the mind protects us from trauma."

Children responded well to Anne's quiet voice, the kind hazel eyes, to what one child had once described as her smiley face. But Kathleen only jerked her head in a nod and did not look comforted.

"Did you lose somebody in this fire?" Anne asked.

Another nod.

If Kathleen was dealing with such a terrible load of grief, her little girl would be, too, which explained Rosemary's call.

"You're doing the right thing to get professional help for your daughter," Anne said. "It's important for you, too, of course. I'm sure Rosemary has recommended somebody—"

She broke off because Kathleen turned abruptly toward the Toyota. Tears ran down her face, and her shoulders heaved, but she made no sound as she gripped the bottom frame of the open window and stood there, arms braced, fighting for control.

Involved in the conversation with Kathleen, Anne had paid little attention to the two people who had been standing outside the house next door except to note that they were out of earshot. Now she became aware that the woman had gone inside the house, but the man was standing at the back of a white Nissan pickup, staring at Anne and Kathleen with ill-concealed curiosity.

"Come on," Anne said. "Let's get out of here. Where are you staying? I'd be happy to drive you there. You can spend some time with your daughter. I'll have a chance to meet her, and we can all talk.''

''Can't—''

''Why not?'' Anne asked, but even as she said it she began to understand and dread the answer to her next question. ''Where's your little girl, Kathleen?''

''Here.'' She took a breath, and the rest came in a rush. ''My Rachel burned to death in that house two days ago.''

ANNE INSISTED ON DRIVING THE TOYOTA. KATHLEEN huddled beside her, saying nothing except to give directions to the Sunrise Motel down on Van Buren Street. Although she made no sound, tears ran constantly down her cheeks as though a tap had been turned on that she couldn't shut off. She held a box of tissues on her lap during the drive, sopping up the tears, adding the wet tissues to a trash bag already overflowing with the soggy pink Kleenex.

The motels lining Van Buren had once been a preferred destination of tourists and business travelers, but tastes change; time moves on. Today's businesspeople had hefty travel allowances; well-heeled tourists opted for the tonier resorts of Paradise Valley and Scottsdale.

The Sunrise Motel had probably been on the lower end of the scale even in the area's heyday. Now it was run-down and deserted except for a maid who pushed a cart loaded with linens and cleaning supplies, seeming to be in no great hurry as she worked her way around the one-story, U-shaped building.

The maid hadn't made it to Kathleen's room, and the small dark unit offered nowhere to sit except for one uncomfortable chair and the unmade bed. There were a couple of white resin lawn chairs outside, however, positioned under a narrow overhang, facing the pool.

At Anne's suggestion, Kathleen willingly sat in one of the chairs and waited while Anne walked back to the office, where she had spotted a Coke machine. Anne's first prescription would have been a meal, but since Kathleen had refused a late lunch, sugar and caffeine seemed the next best thing.

Anne brought back the can of pop and sat quietly beside Kathleen while she took a few sips. The tears had finally stopped. Her cheeks looked red and raw. Anne still hadn't seen her eyes, hidden behind the dark glasses.

"Do you feel like talking now?" Anne asked.

"Not really, but I guess I'd better."

She took another swallow from the can and stared out at the pool where water rippled in a mild breeze, lapping against walls crusted with algae so thick it looked like acid-green barnacles.

Since Rosemary wanted Anne to keep an open mind until she heard Kathleen's story, Anne waited, exhibiting only calm patience, even though a corner of her mind was preoccupied with the logistics of getting back to her car and driving to her scheduled stint at a local abuse clinic by two o'clock, less than an hour away. She still had no idea what Kathleen wanted from her, or how long it would take for her to put that request into words. Grief was an untidy emotion, one that could not be shoehorned into a convenient time slot.

Kathleen took a last sip, put the can down beside the chair, and squared her shoulders. "Randy, my ex-husband—well, we're not divorced, so I guess he's really not my ex—about a month ago, right after Christmas, he and his mother took Rachel and just disappeared. I had no idea where they were until he called and said she—that there was a fire and she—" Kathleen shivered and hugged herself, even though it was sheltered and warm where they sat. "I'm sorry. I can't do this. It's too hard, spilling my guts to you when you'll probably say you won't help me. So why don't I come right out and tell you what I want you to do?"

"All right," Anne said. She could understand that the woman might not want to make such an emotional investment right now. "Whatever you're comfortable with."

"I need to know what happened to my baby before she died, Dr. Menlo. The last time I saw her, she was so upset. She begged me not to leave her. I told myself she'd be okay as soon as I left; I'd see her in a few days; Randy had his faults, but he loved her. The usual stuff.

"Now I can't get it out of my mind. I'm haunted by her little face and the feeling she was trying to tell me something. I picture what she looked like, go over and over what she said. What was I not seeing? What didn't I hear?" She gripped the arms of the chair, and her voice thickened with anguish and rage. "Am I just blowing this out of proportion, or was Randy—somebody—some sick son of a bitch molesting my child?"

So this was what Rosemary thought Anne could do, a psychological autopsy of a dead six-year-old. Well, Rosemary had been right about one thing: Anne didn't thank her for putting her in this situation.

Choosing her words carefully, Anne said, "It could very well be that you're distorting what happened the last time you saw Rachel. It would certainly be understandable if you're not thinking clearly right now. In any case, there are other people—specialists in profiling—who could do a much better job for you."

Anne deliberately sidestepped voicing the correct term. The woman was strong, but right now she didn't need the pictures that the expression *psychological autopsy* would conjure up.

"Then you won't do it," Kathleen said.

Anne thought of all the other questions that needed to be answered. Why did Randy Graley have custody of Rachel? What caused the fire? Was it an accident, or was something more sinister involved? And how would Kathleen deal with it if her suspicions proved to be right?

She also thought about the fact that for now her own life was, more or less, on track and she really didn't need to become involved with a case like this; make no mistake, this would not be something she could reduce to notes in a case file and leave at the office.

The sensible thing was to offer to recommend somebody else and walk away. Instead she heard herself saying, "I don't know. I'll have to think about it."

Once again, it seemed that Rosemary Beiderman— teacher, friend, and therapist—knew her better than Anne knew herself.

two

THE SUNNY ROOM IN THE ABUSE CLINIC WAS FULL OF pleasant, ordinary smells: graham crackers, apples, crayons, the salty-sweet odor of children's sweaty bodies. Still, the stench of the fire that killed little Rachel Graley lingered with Anne as she tried to concentrate on the four little patients who sat with her at a low, round table, scribbling away. All girls, they ranged in age from four to seven. Each had suffered both physical and mental torture at the hands of those who should have loved and protected them.

At Anne's suggestion they were drawing how they were feeling today. Not artistic renderings, just squiggles and symbols. Two of them scrubbed the paper with red, orange, and purple in fierce slashes. Another had taken the barrettes from her hair to hide behind the curtain of dark hair and fill a page with straight black lines.

The fourth one, Amber, first swirled blue color; now she added brown marks like broad *W*s and looked up to whisper, "Birds." Then, for the very first time, she smiled at Anne, just a quick flicker that made Anne's heart turn over.

As the hour went by, Anne knew this would be the only miracle today. Progress in these cases was painfully slow.

She accepted that. No matter. Although she dreaded the sessions, she was committed to the work.

"It will become easier in time," Rosemary had said. "But I won't lie to you, Anne. These are the ones that teach you about pain."

As usual, Rosemary was right.

After Anne said goodbye to the four girls, promising to see them again on Friday, she sat at the low table, glanced at her watch, then opened the clinic folders. She would spend a few minutes to make her notes and then she could leave. Was there enough time to stop at Rosemary's on the way back to the office, or should she simply call again from the car?

When Anne had telephoned earlier, Norman Beiderman had said his wife was resting. Rosemary was in the advanced stages of multiple sclerosis, and Norman took his job as gatekeeper very seriously. If Anne hurried and finished the paperwork, maybe she could manage a quick visit. She preferred that to phoning. But one way or the other, if she was to keep her promise to give Kathleen a quick response, she needed to speak to Rosemary as soon as possible.

To tell the truth, Anne wondered why she didn't just bow out right now and save herself a lot of grief. Rosemary must think she was ready to handle something like this, but Anne wasn't so sure. And Bern was bound to object. There was no way she could keep this from him, even if she tried. He was still living with her at her house in Cave Creek, their temporary arrangement having slipped into an uncertain permanence.

The relationship had been off and on for several years for lots of reasons. One was that Bernard Pagett was a detective in the homicide detail with the Phoenix Police Department. Last summer he had talked her into working with the police, calling her in on his own case that involved a young boy found at a murder scene. When that case turned ugly, it had nearly cost both of them their lives. Now Bern was as dogged in his determination to keep her away from police work as he had been earlier at dragging her into it.

As far as Anne knew, Rachel's death had been a terrible accident. Still, knowing how overprotective Bern was these days, she had no doubt what his reaction would be.

She sighed.

One thing at a time. She had yet to write a note in the folders. She began to remedy that, but had only just completed her first entry when somebody tapped lightly on the open door and said, "Anne?"

It was Joyce Levy, one of the permanent clinic staff. She was slender, small-boned, with a mouse-brown pageboy going gray and pale blue eyes behind glasses with gold wire rims. With her straight neutral-toned skirts worn with Peter Pan collars in summer and sweater sets in winter, she looked as though she belonged in a private New England school, although Anne knew she had been born here and had spent most of her life in Phoenix. Today her buttery-yellow sweater topped a light tan skirt.

"Do you have a minute?" Joyce asked.

"Sure," Anne said, seeing the window of opportunity to visit Rosemary closing fast.

"One of the CPS foster parents brought in a little girl," Joyce said. "Everybody else is tied up."

"I have to be back at my office for an appointment at four. I can only stay maybe half an hour. I'm not sure if that's long enough—"

"Well, it's a start, isn't it?" Beneath Joyce's sweet schoolmarm exterior lurked the steely purpose of a combat general. Her job was to squeeze as much time out of her volunteers as possible, and she was good at her work.

Without giving Anne a chance to reply, she gestured to the folders and said, "Finish those up, and I'll take you to meet the child." Then she hovered while Anne scribbled her notes, launching into a briefing as Anne closed the files and stood up.

"The child says her name is Chrissie. The police picked her up yesterday, wandering around on Broadway somewhere around 32nd Street. They figure she came from a homeless camp near the river."

Anne knew there were places along the Salt River where the homeless tried to survive the cold desert nights in tents or makeshift cardboard shelters.

"She was dehydrated and dirty," Joyce went on. "Probably hadn't eaten for a couple of days, but no real physical problems. The doctor thought there might be some level of retardation. CPS placed her in a home." In Phoenix, Child Protective Services had no large multi-bed facility. They did the best they could with a network of foster care.

"What about her parents?" Anne asked.

"That's the problem. She's not saying much except for her name and that she's five years old. Appears she was abandoned."

Joyce waited for Anne to go through the door first, then walked with her down the hall. Side by side, Anne always felt a momentary surprise to find that Joyce wasn't much taller than she was, maybe five-two.

"Do we know what kind of abuse is involved?" Anne asked.

"Actually, we don't know anything," Joyce said. "The doctor didn't find any obvious signs. It's gotten to the point where I think the fosters just assume abuse in a case like this."

Out in the reception area Chrissie crouched on a sofa next to a big, blond, soft-looking woman. For just an instant Anne saw the little girl tense, and her face lit up with expectation and hope as Anne and Joyce came into the room. Then she slumped back down, the hope quickly gone.

Her red T-shirt and blue overalls looked new and a size too big. Two ribbons—faded pink, limp, and fraying— were tied in bows and pinned in her hair. If you didn't know the circumstances of how she was found, you might mistake the tanned skin and sunstreaks in her dark brown hair for signs of a healthy, skinny child who loved to play outdoors. It was the brown eyes that said otherwise, startlingly large in the thin little face, eyes too old for their five years. A purple bruise smudged her right temple.

Joyce introduced the woman as Rena Trent.

"I'm usually pretty good with little ones her age," Rena said. "She let me clean her up last night and put her to bed. Poor little thing was so tired, she conked right out. But today she fought me about everything."

"Has she said anything more?" Joyce asked.

"Just no—she says that a lot—and she wants her mama."

Chrissie looked up at Anne, her little chin set with determination. Rena might not like dealing with Chrissie's defiance, but Anne saw it as a positive sign.

"I had to wash her hair," Rena went on. "It was filthy. She had a real tantrum about that, mostly about those hair ribbons. I was going to throw them away, but she had such a fit. Banged her head, grabbing for them and thrashing around. That's how she got the bruise. I wanted you to know about that."

"All right," Joyce said and shot Anne an inquiring look.

Anne's half an hour had shrunk to twenty minutes. She made a quick judgment. There was nobody else in the reception area. Clearly this child didn't need to adjust to more strange places or to be separated from Rena Trent right now. While Chrissie would not have had time to become firmly attached to Rena, the woman was still less a stranger than Anne or Joyce, and the little girl needed whatever small security she could get.

Anne sat down next to the child and said, "Hi, Chrissie, I'm Anne."

Chrissie looked straight ahead and said nothing.

"I'd like to sit here with you while Rena and Joyce talk

about some things, okay? They'll be right here in the room."

Still nothing.

Taking the hint, Joyce said casually, "Come on, Rena. I have some papers for you to sign."

At least Chrissie didn't jump up and follow them as they went over to the reception desk. There was a basket of toys on the floor next to the sofa, storybooks piled on a table. Anything there Anne could use? Somehow, she didn't think so.

She sat in silence for a moment, looking down at the top of the little girl's head. Her hair, smelling of baby shampoo, was parted in the middle and held back by two bobby pins that were stuck through the grubby bows. Even her scalp was tanned.

"When I was a little girl," Anne said softly, "my mom used to put my hair in these ponytails on either side of my face, only she called them puffballs."

As she said the words, Anne could remember the feel of the brush, her mother's hands smoothing back the short curls, the rubber bands tightening.

"She used to tie ribbons on my puffballs. I liked blue best. Does your mom make ponytails for you?"

Chrissie still didn't look at Anne. She huffed out a little sigh and said, "Unh-uh. Mama does plaits."

The drawl and that last word suggested that Chrissie and her mother came from where? Texas? Maybe Tennessee or Kentucky.

"Would you like me to fix your hair for you?" Anne asked. "I bet I'm not as good as your mom, but I'll do the best I can."

Chrissie hesitated, then turned so her back was angled more toward Anne. Quickly Anne delved into her purse for a wide-toothed comb. She took out the ribbons, untied the bows, and handed them to Chrissie, saying, "You hold on to these."

Then she began combing, trying to be careful. Rena's

shampoo had cleaned Chrissie's long hair well enough, but
there were knots in places, one of these yielding a sandbur.
Chrissie endured stoically as Anne divided the hair down
the back, sectioned the first side into three tresses, and
began to braid them together, the strands alive and slippery
against her fingers.

No matter what kind of person Chrissie's mother was,
whatever her reasons for leaving her daughter, at least she
had loved this child enough to perform this small ritual.

"I know it's been real scary for you, honey," Anne said
as she tied a ribbon on the first pigtail and began to braid
the second. "But we're going to take care of you and try
to find your mom. But you need to help us, okay?"

The slightest nod of the small head.

"Do you know your mommy's name?"

"Mama."

"A name that other people call her," Anne said.

"Don't know."

"Do you have another name besides Chrissie?"

"Sometimes Mama says Christina Louise."

She said it *Chris-TEEN-a Lu-EEZE* in what must have
been a good imitation of a mother's exasperation at a
naughty little girl.

"What about your daddy? Is he here with you?"

"He didn't want us," Chrissie said flatly.

These are the ones that teach you about pain, Rosemary
had said—right again.

"How about your grandma or grandpa?"

"Mama said I got a granny," Chrissie said. "She lives
in a house with great big trees, but I never seen it."

"Do you and your mama have some friends?"

"Just Harlan. He watches me sometimes when Mama's
not there."

And where did her mama go? To work? Off with a
boyfriend? With this man Harlan? Anne knew it was not
unusual for a mother to put a sexual relationship with a
man ahead of the needs of her child. One woman in South

Carolina had killed her two little boys because her lover didn't want children.

Anne attached the second ribbon, very much afraid the tenuous link she'd forged with the little girl would now be broken. But Chrissie moved just close enough so her body pressed lightly against Anne.

"I tried to be good," Chrissie whispered. "I tried real hard."

"Oh, honey," Anne said. "I know you did."

"Mama said stay with Harlan and be good. She said she was gonna bring me a cheese sammich and some 'nilla wafers. But Harlan went off 'cause he needed a thunderbird, and I was so scared. I stayed in our box and I waited and waited, but Mama didn't—she didn't come—back."

Anne could feel the little body trembling. Chrissie leaned heavily against her and began to sob. All Anne could do was gather the child into her lap and hold her, whispering comforting sounds. She told the little girl that none of this was her fault, that everything would be all right, when all the while she had the bleak feeling that things might never be right again for this poor child.

Then, as much as she hated to leave Chrissie, Anne reluctantly gestured for Rena and Joyce to rejoin them. Still crying, Chrissie clung to Anne only briefly before she went to Rena.

Anne touched the hair she had smoothed back from Chrissie's face. It was wet with tears. "I'll come to see you, sweetheart, I promise. And we're going to try to find your mama, okay?"

But Chrissie had already shut down. She turned away, pressing her face against Rena's neck.

"Did you get anything?" Joyce asked as she walked Anne to the door.

"Well, I doubt that she's retarded," Anne said, then passed on what Chrissie had told her, which was precious little, but maybe the police could find the man named Harlan and get some information from him. If the man was

Chrissie's mother's boyfriend, she appeared not to have left with him. Finding out if the child had been abused would have to wait for another session, although experience had conditioned Anne to expect the worst.

Back in her car, Anne sat and stared out at the late-afternoon sunlight, spilling across the Camaro's hood, bright as corn pollen. All the loss she'd observed today weighed her down like so many stones in a sack. Those four little girls in the clinic had lost their innocence and trust; Chrissie had lost her mother; Kathleen had lost her daughter. All of them looked to Anne for help, hope, solace.

How could she turn away?

The Beidermans' line was busy; Norman detested call waiting and refused to have the service. After a moment of hesitation, Anne dug out the note containing the number of the Sunrise Motel.

Kathleen Graley answered on the second ring.

After identifying herself, Anne said, "I'm still not sure I'm the right one for the job, but if you want me to do it, I'll try to find out what was going on in Rachel's life before she died."

three

BERN PAGETT PULLED ON A PAIR OF DISPOSABLE GLOVES
and looked at the dead man sprawled in the alley, struck
not so much by the ugliness as by the dreary, routine,
absolute banality of the murder scene.

There wasn't any doubt who the killer was. Handcuffed,
he stood about ten feet away just outside the yellow tape
with Will Hanson and a patrolman who had been the first
officer to arrive on the scene. The skinny, filthy, bearded
man—Bill Moultry, he said his name was—looked eerily
like a blood-spattered twin to the nameless corpse.

Moultry leaned against a brick wall that had been used
as both a repository for graffiti and a urinal and launched
into a rambling confession, not his first, according to the
patrolman who interrupted to say, "I read him his rights,
but he won't shut up."

Will, an overweight hound dog of a man with sad,
baggy eyes, just listened patiently.

"I axed him to share," Moultry was saying, his hoarse,
whiny voice rising above the background monotone of a
police radio in the patrol unit. "I axed him please. I wuz
real nice about it. Ax Bunny, he'll tell you I wuz nice.
'Fuck off' is what the asshole said. Wouldn'a hurt him
none, would it? Had that great big jug. Got me mad is all.

Got me fuckin' furious, he wuz so mean about it. So I stabbed the son of a bitch, is what I did.''

Will was lead investigator today, in charge of interviews. Bern's job was to collect the evidence. Collection was still necessary even though they had the killer, the weapon, and maybe a witness—assuming they could find this guy Bunny.

These days the department wanted everything done by the book. This was especially true because you never knew when some open-and-shut case of one wino stabbing another might suddenly become a media circus, with a hotshot lawyer claiming everything from police conspiracy to a gangland slaying, or, when all else failed, contending the victim committed suicide by stabbing himself fifteen times until he finally nicked a femoral artery and bled to death.

Bern ducked under the tape and stood there for a second, assessing the alley that was located only three blocks from the Police and Public Safety Building, an irony sure to be noted by the reporters.

Bern was just shy of six feet and losing a few more strands of his dark hair every day. He'd begun to feel extra weight collecting into a paunch, but a brush with death a few months ago and a long recovery had remedied that problem, rendering away enough body fat so that he looked downright gaunt. After a stretch of desk duty, he was finally back in the field.

"Everything's just fine," he'd told the department psychologist, told his own live-in psychologist, too. And what he said was true—except he found he wasn't so successful these days at removing himself, at maintaining a cool, objective distance.

But he was working on that, working on his defenses as he dismissed the typical debris in the alley: newspapers, cigarette butts, a broken hypodermic needle. He picked up a plain but efficient kitchen knife with a narrow six-and-a-quarter-inch blade and bagged it; tried to ignore the fixed, staring eyes of the dead man and the coppery stench of blood that overlaid a miasma of other odors. He was doing okay, too—until he moved in closer to the body.

The wine coveted by Bill Moultry had spilled from the broken bottle and lay in puddles like thin, dark blood. The smell of the wine overpowered everything else, coiling up into Bern's head. Suddenly he was lying on summer-hot earth, the night sky overhead crusted with stars, pain in his head where the woman had smashed him with her wine bottle, pain in his ribs where she'd kicked him—amazing, breathtaking pain—lying there watching that mountainous shape on the porch and knowing that if he moved. . . .

"Bern?"

Will's voice wrenched him back to the present, the shift so violent he felt dizzy and sick.

"Bern, you okay?" Will persisted.

"Yeah, sure," Bern said, and knew he sounded shaky.

Will had come under the tape to hover over him, a worried frown on his face. Bern realized he was crouched on all fours in the bloody, wine-spattered muck of the alley.

"I'm fine," he muttered, standing up, the muscles in his legs quivering, his heart racing.

"The hell you are," Will said. "What's wrong?"

"Nothing—just—a little dizzy. My blood pressure's on the low side these days." He tried for a grin. "One of the few benefits of my hospital stay."

"Well, you scared the shit out of me," Will said. "Why don't you go sit in the car? I'll finish up here."

"No." Bern practically shouted the word. He knew the surge of irritation was unreasonable, but couldn't keep his hackles from rising or keep the surliness out of his voice. "Dammit, Will, leave me alone. I'm perfectly capable of picking up a few lousy pieces of evidence."

"Yeah, sure. Sorry."

Will lifted his hands as he said it and backed off, but he still eyed Bern dubiously as he ducked under the tape and went to confer with the officer who now had Moultry in the patrol unit, ready to be transported.

Christ, Bern thought, feeling cold sweat trickle down his back.

Maybe he was coming down with something. There was a flu bug going around the squad room. Or maybe lack of sleep was to blame. He never rested well in Anne's house in Cave Creek, backed up against those miles of wild mountains. It was as though he had to constantly stay on guard to make sure nothing was creeping up on him. Lately, when he did drift off, his sleep was filled with vivid nightmares.

Perversely, however, what Bern wanted right now was to finish this call as quickly as possible, make the long drive north, and spend a quiet evening out on the edge of nowhere with Anne. He knew that was not going to happen when he saw Will trudging back from the patrol car.

"We need to wrap it up," Will said. "Remember that call we got from Steve Gainey a couple of days ago?"

Gainey was an arson investigator with the Phoenix Fire Department who had been called to a house fire over on Carolton in the Arcadia district involving the death of two people. As standard procedure, homicide had been notified and put on standby until an arson was declared.

"Has Steve called it?" Bern asked.

"Yeah," Will said, which made the case a double homicide.

"Am I lead?"

Bern didn't like the small hesitation or the speculative look in Will's eyes. Will shrugged. "Your turn."

"Then what are we waiting for?" Bern asked curtly. "Let's go."

"Hey, Duke. It's me," Anne called out as she let herself in the front door.

At the sound of her voice the fierce barking, audible outside the house, changed to an ominous rumble coming from the direction of the kitchen.

Bern had called while Anne was with her last patient to

leave word that he was going to be tied up for a while, so she'd had to make a trip home to tend to the dog before she went to meet Kathleen Graley.

Now Anne left her purse and keys on a hall table and went on back to the kitchen area where an expandable gate stretched across the entrance. Duke stood on the other side of the wire-mesh barricade, legs stiff, head lowered, ugly yellow teeth bared. A mix of Doberman and black Lab, he bore clear physical signs of a life of brutal mistreatment: a drooping ear, a kink in the tail where it had been broken, a fresh ragged scar on his belly.

"Hey, boy, did you think we forgot about you?" Anne kept her tone calm and friendly as she took down the barrier. Still growling, Duke backed away, retreating under the kitchen table.

Although Duke had never once made a mess in the house, the room had a distinctly doggy odor. A bath was in order and soon, although Anne was not looking forward to the experience. Bern had taken Duke to the groomer once, after the dog's wound healed. That bath had required all three people who worked in the shop plus a muzzle, and Bern had been told that never, under any circumstances, would they bathe the animal again.

Anne kept up a soothing patter as she went over and opened the back door. Duke eyed the door, measuring his need against his desire to avoid walking so close to her.

"Well, come on," Anne said. "I made a special trip home, but I'm in a hurry, so don't take all day."

Gathering his courage, the dog rushed past her out onto the wooden deck, then bounded down the steps to the rocky yard below. Anne followed him and stood by the railing, watching as he hurried over to the edge of the yard and relieved himself.

Anne had never intended to have any kind of a pet, much less a dog as unattractive and surly as this one. Bern had rescued Duke from the pound because, she supposed, he identified with the animal since both had been damn near killed by the same vicious woman.

Both man and dog might have healed; however, Anne wasn't sure she and Bern had made much progress in changing the animal's hatred and distrust of people.

She gave him five minutes to sniff around the area where the yard angled steeply upward toward the wild hillside. Duke came reluctantly to her call, sidled past her into the kitchen, and retreated back under the table while she filled his water dish and poured out some kibble.

By nature, Anne was a lot more optimistic than Bern. If she suspected they'd never have more response than guarded hostility from this dog, Bern must feel the same way, but they never talked about these doubts. As Anne put the gate back across the kitchen entrance, she thought she knew why.

Somehow the dog had become a symbol of the relationship between her and Bern. Giving up on the dog would mean they were giving up on themselves, and neither was willing to do that. They loved each other; that much was never in question. So why were things always so hard?

When Bern had moved in with her after his stay in the hospital, communication between them had been open and easy. Now Bern had shut down again. Something was wrong; that was obvious. He wasn't sleeping well. He looked haggard and remote. But when she tried to question him, she got either polite reassurances or curt turn-offs.

Back in the car, heading toward Phoenix, her worries about Bern gradually gave way to thoughts of little Christina and then to Kathleen Graley. Anne still hadn't spoken to Rosemary, and there was no point in calling now. Norman always put on the answering machine during the dinner hour.

To tell the truth, Anne was having second thoughts about working for Kathleen. She'd acted on impulse; now she wondered how she could have been so rash. Simply finding the time was going to be a problem. She had commitments, both to her own patients and to the children at the clinic. She would explain that to Kathleen. If her schedule presented a problem, well, at least it might give Anne a graceful out.

As she drove, the sun vanished behind heavy clouds that loomed in the west. Street lights winked on here and there, tentacles of the city reaching farther and farther out. A sudden gust of wind stirred up dust that peppered the car like fine sleet. She had to swerve to avoid a tumbleweed that was a quarter of the size of the Camaro.

Winter darkness had settled in by the time Anne arrived back at her office, and a cold breeze sent her hurrying across the parking lot, where only a few cars remained. Peggy had left a light on in the suite Anne shared with two other psychologists. The offices were silent and empty as Anne came in and locked the outer door. A note on her desk from Peggy read: *Turkey sandwich and salad in the fridge. Coffee ready to go.*

There were few truly indispensable people in this world. Anne was sure Peggy Rettig was one of them. Not only did she keep their business running smoothly, she mothered all three of her employers as well.

The coffeemaker was in the storage room. Anne went there to switch on the machine. Savoring the fragrant smell, she collected the first of the brew in her mug, then removed the food from an undercounter refrigerator and took it back to her office. A glance at her watch told her she had fifteen minutes to eat before Kathleen arrived.

She sat at her desk and unwrapped her supper. Peggy, bless her, had straightened up the play area that occupied about half of the rectangular room.

Toys and hand puppets were stowed in the red and yellow plastic baskets that lined open wood shelving. The sand tray and Puncho were back in the closet along with the rest of the toys and art supplies. Brightly colored floor pillows were neatly stacked. Peggy had even wiped down the low table that was used for painting and play therapy, a sturdy oak workbench Anne had found at a garage sale, perfect once she had sawed off the legs.

The rest of the furnishings consisted of a small sofa, two wing-backed chairs, and some lamps and tables. Her desk was placed in a corner, out of the way and certainly not meant to be the focus of the cheerful, comfortable room. The walls held posters from the Phoenix Zoo as well as pictures of blooming saguaro and brilliant orange Mexican bird of paradise.

Anne had finished her salad and was just starting the sandwich when somebody rapped loudly on the outer door in the reception area. Assuming Kathleen had arrived a few minutes early, Anne hastily wrapped the sandwich and went to unlock the door.

But it wasn't Kathleen who stood on the other side of the door, visible through the glass. It was Bern. Anne let him in, along with a cold blast of wind.

"I called the house," he said. "When you weren't there, I decided to swing by here."

"I wish you'd had me paged," Anne said. "I'm meeting a client—"

She broke off, suddenly aware it was Bern the cop towering over her, his voice clipped and cold. She also sensed a panic behind the glacial exterior that bordered on terror.

"You're upset," she said. "What's wrong?"

"I just got called in on a double homicide. Imagine my surprise when your name was mentioned."

"*Homicide?* What are you talking about?"

But Anne felt a chill surge of intuition and was suddenly sure she already knew what his answer would be.

four

CONFIRMING ANNE'S PREMONITION, BERN SAID, "LITTLE girl named Rachel Graley ring a bell?"

"The fire," Anne said, feeling sick. "Was it—?"

"Arson," Bern said.

"And you said a *double* homicide?"

"I sure did. Now, you mind explaining why you got involved without telling me?"

"Wait a second," Anne said, fighting back a flare of anger. "Not that I feel obligated to report everything I do to you, but I would have told you when I had the chance. This all came up today, and we haven't spoken to each other since breakfast."

"Today?" Bern said, some of the wind abruptly gone from his sails.

"Yes. And arson wasn't mentioned." In addition, Kathleen had left out the fact that somebody other than Rachel had died. "Who was the second victim?"

"The housekeeper. A woman named Rufina Vaughn. Mrs. Graley sure didn't tell you much."

Anne tried for patience, in spite of her irritation, because she understood Bern's reaction and knew he was afraid she might, once again, put herself in danger. She said, "We spoke only briefly. We were going to have a meeting this evening. As a matter of fact, she should be here any minute. But you knew that, didn't you?''

''She left a message at her motel saying she could be reached at your number. I don't get it, Anne. You work with children. What exactly does Mrs. Graley want you to do?''

''I can't tell you, not without discussing it with her first. And glaring at me won't change my mind.''

Bern had a retort ready, but before he could use it, Kathleen Graley pushed open the door and came inside.

She was shivering in spite of a black nylon ski jacket worn over her rumpled beige slacks and green knit top. The wind had tousled her hair into curly tendrils around her face. It was the first time Anne had seen her without sunglasses. Ordinarily, Anne thought, her eyes must be her best feature—large, a beautiful china blue—but now they were bloodshot, the lids red-rimmed and swollen.

''Sorry,'' Kathleen said with a glance at Bern. ''If I'm interrupting—''

''You're not,'' Anne said. ''Bern was just leaving.''

''No,'' Bern said, ''I think I should introduce myself. Bernard Pagett. I'm a detective with the Phoenix Police Department. You're Kathleen Graley?''

''Yes. Why?''

Bern said, ''I've been assigned to investigate your daughter's death.''

''I thought it was just the fire department that was investigating.'' Kathleen's puzzlement was quickly turning to dread. ''They told me it was probably a gas leak. An accident. It was—wasn't it?''

''Why don't we sit down,'' Bern said, indicating the chairs in the reception area, but Kathleen was shaking her head.

''No, *tell* me,'' she said with terrible urgency. ''Tell me right now.''

Anne took a step closer, instinctively wanting to protect Kathleen and knowing she couldn't.

"Sorry," Bern said, "I can't give you specifics, but there's evidence the fire was deliberately started."

"It was *deliberate*?" The word seemed torn from her insides. She looked around in panic, suddenly gray and ill. "Where's—? I need—"

"Over here," Anne said, grabbing her elbow and steering her toward the bathroom.

After Kathleen stumbled inside, Anne closed the door and moved a few steps away. From behind the bathroom door came the muffled sounds of Kathleen's retching.

"Ah, Jesus." Bern backed up and slumped down in a chair. "Sometimes I hate this fucking job."

"She's had quite a shock," Anne said. "You're not planning on questioning her, are you?"

"It has to be done."

"But not tonight," Anne said firmly. "Aren't there other people you can talk to? Her husband, for instance?"

"Sure, if I can find him. People are too damned mobile. They're never where they're supposed to be."

He looked tired and drawn. She knew he'd already put in a twelve-hour day. "Then please, Bern, go on home."

"Yeah, maybe I should." He got to his feet, stood there, and stared back toward the bathroom. "I can't talk you out of this, can I?"

"She needs me, Bern."

He reached out to brush her cheek with his fingertips. "Ah, Annie," he said, with just a hint of a rueful smile, "don't we all."

KATHLEEN HAD TAKEN OFF HER JACKET AND LAID IT NEXT to her. She sat on the sofa in Anne's office, hunched forward, arms across her chest, hugging herself. From the opposite chair, Anne watched Kathleen anxiously. Something about the way the light fell on the planes of her face gave Anne a chill, the skull so visible beneath the flesh.

"Are you sure you don't want me to take you back to your motel now?" Anne asked.

Bern had left before Kathleen came out of the bathroom, asking Anne to relay the message that he'd see Kathleen at nine A.M. tomorrow.

Kathleen shook her head. "Sitting around in that miserable room, doing nothing, I'll go crazy. God, you think something is so awful it just couldn't be any worse. And then you find out—it is." Her voice broke on the last word, and she squeezed her middle tighter as though she were holding herself together. "Sorry, it's just—so damned *hard*—"

"I know," Anne said. "Take your time."

"I wish Detective Pagett had stayed. I need to ask him—do they have any idea who did this? Does he think Randy—? No, Randy wouldn't, he just *wouldn't*—"

"You suspect he may have abused Rachel," Anne pointed out quietly.

"*Suspect*," Kathleen said. "God, I hope—I *want* to be wrong. But I keep thinking about what he said to me when I got here. He was full of excuses. He kept saying, of course he hadn't kidnapped Rachel—how could I think that? He and Sharon—that's his mother—just hadn't gotten around to calling me and telling me where they were. Jesus, the man is such a total shit. I think he's capable of almost anything, so why am I having doubts?"

"But you are," Anne pointed out. "Let me tell you something, Kathleen. Bern's very good at his job. If anybody can find out who killed Rachel, he can. I didn't pass on what you've told me, what you suspect, but I really think he ought to know."

"Of course," Kathleen said. "Yes, tell him, or I will. This changes everything, doesn't it? I mean, what I asked you to do. If Rachel was—if she was *murdered*—then maybe it was because Randy—because he was trying to *hide* something."

"It's possible, if your suspicions are right," Anne said. "But there are other explanations. The housekeeper—Mrs. Vaughn—could've been the intended victim, not Rachel.

Or the arsonist might have thought the house was empty.''

"I guess so. But whatever happened, I still want to find out about Rachel, about my baby.''

Her eyes gleamed with a desperate intensity, her need to know all the agonizing facts fueled by her feelings of guilt. Anne knew Kathleen was trying to make sense out of a terrible, senseless act, attempting to integrate it into her life.

"Please, Dr. Menlo,'' Kathleen said, "will you help me? I guess you'd have to work with the police. Is that a problem? Can you do that?''

"Well, I've worked with them before,'' Anne said. "What I think you ought to consider is that I may very well be duplicating their investigation. As a matter of fact, when Bern hears about your suspicions, I can almost guarantee he'll want to dig into all this. It's a sad fact of life that the people closest to a victim are the highest on the suspect list.''

Before Kathleen could reply, Anne's beeper went off. She recognized Rosemary's number on the pager display.

"Go ahead,'' Kathleen said. "I can wait if you want to make a call.''

"I do,'' Anne said. "Think about this, will you? I won't be long.''

She went out into the reception area, closing the office door behind her, and called Rosemary from the phone on Peggy's desk.

"I'm sorry you had trouble reaching me,'' Rosemary said. "Norman only just now gave me the message. Did you speak with Kathleen Graley?''

"Yes.'' Anne told her about the meeting at the house that had burned with Rachel inside.

"Oh, Anne, I had no idea she intended to do something like that. It must have been a difficult situation.''

"Well, more for her than for me. But it was graphic. And compelling. If she thought it would affect my decision, she was right.''

"You'll help her, then?"

"I agreed to, although now I find out it's a lot more complicated. Did you know another person died in the fire?"

"Yes. A housekeeper, I think."

"Well, Kathleen wasn't aware of it when she spoke to you, Rosemary, but the fire was arson."

"Lord," Rosemary said in dismay. "If I'd had any idea, I would never have gotten you involved."

"It gets worse," Anne said. "Bern's handling the case."

"Then maybe you should withdraw. Let me recommend somebody else to Kathleen." Rosemary paused, then asked, "Or is it too late for that?"

The accuracy of the guess told Anne once again just how well Rosemary understood her.

"Probably," Anne admitted. "Although I've suggested she simply let the police handle everything. She's here now, in my office. What did she tell you about herself? In case I don't withdraw."

"In case you don't," Rosemary said dryly. "I can't add much."

What she had learned was that Kathleen was in graduate school at UCLA, majoring in biochemistry. A friend of Rosemary's worked in that department—Daniel Dees. He was with Kathleen when she got the news about Rachel. Daniel gave Kathleen Rosemary's name because he thought she was going to need somebody to help her in Phoenix.

"When she called and was so distraught, I couldn't say no," Rosemary went on.

This didn't surprise Anne. Even wheelchair-bound, even with all her chronic health problems, Rosemary would have a hard time turning away somebody in such distress.

Rosemary said, "So she came here, and we talked. It quickly became apparent that she wanted something other than grief counseling, and it was obvious to both of us I couldn't do it. We didn't get into much detail. If you want me to, I'll talk to Daniel about her."

Anne thanked her for the suggestion and promised she would be in touch. Back in her office, Kathleen crouched on the edge of the sofa, tension visible in her body.

Anne felt a twinge of unease as she sat back down and studied Kathleen. She asked, "Have you thought about what I said?"

Kathleen jerked her head in a nod. "But I haven't changed my mind. The police have lots of fish to fry, Dr. Menlo. I want somebody devoting time just to Rachel."

"All right, then. I guess we have a lot to discuss."

But Kathleen jumped up and reached for her coat and her knapsack purse. Anne could almost see the raw pain and anger simmering beneath her skin.

"Could we do it tomorrow with Detective Pagett? So I won't have to go through everything twice."

"Kathleen, listen to me," Anne said with growing alarm. "I think I know what you're feeling—"

"No," Kathleen said, jamming her arms into the coat sleeves, slinging the straps of the purse over one shoulder. "You don't."

"You're right. I couldn't possibly know. But I understand you want to strike out at somebody, anybody, to ease the pain." And Anne had a good idea who Kathleen's first choice of target would be. "Don't do it. Go back to the motel. I'll have Dr. Beiderman prescribe something for you."

"Sleeping pills? She already did."

"Then take them," Anne said. "Rest. We'll deal with all this tomorrow with Bern."

"Sure," Kathleen said with no conviction and a quick, tight smile that was just a stretch of her lips across her teeth.

She hurried from the room, already across the reception area by the time Anne exited her office. As Kathleen pushed the front door open, Anne could read her face and see the seething turmoil giving way to rage.

One thing she knew for sure. Kathleen Graley did not look like a woman heading back to her motel for a sleeping pill and a good night's sleep.

five

THE GUSTY NORTH WIND BUFFETED THE JEEP AS BERN left the parking lot outside Anne's office and drove slowly over toward Seventh Avenue.

The cold dryness of the wind made the air crackle. He could feel it, like ground glass inside his sinuses. Everything was charged with static, making the hair on his arms rise.

Streetlamps glowed as brightly as usual. Houses and offices were lit; neon blazed. Still, tonight he could sense how thin that lighted veneer of civilization was, just an artificial membrane between him and the endless darkness beyond. The feeling stirred an atavistic fear that sent adrenaline surging through his body.

He found himself gripping the steering wheel, alert for gunfire, screams. Christ, maybe even the bellow of mastodons.

He braked as the traffic light on Seventh turned red, and sat there, telling himself Anne was right. He ought to head home, go to bed early. Sleep.

Yeah, fat chance, all pumped up like this. Paperwork at headquarters, then. Or take another crack at finding Randy Graley and his mother, Sharon, at their hotel in Scottsdale. Maybe track down Rufina Vaughn's family.

Simple choices.

Yet he didn't move as the signal changed green, to red, and back to green. He sat, frozen with indecision, until a car pulled up behind him, honking indignantly while the light cycled again. The Cherokee leaped as Bern stamped the accelerator, jerked as he hit the brakes. Tires squealed as he made a U-turn.

Feeling shaky, disconnected, and out of control, he crept slowly back to the parking lot outside Anne's building. There he stopped a few spaces away from her Camaro which was parked beside the old Toyota that must belong to Kathleen Graley. His fingers were clenched so tightly on the steering wheel it was an effort to let go, and it took a conscious act of will to shut off the engine and kill the headlights.

Then, with the wind rocking the Jeep, he stared at the lighted window of her office, knowing that something was very wrong with him, afraid to examine the possibilities.

He had only about a minute to think about his problems before Kathleen Graley hurried from Anne's building. The wind whipped her hair and flapped her unzipped coat as she got into the Toyota and drove away. Almost immediately Anne came out, locking the office.

Bern wasn't sure if he'd intended to wait for her, or if he had just come to sit, reassured somehow by being close to her. Whatever his intentions, she had spotted the Cherokee, and now he was caught.

While he readied the lie that would explain what he was doing sitting here like an idiot in the dark, Anne rushed over, opened the Jeep's door, and climbed inside. In the light of the dome lamp he could see the worried look on her face and knew right away her worry wasn't for him.

"What is it?" he asked.

"Do you know where Randy Graley is staying?"

"Over in Scottsdale." Randy and his wife weren't living together, and Rachel had been in her father's care when she died. Any fool could add that up, even one who didn't have his head on straight. Bern put his worries and Anne's part in all of this on hold and asked, "Trouble?"

"I hope not." Anne shut the door and reached for the seat belt. "I should have stopped her, Bern."

He started to say there are times when life is a goddamn steamroller and you're going to get flattened no matter what. Thing was, he wasn't sure if he was talking about Kathleen Graley's situation or his own.

So he kept quiet and stuck to getting them across town as quickly as possible, while Anne told him what she knew about the Graleys and about Kathleen's suspicions.

THEY DIDN'T SEE KATHLEEN'S CAR ON THE WAY TO Scottsdale. Of course, Bern was plotting the most direct route, one that a stranger to Phoenix probably wouldn't take. Or maybe Anne was borrowing trouble, and Kathleen was on her way back to the Sunrise Motel. Anne hoped this was true, but she really didn't think so.

She was still puzzled as to why Bern had been sitting out in front of her office, but there would be time for questions later. Right now she concentrated on briefing him, which reminded her how little she knew about these people. The important thing at the moment, however, was Kathleen's anger toward her husband and the ugly questions that fueled that anger.

As soon as Bern heard about that part, he got out his cellular phone, asking tersely as he punched numbers, "Do you know if she has a gun?"

"What?" Anne said. "No. I've no idea."

She hadn't even thought of such a thing, although she should have. Everybody from eight-year-olds to grandmothers packed weapons these days. All the same, it appalled her that guns were so routinely assumed to be a possibility.

But that's what Bern was doing as he asked Phoenix PD dispatch to have a patrol car meet them at the Holiday Inn. At this time of night traffic was light, even in Old

Town Scottsdale, and Bern drove fast enough to keep
Anne clutching the armrest with her heart rate accelerat-
ing.

The last few miles passed in silence. In profile, Bern's
face was all angles and bone, almost a stranger's face, a
realization that sent a tremor of unease coiling through her.

He's just lost weight, she told herself.

The reasonable rationalization allowed her to put aside
her disquietude as they turned into the entrance to the Holiday Inn and parked in a yellow zone out front. Seconds
later a patrol unit pulled up behind them.

Near the Civic Center, on the edge of Old Town, the
hotel complex was made up of several units, two-story
buildings of weathered wood and adobe sprawling amid
landscaped grounds, tastefully lit now in the chill darkness. Not the Ritz, but a long way up from the Sunrise
Motel.

The patrolman, young and compactly muscular, said he
was Toby Jessup. Bern gave him a concise summary as
they went up a short flight of steps to the lobby entrance,
leaving Jessup to speak to the bell captain while Bern went
inside with Anne.

Bern's gold badge brought the manager scurrying out.
Mr. Vasquez was short, overweight, dark, and dolorous.
After querying the staff, he reported that nobody had come
in asking for either of the Graleys. Anne understood this
didn't mean a whole lot. Kathleen might already know
Randy's room and might have gone directly there.

Behind the high front desk, Vasquez frowned at a computer display, checking registration. "Let's see—Graley,
Randolph and Sharon. They have adjoining rooms." He
gave Bern the two room numbers and fumbled for the
passkey that Bern had also requested. "I ought to come
along. There's not going to be any trouble, is there?"

"I hope not," Bern said. "But we'll handle it. You call
the rooms. Tell both the Graleys not to let anybody in until
we get there."

Vasquez didn't argue. He picked up the phone immediately as Anne trailed Bern to the door, where the patrolman was standing by.

"You stay here," Bern said to Anne in a tone that
brooked no argument, and then conferred briefly with the
bellman on the location of the rooms.

Bern and Officer Jessup left and walked swiftly in the
direction the bellman pointed, outside and across to a unit
on the other side of the entrance drive.

Behind her, Anne heard the manager say, "Not answering. Jesus, I don't need this."

All kinds of ghastly scenarios went through Anne's
mind, but she realized that in most of them, Kathleen was
on the receiving end of any pain being dished out. Bern
wouldn't like it, but Anne left the lobby, quickly crossed
the drive, and went along a covered walkway to a flight
of stairs. She could see Bern and the officer up at the top
on the landing, turning left.

The stairs and the landing were open, breezy and cold.
Forget the Chamber of Commerce brochures and the typical non–desert dweller's preconceived notions; it felt like
winter.

Bern and Jessup were pushing through a glass door, the
patrolman going first. Beyond them, Anne saw a long,
dimly lit hallway. Moving quickly, she slipped through the
door before it swung shut.

Both men rounded on her, Jessup's hand on his weapon.
Bern said, "Dammit, Anne—" then broke off as they all
saw the woman about six doors down.

It was Kathleen Graley. She must have made good time,
too, even if she didn't know the city. She was leaning back
against the wall. Nothing casual about her posture. The
wall was holding her up. The number on the door opposite
where she stood was the number the manager had given
Bern for Randy's room.

When Anne tried to go past Bern to get to Kathleen, he
put out his arm, barring her way.

"Randy's not in there," Kathleen said dully, her face shadowy in the dim light. "Or at least he's not answering the door. Neither's Sharon."

Her knees seemed to give way. She began a slow, heavy slide down the wall and ended up sitting on the floor. Her knapsack purse slipped off her shoulder to lie beside her. Anne tried to go around Bern, but he continued to block her until Jessup reached Kathleen and picked up the purse. Kathleen's hands were in plain view—weaponless.

After a quick check, Jessup shook his head to Bern and replaced the purse as Bern went down on his heels beside her.

"Kathleen?" Bern said. "Are you all right?"

She looked past him, up at Anne.

"I guess they're out to dinner," Kathleen said. "Sharon never eats before eight o'clock. I forgot about that." She looked back to Bern. "Does he know yet? Does Randy know you found out the fire was arson?"

"No," Bern said. "Not yet."

"I was going to do it myself, but now—please, Detective Pagett, let me stay. I want to see his face when you tell him."

Bern hesitated, and Anne knew that Bern the cop was making a cold calculation, weighing the shock effect of telling Randy about the fire that killed their child with his wife's accusing eyes fastened on him.

"I don't think that's such a good idea," he said with a touch of regret in his voice. Then he stood and held out his hands to her. "Come on. You look exhausted. I'll have Officer Jessup take you back to your motel."

"Bern's right," Anne said gently. "I understand your need to confront your husband, Kathleen, but—"

Anne intended to say, "Now's not the time," but she broke off as the glass doors swung open with a fresh gust of cold wind and a man and a woman came into the hall. Anne guessed who they were even as Kathleen ignored Bern's outstretched hands and scrambled to her feet.

Toby Jessup read the situation, too, and moved swiftly to place himself between the two approaching people and the rest of the small group crowding the hall.

Randy Graley had turned toward his mother to say something, the words just a baritone rumble. Sharon saw the waiting group first. She reached out to put a warning hand on her son's arm and stopped, staring at them.

Even in the poor illumination, Anne was struck by the resemblance between the two, a genetic echo of bone structure and body movement rather than specific details. Both were tall; in heels Sharon was almost the height of her son. Randy was lean, Sharon fashionably gaunt. Even the way their hair lay short and sleek against their heads looked similar, although Randy's was a dark brown and Sharon's was almost white.

"Kath?" The light was good enough to read a whole gamut of emotions on Randy's face, ranging from surprise to wary dread. "What's going on? What are you doing here?"

The patrolman grabbed Kathleen as she rushed at her husband, shrieking, "What did you do to her, you bastard? Did you set the fire yourself? *What did you do to my baby?*"

Randy backed away, up against his mother, who stood her ground still as stone. Even in the inadequate light of the hall, Anne could see that the color had drained from Randy's face. Shock at hearing the dreadful circumstances of his daughter's death? Or fear at being found out?

Jessup had a firm grip on Kathleen and was saying, "Come on, ma'am."

To Anne, Bern said, "Take care of her, will you?"

Anne picked up Kathleen's purse and followed Jessup as he hustled Kathleen down the hall past Randy and Sharon and out through the glass doors. Behind her, Anne could hear Randy asking, "What the *hell* is she talking about? Has she gone *nuts*?", and Bern identifying himself in that cool, authoritative voice that meant his suggestion to go inside and talk about it was an order and not really up for consideration.

Out in the chill night breeze, Kathleen's rage quickly fizzled. She sagged against Jessup's sturdy body the way she'd been leaning on the wall outside Randy's door.

At the top of the stairs, she said, "I want you to stay, Dr. Menlo. Please. Be there when Detective Pagett talks to Randy."

"I can interview Randy later. Right now, I don't think you should be alone."

"I'll be all right, really. I'll just go back to the motel and wait to hear from you."

"I'm not sure you should be driving."

"Don't worry," Jessup said. "I'll take her."

"But I have my car," Kathleen began.

"I'll bring it to you," Anne promised.

Kathleen pointed out the old green Toyota parked over in a corner in back of the unit and gave Anne the keys. Something about the way she let Jessup lead her away, mute and docile, triggered a memory for Anne: a vacation with her parents when she was eleven, up in the California gold country, just the three of them. Her brother, sixteen-year-old Kevin, had stayed home to work his summer job.

It had been late afternoon, the sun lazily sinking behind stands of pine trees, the shadows long and rapidly growing purple. The Menlos were just outside of some small town, its name long forgotten, Anne in front with her dad because she was feeling a little carsick on the curvy road.

She saw just a blur of movement as the three deer bounded from the camouflage of shadow into the road, two does and a fawn. Even though Sam Menlo was driving below the posted limit, instantly slammed on his brakes, and steered hard right, they all heard the sickening thump of metal striking flesh.

She remembered her father's litany of grieving curses as he jumped out to find the fawn down on the pavement, one delicate leg bent at a horrible angle, a gash opened up in the velvety flank. Ignoring the blood that stained his clothes, Sam had scooped up the baby deer and brought it into the backseat of the car, held it while Anne's mother drove into town to find an animal hospital. Anne could still see that small, wild thing lying so docilely in her father's arms, its huge eyes full of stunned pain.

Kathleen had that same look. She hadn't suffered physical injury; her pain was all inside, the worst kind of torment.

And now Anne remembered something else: neither her father's concern nor the veterinarian's efforts had made any difference that night so many years ago.

The little fawn was dead by morning.

six

BERN NOTED THAT NOBODY HAD CRACKED A DOOR TO look out and see what was going on in the hall. Either Randy and Sharon Graley had this end of the unit to themselves, or the other guests had allowed their survival instinct to outweigh their curiosity—pretty smart these days when raised voices can like as not be followed by shotgun blasts.

As for himself, Bern was glad to be leaving the drafty, poorly illuminated hall, although he would have been a damn sight happier if he'd called Will Hanson at the same time he requested a patrol car. Now he was going to have to question both the Graleys by himself.

Not that he couldn't handle it. Whatever had been wrong with him earlier tonight was gone. Considering what he'd been through last summer, he was allowed some minor aberration in his behavior once in a while, wasn't he? Right now he was just tired and hungry but quite capable of doing his job in that state. As a matter of fact, during a good percentage of his time in the department, he'd done his job in that state.

Sharon Graley went in first and flipped on light switches. The room was not overly large or lavish, but it had good, bright illumination that allowed Bern to get a better look at mother and son. Bern thought that Randy missed handsome by a good margin, and he'd bet Anne would agree. Bern would also bet that Randy had always relied on an easy, boyish charm that was at this point wearing thin. Pretty soon there'd be no hiding the mean glint in his nondescript hazel eyes or the sullen set of his mouth.

Bern felt better equipped to judge Sharon. Not beautiful. He thought she never had been, but she was certainly attractive. She had that shade of silver-gray hair that looked so striking on women with youthful faces—although he had to wonder if that smooth, unlined skin had been surgically enhanced or if she was truly impervious to the effects of gravity and age.

It struck him that they were both extremely neat with their grooming, maybe even fastidious in their somber-hued clothes. Randy's chocolate-brown jacket looked just out of the cleaner's bag. He wore no tie, but the top button of his cream-colored, oxford-cloth shirt was buttoned, his pants had a knife crease, and his oxblood-brown loafers gleamed. Sharon wore an expensively simple charcoal-gray dress, long-sleeved with a banded collar, and carried a coat made of some silky black lightweight fabric.

While they might be meticulous about the way they looked, the same couldn't be said for the condition of the room. It was Randy's room, according to the number given to Bern by the manager, and confirmed by the ties, shorts, trousers, and shirts strewn around the rumpled bed and draped carelessly over the two chairs that flanked a round table.

The table held a bottle of Scotch and a bottle of sherry, glasses, and an ice bucket. Randy took off his jacket and tossed it on the bed, then unbuttoned his shirt sleeves and turned up the cuffs in two neat folds as he headed for the liquor.

"Randy," his mother said, mildly reproving, but he ignored her, poured a double shot of Scotch into a glass,

and downed it while she turned to Bern. She had a
straight-on, unblinking gaze, eyes a definite shade of green
that probably owed something to contact lenses. "You'll
have to excuse him, Lieutenant—was it Paige?"

"Pagett. *Detective* Pagett," he added, although after
Columbo all homicide detectives were called Lieutenant
and there was damn little they could do about it. "If you'd
like a drink yourself, Mrs. Graley, go ahead."

"You sound like I'm going to need one," Sharon said.

That's just what he thought, but a second look told him
he was wrong, that Sharon Graley was equipped with her
own brand of body armor beneath her chic dress. She
would experience grief and rage like everyone else, but
she would allow herself all those major emotions only in
carefully measured doses.

Somebody rapped on the door. Instincts still on alert,
Bern said, "I'll get it."

It was Anne. "Kathleen wanted me to sit in on this,"
she said quietly, for his ears only. "Is that okay with
you?"

He hesitated. Strictly speaking, she wasn't officially a
part of the case and shouldn't be there. Knowing Anne,
however, he was not going to be able to talk her out of
profiling little Rachel for Kathleen. Better if he allowed
her to sit in on his interview rather than going it alone.

"Okay," he said and let her in.

BERN KEPT THE INTRODUCTION BRIEF AND VAGUE, LEAV-
ing off Anne's title. If the Graleys wanted to assume she
was another detective, Anne was certainly not going to
point out their mistake. At any rate, she thought they were
too concerned with what had happened out in the hall to
do much speculating about her status.

"Ms. Menlo," Sharon said politely enough, although
Anne thought she caught a dismissive note in Sharon's
tone. "What was that all about out in the hall, Lieutenant
Pagett?

I know Kathleen is having a hard time right now, we all are, but the things she was saying...."

Her voice trailed off, her glance flicking from Bern's face to Anne's. But Randy, fortified with Scotch, put the question more succinctly. "What the fuck did she *mean*, did I set the fire? It was an *accident*."

"I'm afraid not," Bern said. "We don't know exactly how it was done yet, but it was definitely arson."

Randy stared at Bern and Anne, either really shocked or doing a good job of faking it. "No, that can't be— arson? *Jesus*. And Kathleen thinks *I* could've done something like that? My God, with *Rachel* in the house?"

Anne thought she saw shock in Sharon's eyes, too, before she darted a glance at Randy. And how to read that glance—concern? Surprise? Or the doubt of a parent who knows her offspring well enough not to rule out the possibility that he'd done just what Kathleen suspected?

Sharon immediately turned back to demand of Bern, "Are you accusing my son of this?"

"No, ma'am, I'm not. We're just beginning our investigation."

"Good. Because he adored Rachel; we both did. And Kathleen knows it. These wild accusations of hers—well, it's obvious she's totally out of control."

"She's flipped out," Randy declared, reaching for the Scotch bottle and pouring another jolt. "Jesus Christ, just *thinking* I could do something like that." He downed the drink in a long swallow as the phone rang.

Sharon answered it, saying, "Yes—yes, they're here. No, we're fine, but thank you." Hanging up, she said to her son, "The manager says Lieutenant Pagett and Ms. Menlo came looking for Kathleen because they knew she was coming here and were afraid we might be in danger."

"From Kathleen?" Randy said, astonished, as though he honestly couldn't picture his wife being dangerous.

"Yes, Randy. Of course, they don't know her the way

we do." Sharon turned to Bern. "I honestly don't think you had to worry, Lieutenant—"

"Detective," Bern said, beginning to sound a little annoyed. "My boss is the only lieutenant in the unit."

"*Detective* Pagett," Sharon amended. "We appreciate your concern. And yours," she added to Anne.

"We get paid to be concerned," Anne said, which certainly described both their jobs.

"And to ask questions," Bern said. "I'll need to speak to you and your son separately, Mrs. Graley, so if you'll step into your room, I'll talk to Randy first."

"Is that really necessary? Randy's been in shock. I doubt he's thinking straight."

Anne thought she was right, especially if Randy had another drink. And judging from the way he was eyeing the bottle, that was a distinct possibility.

"Sorry," Bern said, polite but implacable. "It's routine. But I'll take his mental state into account."

Sharon looked at him as though she'd like to know what *that* meant, then shrugged in capitulation. But before she left she capped the Scotch and took it and the sherry with her, ignoring the way Randy glowered at her.

After she closed the door to the adjoining room, Bern picked up the other chair and positioned it so that when he sat down he was practically knee-to-knee with Randy. Anne perched on the end of the bed.

The liquor had slackened Randy's face and put a mean glint in his eyes, but Anne glimpsed a facile charm and boyish good looks, things that must have attracted Kathleen. Was he really capable of the things that Kathleen suspected him of doing?

"I don't know what you want from me," Randy said sullenly, articulate enough in spite of the Scotch. "Ask the fire department. I got home about five-thirty, just before dark, to find the street blocked off and my house burned to the ground. Nobody could tell me anything about Rachel. They had to wait until the rubble cooled off to look—'' He stared down at his empty glass as though he were trying to will it full again, his face full of pain and grief. ''I don't know anything except my little girl is dead, so what could I possibly tell you?''

''How about why you took your daughter and vanished without a word to your wife?'' Bern said. ''That seems like as good a place as any to start.''

''Oh, I'm sure you got an earful already,'' Randy said, shifting instantly to the defensive. ''I know what Kathleen's telling everybody, that I kidnapped Rachel, my own *daughter* for Christ's sake. Bet she's not telling you how she dumped Rachel, is she? Getting her Ph.D., that's what's important, not her little girl. I mean, it's not like UCLA's in Alaska. A lot of people commute from Orange County; they do it every day. But not Kathleen. She might lose an hour's sleep, might not be there to suck up to old Professor What's-his-name.''

Randy suddenly caught himself, shooting a look of earnest contrition at Anne, appealing to her rather than Bern. ''Sorry. I know I ought to be more understanding, but it hurts to hear that stuff.''

''I'm sure it does,'' Anne said, careful to keep her tone nonjudgmental. There were two sides to every story; however, she couldn't imagine anything that would excuse what Randy had done.

''So what really happened?'' Bern asked.

''This business deal came up suddenly here in Phoenix. Mom and I had to move on it fast.''

''What business are you in?''

''Real estate. There were so many last-minute things to do—I don't know. Kathleen and I hadn't been communicating very well, anyway. I figured she'd hardly miss us. I'd call as soon as we got settled. But what with one thing and another—'' He broke off and had the grace to look uncomfortable, if not guilty.

Anne said, ''You didn't call Kathleen until after the fire, after Rachel was dead.''

"Yeah, I know it *sounds* bad—" Randy shifted uneasily, his glance skating off her face to Bern's. "I hope you're not paying any attention to these crazy things Kathleen's saying."

"Oh, I listen to everything," Bern assured him. "Tell me about the day of the fire. Where were you?"

"Jesus, I can't believe this. You *do* think I had something to do with it."

"Just routine, Randy. I'll be asking everybody."

"Well, Mom'll tell you. I was with her, looking at some property. Way out someplace. Apache Junction? Mom would know. We left at nine-thirty, as soon as Rufina got there."

"You know many people here in Arizona?" Bern asked. "Done much business here?"

"No. Why?"

"How about back in California? Any business deals gone sour? Made any enemies?"

"*No*. Not like that. I mean sometimes people get unhappy. Most of them have an inflated idea of what real estate's worth. But to burn down my house and kill my daughter? No way."

Bern asked a few more questions, but it was obvious they were going to get nothing more out of Randy. What was not so clear to Anne was how to read the man. He seemed truly indignant at any suggestion that he might have been responsible for Rachel's death, and genuinely grief-stricken. But Anne, of all people, understood how malice hides beneath the facade of normalcy and that grief does not exclude the possibility of guilt.

IN THE OLD TOYOTA ON HER WAY TO KATHLEEN'S MOTEL, Anne wished she had something definitive to tell her client. She also wished she'd been able to sit in on the interview with Randy's mother, but she had to deliver Kathleen's car, and she wanted to make sure Kathleen was all right.

The Sunrise Motel may have looked deserted during the day, but there were plenty of vehicles in the lot now. Anne found a space as close to Kathleen's room as possible. Before she left the Toyota, she called from her cell phone and requested a cab to pick her up in thirty minutes.

Outside she caught a whiff of chlorine from the pool, the smell quickly overcome by the unmistakable odor of take-out chicken. Thin doors leaked the sounds of canned laughter and television gunfire. Kathleen's set was on, too, and Anne was happy to hear it.

The set was switched off almost instantly when Anne knocked. From Kathleen's intense expression when she opened the door, the sitcom had provided only minimal distraction. She hadn't changed into nightclothes, and if the bed was mussed, it was from sitting, not lying down to rest.

"What happened?" she asked before Anne was barely inside.

"Let's sit," Anne said, putting her purse and Kathleen's car keys on the lamp table.

She put the one straight chair beside the bed for herself, shrugged off her coat, and waited for Kathleen to sink down on the edge of the mattress.

"You have to understand something," Anne said. "Most people register the appropriate emotions when they hear dreadful news—especially the ones with the most to hide."

"So you didn't get anything?"

From the level of Kathleen's disappointment, Anne knew she had counted heavily, way too heavily, on some telling reaction from her husband and on Anne's perceptions.

"No," Anne said. "You have to prepare yourself, Kathleen. What you've asked me to do may not be easy, and in the end there may not even be clear-cut answers to your questions."

"He's hiding something," Kathleen insisted. "I saw it in his face."

"I think so, too," Anne said.

"So what happens next?"

"We talk—you and Bern and I. He'd like you to come in tomorrow morning. Can you do that?"

"Of course."

"All right. We'll start there. For now, it's very important that you get some rest. Think of this as a battle. If you don't take care of yourself, you won't stand a chance of winning."

This seemed to be the right note. Kathleen went into the bathroom and put on a flannel nightshirt, red with teddy bears in Santa caps. When she came back, she brought a cup of water, tipped out one of the sleeping pills Rosemary had prescribed from the small plastic vial, and swallowed it.

Anne turned back the covers. Kathleen sat on the edge of the saggy motel bed and smoothed the nightshirt fabric over her knees, looking ready to weep again.

"Rachel gave this to me for Christmas," Kathleen said. "She was so proud that she had picked it out herself."

Outside, a horn tooted. Anne peeked out the curtained window. "My cab's here, but I can have them send another one later. Would you like me to sit with you for a while? Until you get sleepy?"

Kathleen shook her head, making a visible effort to pull herself together. "No, you go on. It's getting late. I'll be— I was going to say okay, but that's a lie. But I think the pill—on an empty stomach—it'll hit me pretty quick."

"All right, then." Anne picked up her coat and purse. "I'll see you in the morning. Come and turn the deadbolt."

At the door with the wind plucking at the full sleeves of her daughter's Christmas gift, Kathleen asked, "Anne, do you know about chaos theory?"

"I know it." The theory postulated the significant end

result of an insignificant event: A butterfly flaps its wings, and the motion eventually changes global weather.

"It's true," Kathleen said. "You do something—one stupid thing—like meeting somebody—and everything changes forever."

"Yes," Anne said, knowing how true this was from her own experience. "It happens that way. Good night, Kathleen."

Outside, Anne heard the bolt click and the security chain slide into place. But the lights didn't go out. They were still on as Anne got into the cab and rode away. Maybe the sleeping pill had kicked in, leaving Kathleen too groggy to turn off the lamp, but Anne suspected otherwise.

She knew there were times when everyone is afraid of the dark.

seven

SHARON GRALEY'S ROOM WAS A MIRROR IMAGE OF Randy's, with the bathrooms placed back-to-back. Unlike her son, however, Sharon kept everything in perfect order. There was no sign of the confiscated Scotch and sherry. Instead, her round table held a small steaming pot of water—the kind of pot provided by the motel—two white plastic mugs, and a box of herbal tea bags.

She sat in one of the two chairs, made a hostesslike gesture to the other, and asked, "Tea, Detective Pagett?"

Bern surveyed the box that promised a "truly natural" assortment and said a polite "No, thanks." The stuff tasted like perfumed weeds to him. Give him good old orange pekoe any day.

"Is Randy all right?" Sharon asked, selecting a tea bag and putting it in her mug.

"I think he'll survive," Bern said dryly.

"Sometimes I wonder. You've no idea what we've been through."

"Yes, ma'am, that's certainly true."

The smell of lemon and mint wafted up as she poured water into the cup.

"I'm sure he told you what a terrible shock it was, coming home, the smoke, that terrible smell, all the fire engines. When we realized it was our house that was burning, Randy jumped out of the car and started screaming. The firemen had to physically restrain him. They told us Rachel was found in her bedroom. Do you know if that's true?''

"Yes, ma'am, that's where she was."

"So maybe she was asleep and never woke up," Sharon said, but was not comforted by the thought.

"That's possible," Bern said.

"We lost everything," she said. "Of course, there was insurance, so the material things can be replaced."

"What about on Rachel?"

She drew back as though he'd slapped her. "You mean *life* insurance? No, we don't profit from Rachel's death, Detective Pagett, if that's what you want to know."

"It's a question I have to ask, Mrs. Graley." As was the next one about their whereabouts the afternoon of the fire.

Sharon sipped tea and said she would supply him with addresses of the properties out in Apache Junction. And no, she could think of nobody who harbored the slightest trace of ill will toward her and her son except for Kathleen, and she was, of course, out of her mind with grief and not thinking rationally.

"It has to be some crazy person, a firebug, don't you think?"

What Bern the cop thought was that people who were leading law-abiding lives wouldn't suddenly up and leave all those kind, friendly folks back in Orange County, California. *Vanished* was the way Kathleen had described their leave-taking. Tomorrow he'd start digging into the Graleys' backgrounds; tonight, he knew damn well he wasn't going to get anything except more evasive answers to his questions.

"You look tired, Detective Pagett," Sharon said. "Surely you don't always work this late."

"More often than you might think," Bern said as he

stood up. "I'll want you and Randy to come down to headquarters and give us a formal statement. Maybe tomorrow afternoon."

"Well," Sharon said, sounding vague and noncommittal, "things are so unsettled right now. I don't know exactly what our plans are."

A good deal of the time Bern was a firm believer in all the freedoms guaranteed in the Constitution, although like most cops he was bitterly opposed to those Supreme Court interpretations that made it hard to catch the bad guys and damn near impossible to keep them locked up. Once in a great while, like now, he thought the old Soviet system of internal passports wasn't such a bad idea.

He put some steel in his voice. "Just be sure you stick around for a few days while we investigate."

The Phoenix Police Department's budget was shrinking while the city's population and crime rate were expanding. Bern might have a gut feeling that there was a good chance the Graleys would cut and run by morning, but, given budget constraints, gut feelings weren't cause enough for twenty-four-hour surveillance.

Extracting a card from his pocket and handing it to her, he added, "Call me if you decide to change motels."

"You mean don't leave town, don't you?" Sharon asked with a touch of sarcasm.

"Yes, ma'am," Bern said. "That's exactly what I mean."

THE LIGHTS WERE ON IN THE LIVING ROOM, CONTROLLED by an automatic timer, when Anne arrived home. In the kitchen, behind the expandable gate, she could see Duke's eyes glowing in the dark room and hear his low rumbling growl.

He retreated under the table when she flipped on the light and took down the gate. Strangely enough, although Anne had felt some uneasiness around the dog, she'd never been afraid of him.

"Hey, boy," she said. "Not much fun being here alone all the time, is it? Need to go out?"

The wind was even stronger out here away from the city, gathering force as it blew down over the mountains. She gripped the rear door tightly to keep it from slamming back against the cabinets. Duke sidled past her, his ears flat against his head. She followed him out and closed the door behind them.

She had kept her jacket on. Now she pulled it more tightly around her as she stood on the deck, but was soon shivering as she waited for the dog. Overhead, the sky was thick with stars, the starshine so bright that everything gleamed, silver on black. The brushy hillside shifted and rippled in the wind, alive with luminous light.

Finished with his toilet, Duke prowled along the back perimeter of the yard at the base of the hill. Suddenly he froze and stared up at the pile of boulders that lay about halfway up. He growled, that low vibration deep in his throat.

Something up there. Anne saw it, too, although she couldn't make out more than just a flicker of movement. In back of the boulders a rocky ledge had been hollowed out to form a natural basin. The previous owner of Anne's house had installed a water line up the hillside to keep the basin filled. He had even made this practice a condition of the sale to Anne.

An early-morning vigil, at the time most of the animals came to drink, had come to be one of the joys of her life. She'd seen coyotes, javelina, jackrabbits, even an occasional bobcat. But there wasn't enough light to see what was up there now.

Afraid the dog would bolt up into the brush, she called sharply, "Duke, come on, in the house."

Like a small child asserting his independence, he stayed where he was for several seconds before he came, reluctantly, up onto the deck.

"Good decision," Anne said, opening the door. "Believe me, you don't want to tangle with a wild pig or a pack of coyotes.''

In the kitchen Duke withdrew back under the table and watched her while she took out a pitcher of orange juice and poured herself a glassful.

''Poor fellow,'' she said. ''Cooped up in here.''

The situation couldn't go on this way much longer. It wasn't fair to the dog. If he was going to become a permanent addition to her household, she would have to fence the yard. And accept the fact that with a dog so close, most wild animals would stay away from the water basin.

She sighed as she sipped the juice. Of course, the real issue was her relationship with Bern. But was she ready to deal with their problems?

She would have to, and soon, but not tonight.

ANNE WAS ALREADY IN BED WHEN BERN GOT HOME. HE shushed the dog and went quietly down the hall to peek in the bedroom. The lamp beside the bed was on, turned down low. Anne stirred, lifted her head, and said groggily, ''Bern?''

''Yeah, babe, go on back to sleep.''

'' 'Kay,'' she said and snuggled back into the pillow.

Out in the kitchen, he wrinkled his nose at the slight kennel smell, said, ''Hey, mutt, guess it's just the two of us,'' to the dog who was growling ominously beneath the table, and went to stare into the refrigerator. He hadn't eaten dinner—too busy—and when he got a break, his appetite had disappeared. He still wasn't hungry, but he had a definite hollow feeling and knew he should eat.

He took out a block of cheddar and a can of Budweiser, went back to the table, and sat down. He popped the tab on the beer and contemplated the cheese. Unless he planned to gnaw on the stuff, he'd have to get up and find a knife and a plate.

''Not worth the effort,'' he said and pushed it away.

One good thing about having an animal around—you

could voice your thoughts without being accused of talking to yourself. He sipped the Bud and stretched out his legs. Duke responded to the movement by revving up his growl, and when Bern leaned over to look under the table, Duke bared his ugly, yellow teeth.

"Wonderful," Bern said.

What the hell had he been thinking, bringing the animal here? When Bern was growing up, his dad would never give in to his desperate desire for a dog. Wade Pagett always saw the downside of every situation. While young Bern visualized adoring puppy eyes and wet puppy kisses, his father thought only of smelly accidents on the living room rug, hair storms engulfing the furniture, and disgusting canine sexual habits.

So now Bern supposed he could blame his lapse of judgment on his boyhood yearnings. All those dog movies hadn't helped either, the ones where kindness eventually tamed the most savage of beasts.

So now what should he do?

Give up and take the dog back to the pound?

Just the thought triggered a wave of despair so profound that he sat immobile in the kitchen chair for several long minutes, incapable of lifting the beer can, and knowing even if he did he wouldn't be able to swallow.

Go to bed, he ordered himself.

He was exhausted, and who wouldn't be after this long, unending bitch of a day.

When he finally hauled himself upright, he felt so weighed down with fatigue, that he could barely lift his feet, and shuffled like an old man down the hall.

Lying next to Anne, breathing her warm fragrance, he registered that the digital clock on the bedside table read 11:05, and then he fell asleep instantly, like plunging into deep, warm water.

Just a short respite, and then the dream came, so vivid he could feel the hard, hot earth beneath him and smell the powerful blend of spilled wine, dog feces, and crushed sharp-scented weeds. A bright night sky arced overhead. Pain clanged in his head and raged in his chest.

Had to get to his gun. . . . No, couldn't. *She* had it, Florence Mosk, that mountainous shape on the porch, and all he could do was lie there—helpless—and wait. . . .

He jerked awake, heart drumming, his body slicked with sweat.

The digital clock read 3:10.

Christ.

His body ached with his need for sleep. He'd read an article on insomnia that said lying calmly and resting was almost as good as sleeping. But what if your brain had mistaken dreams for reality and given you a shot of adrenaline, guaranteed to leave you in a twitchy state of hyperalertness?

He knew one thing. If he got up, he'd be prowling around the rest of the night. He forced himself to lie still and take several deep breaths. Outside, the wind had died down. Inside, the furnace had cycled off. The house seemed enclosed in a bell jar of stillness.

He had an instinctive distrust of this kind of silence, maybe passed down by ancestors who had lain awake listening for the muffled pad of saber-toothed tigers or the stealthy whisper of Apache moccasins.

No tigers or Apaches here. Instead he heard the click of Duke's toenails as he restlessly prowled the kitchen. Maybe the poor beast had his own nightmares.

Beside him, Anne turned over, the movement bringing her close enough so her leg rested against his, and he could feel her breath warm against his shoulder. If he put his arms around her, drew her close, touched her. . . .

What was it his dad used to say? *Don't start something you can't finish.*

Bern slipped out of bed carefully, went to pace the dark, silent house, and didn't return to bed until shortly before dawn.

eight

BECAUSE ANNE HAD AGREED TO WORK WITH KATHLEEN Graley, what had been a lightly scheduled morning was now going to be hectic, so she planned to leave early to try to get a jump on things at the office. Bern came rushing into the front hall just as she was collecting her keys and purse from the hall table and getting ready to leave. He mumbled something about being late for a meeting and hurried out.

She grabbed the door before it swung shut behind him and called, "What time for Kathleen?"

"Dunno." His words were clipped and a little hoarse. "Call you."

"Good morning to you, too," she fumed as she watched him rocket off down the driveway in his Jeep.

She glanced toward the kitchen where Duke was standing behind the gate. She didn't feel comfortable walking a big dog like Duke, and, anyway, it had been Bern's idea to saddle her with an unwanted pet. So their agreement had been that he would do the exercising. But once again he hadn't allowed himself enough time this morning, and she was pretty sure he hadn't walked Duke the night before. She could swear the dog's eyes held the same longing they had earlier when he'd come out from under the table to watch as she left for her daily bike ride.

Broken promises from Bern and a guilt trip from a dog— *Do I really need this?* she thought as she slammed the door behind her and stalked to her car.

In the Camaro driving to work, her anger slowly gave way to uneasiness as she thought about those few moments in the hallway. Bern was never at his best in the mornings, but the way he looked today went far beyond the night-owl surliness she'd come to expect and tolerate. His face had been all raw angles, with his eyes feverishly bright and sunken back under the brow bone. Even the way he moved was different, his confident gait gone. He looked out of control, unstrung.

Something really is wrong, she thought with dismay.

He wasn't sleeping. She knew that. As a matter of fact, she was pretty sure he'd gotten up again last night, although he'd been careful not to wake her. And she thought again about that strange incident the night before, coming out to find him sitting in his Jeep in the parking lot.

There was something else, too, a niggling worry she'd been brushing aside. She and Bern had not made love for almost two weeks.

Like last night's, his cases often kept him out late in the evenings, so she was asleep when he got home. Otherwise, he pleaded fatigue. Now she wondered if he was suffering impotence and covering it up out of some dumb macho pride.

She'd worried that he had gone back to active duty too soon, but he'd chafed at desk work and convinced everybody—including his doctor, the police psychologist, and Anne herself—that he was ready to resume his regular workload. A detective didn't punch a time clock, however; especially not one in homicide. The job was demanding and draining even to somebody in the best of health.

She would make him sit down and talk about it. She'd insist he have a complete checkup. And if strain and the growing rift between them couldn't be explained by a relapse?

She pushed the thought away as she turned into the parking lot, left her car, and went into the office. The suite was empty and silent. It would be a good forty minutes before Peggy arrived.

Anne plunged right into a stack of paperwork, but she couldn't escape her worry about Bern or escape the nagging question that kept returning, churning her stomach with a sick, chill pain: What if Bern's problems were not simply health-related? Maybe Bern was drifting away, and the love that seemed so deep and sure was not to last forever after all.

WHEN BERN ARRIVED IN THE SQUAD ROOM OF THE HOMICIDE detail, he made a beeline for the corner where a shiny twelve-cup Braun coffee machine sat on a table. What he saw convinced him that at last he truly understood the reason why people commit murder.

The glass pot was empty.

Frank Trusey was there, scooping Colombian espresso into the filter. When Frank moved down from his native Seattle a few years ago, he had immediately tossed out the division's ancient urn and contributed the new coffeemaker, addicting the entire squad to freshly ground flavor and megadoses of caffeine long before Starbucks made its frontal assault across the country.

Frank was skinny with a pointy nose, receding ginger hair, and the beginnings of a ridiculous mustache. He usually had some cheery remark for everybody. If he had one for Bern this morning, he took a look at Bern's face and thought better of it. Instead, he switched on the machine and beat a strategic retreat while Bern picked up a mug, substituted it for the glass pot, and let the first fragrant stream of dark liquid run straight into the cup.

Waiting for the cup to fill, he told himself he might as well have shared Randy Graley's Scotch the night before.

His head pounded, and he felt shaky and sick——all the effects of a hangover without any of the fun of getting one.

His first sip of the dark brew jolted him straight down to his socks——matched, he hoped, although he wouldn't bet on it. He had finally fallen into a deep sleep this morning only to be awakened by the alarm, the sound quickly followed by the realization that he had forgotten to reset the damn thing and was going to be late to an early meeting if he didn't hustle.

Now, he dropped some money into a box beside the coffee machine, took another long swallow, then carried the mug over to his desk where Will Hanson was waiting, well-rested and unhurried.

Will said with concern, "Jesus, Bern, you look like fresh roadkill."

"Late night," Bern said, each word an effort. "I wound up interviewing Randy and Sharon Graley. She here?" He tilted his head toward Lieutenant Jane Clawson's office.

"Yeah," Will said. "We're next in line. Paul and Irene are in there."

"Figures," Bern muttered.

Paul Rodriguez and Irene Wanamaker's case involved the murder of a well-known Phoenix banker's wife. High profile equaled high priority and——a real plus——guaranteed that the media would be kept busy and wouldn't be sticking their noses into the Graley case. It also meant that Bern and Will had to hurry up and wait.

Bern sat down and hunched over his coffee, wrapping both hands around the mug while more blocks of memory fell into place. He had skinned out of the house still damp from the shower, brushing past Anne. He remembered now her shouted question about Kathleen Graley.

He also remembered the angry look on Anne's face. Why was she mad?

Shit——the dog, of course.

"Bern, are you all right?" Will asked.

"Fine," Bern snapped. "Just give me a minute, will you?"

"Yeah, sure," Will said, sounding hurt as he left and went back to his own desk.

Bern took a bottle of Advil from a drawer, shook out the last three tablets, and washed them down with the rest of the coffee. Then he sat for a minute rubbing his throbbing temples.

Last night during those long sleepless hours, he'd tried to figure out some way to talk Anne out of working for Kathleen Graley. Given Anne's stubborn nature, he finally conceded there was nothing he could try that didn't involve bodily harm or imprisonment. All he could do was attempt to control her involvement and that meant a selling job on Jane. And anybody facing that situation better have his wits about him.

He trudged back to the coffee machine for his second hit of caffeine.

"Now let me get this straight," Jane said. "You've been adamant about taking Anne off our list of consultants, you've forbidden anybody around here from even *thinking* about calling her on a case, and now you want to make her an official part of this one?"

"I don't *want* to," Bern said, "but she's going to be mixed up in it whether I like it or not. The department can certainly use her insights."

"And you figure this way you can keep an eye on her," Jane concluded dryly.

The department had just thrown an over-the-hill party for Jane Clawson's fiftieth birthday, complete with black balloons, a black-bordered cake, and a deluge of ribald cards consoling her on her half-century landmark.

She liked to joke that she might be fifty, but she only looked forty-nine. In Bern's opinion she looked much younger, despite laugh wrinkles around her clear blue eyes and a few gray threads in her dark hair. She kept her sturdy body trim by spending her lunch hour on the treadmill in the police gym, and she avoided the coffee machine. Instead she kept a bottle of mountain spring water on her desk to sip.

Today, as always, she looked smartly put together in a tan skirt and a white silk blouse that wrapped in front, the soft V-neck accented by a pin that was an abstract squiggle of gold. A tan jacket hung on a plastic hanger on a hook behind the door.

And, as always, Jane seemed to hum with vitality. Bern wondered glumly if he were the only person in the whole damned department who had trouble getting it together in the mornings.

"Let's say I approve putting Anne on the case," Jane said. "Don't you think there'd be some conflict of interest here? Would Kathleen Graley really want Anne to share information?"

"From what I saw last night," Bern said, "she'll be delighted, especially if there's any truth to her suspicions."

Also, from Kathleen's choice of motel accommodations and the looks of her car, he had a pretty good idea she'd appreciate having part of Anne's fee defrayed by the Phoenix police.

"Well, I can probably justify it," Jane said, "as long as we don't drag this out. Tell me what else is going on."

In the ten minutes since Bern and Will had been in Jane's office, Bern had sketched in the events of the previous evening. Now Will said, "I'm waiting to hear from the arson investigator—Steve Gainey, you know him?"

Jane nodded. "Good man."

"We'll meet him at the house sometime today and have him give us a complete briefing. He had to beg off yesterday. Something came up. We began interviewing the neighbors instead."

"So you don't know the details of the fire yet?"

"Just that they assumed originally there was an explosion from a natural gas leak,'' Will said, ''but Gainey says from the temperature of the fire and the burn pattern, that's not the case.''

''Autopsy report?''

''Not yet.''

''Okay,'' Jane said. ''What about the other victim, the housekeeper?''

''Rufina Vaughn,'' Bern supplied. ''From the fire incident report we found out there's a husband and a son. I'll try to get to them today. One of the neighbors told us the son was at the Graley house the day of the fire. She saw him leave an hour or so before the explosion.''

''The Graleys were renting,'' Will put in. ''Owners are some people named Swales, live out in Sun City. I figured I'd talk to them, make sure we have all the insurance carriers and amounts.''

''What about your other cases?'' Jane asked.

''Nothing that can't wait,'' Will said. ''You, Bern?''

''I'm pretty clear.''

''You closed out the stabbing on the John Doe from yesterday?'' Jane asked. ''No problems there?''

''Oh, yeah,'' Will said. ''It's solid.''

''It better be,'' Jane said. ''That asshole just kicked two more cases.''

She didn't have to be more specific. Bern and Will knew she was referring to Gerald Ellis, the Maricopa County Attorney. An ongoing war raged between the police department and the county attorney's office. The police insisted that Ellis would only prosecute cases he was sure to win so he could look good to the voters. Ellis's response was that he was not going to spend taxpayers' money taking sloppy cases to court.

''Okay,'' Jane said. ''We have to make this one good, guys. Show that asshole what we can do.''

On the way out, Will said, ''Maybe I ought to have Frank check out that guy Moultry mentioned—Bunny?''

''Couldn't hurt,'' Bern said.

Thinking about the stabbing also reminded Bern of the incident yesterday, the one last night, and the vivid dreams. Insomnia, he told himself. Sleep loss did weird things to people. Still, it was about time he talked to a doctor, so he went to his desk and made a late afternoon appointment at the clinic.

He knew his primary reason for doing so was for his health, but he had to admit he was also following the warning that his first patrol partner had said ought to be tattooed on the appropriate part of every cop's anatomy. CYA—Cover Your Ass.

That done, he called Kathleen Graley at her motel and asked her to come in at ten. This would give him time to try to track down the Vaughns, father and son, and see if there was any possibility of connecting with them today.

The appointment with Kathleen confirmed, he called Anne's office.

"Sorry, she's on the other line," Peggy said. "Do you want to wait?"

He was surprised at how relieved he was that he could leave a message and avoid talking to Anne. He hung up to see Will headed over, bearing two oversized glazed doughnuts on napkins, stacked one on top of the other in his left hand. He had a mug of coffee in the right.

"Thought you could use one of these," Will said, putting down his offering in front of Bern.

As a rule, Bern never ate in the morning, but since he'd missed dinner, he thought Will was right. He ought to eat. He was also feeling a little ashamed at snapping at Will.

"Thanks," Bern said. "About earlier—you know how I am in the morning."

"Yeah, no problem," Will said and went back to his desk to munch on his doughnut as he wrote reports.

Bern hoped Anne was going to be as understanding.

ANNE WAS ON THE PHONE WITH THE PEDIATRICIAN OF ONE of her little patients when Peggy arrived. She stopped at

Anne's open door to give her a wave before she went on to her desk in the reception area.

For the past five years, Anne had shared the office suite with two other psychologists, Cynthia Lynde and Andrew Braemer. The three made a practice of getting together first thing on Monday mornings to discuss any problems, an informal ritual that was usually just a half hour of coffee and friendly conversation.

Now, as soon as she finished her phone call, Anne went out to ask Peggy to see if Cynthia and Andy could give her a few minutes as soon as they came in, preferably together.

This break with the normal routine brought a concerned response from Peggy. "What's wrong?" Peggy had just hung up the phone and was finishing a message slip.

"Nothing to worry about," Anne said, "but I'd like to explain to all of you at once. How does the schedule look?"

"Should work if they get in on time."

Peggy took off her reading glasses, let them hang on a chain around her neck, and studied Anne with a worried look on her square, no-nonsense face. Peggy had a college-age daughter of her own. Still, she not only ran the office with maximum efficiency, but mothered the three of them as well.

"If only we could clone her," Andy had said once. "Give her to all our patients."

"Yeah, but then what would we do for a living?" Cynthia had countered.

Peggy wore her brown hair short with straight bangs cut just above her eyebrows. Her clothes never varied: straight skirts, frilly white blouses without jewelry, and sling-back low-heeled pumps. Her only concession to season was to change from long sleeves in winter to short in summer.

"Any of those messages for me?" Anne asked. There were several of the pink slips in front of Peggy.

"A few."

One message was a patient's mother canceling Anne's only morning appointment. A second was from Bern giving Anne the time for the meeting with Kathleen Graley. No need to call back unless there was a problem. The third was from Joyce Levy at the abuse clinic, who would like to speak to Anne as soon as possible.

Anne went into her office to return Joyce's call, sighing as she dialed the number. No doubt Joyce had another emergency, another child who desperately needed help.

Just say no, Anne told herself as the phone began to ring.

Joyce picked up right away, sounding distracted. "Oh, Anne, hi. Hang on for a second, will you?"

Anne could hear Joyce speaking to somebody, the words muffled, probably by a hand over the mouthpiece, but she caught a name: Christina.

"Let me know as soon as you hear," Joyce said, clearly not to Anne. Then, "Sorry—the police. I was just finishing with them."

"What's happened?" Anne asked. "I heard you mention Chrissie. Is she all right?"

"I wish I knew," Joyce said. "You remember the foster mother, Rena Trent? Rena says she looked in on Chrissie when she first got up this morning to get her own kids off to school, and the child was sleeping. That was around six-thirty. She'd been up and down all night, so Rena decided to let her stay in bed as long as she wanted."

Oh, Lord, Anne thought, already anticipating the worst as Joyce went on to say that when Rena peeked in again at eight o'clock to check on Chrissie, the little girl was gone.

nine

Joyce went on to describe how Rena Trent had frantically checked the house and the yard, then driven around the neighborhood. There had been no sign of Christina, so Rena had called the police, Child Protective Services, and then Joyce.

Since it was only ten minutes before nine, Anne thought Rena had accomplished a remarkable amount in such a short time.

"Rena wanted me to tell you," Joyce said. "I know you didn't spend much time with Chrissie yesterday, but if you can think of anything that could help, we'd like to know."

Anne remembered the little girl's body pressed against her, the feel of her hair.

"All I can tell you is that Chrissie's only focus right now is her mother," Anne said. "I'd say that she's trying to find her."

"Assuming the child left on her own," Joyce said.

"Yes, assuming that. Is there any reason to think she didn't?"

"No, although in this day and age the police aren't rul-ing out anything. The child couldn't even tell us her last name. I don't see how she'd find some homeless camp miles away, but I'll pass it along anyway.''

"I wish there were something else I could do," Anne said. But short of getting in her car and joining the search, she didn't know what that could be. "Will you keep me posted?"

Joyce promised she would.

Just as Anne replaced the phone in the cradle, she heard Cynthia and Andy come into the reception area, arriving together. A few seconds later Cynthia knocked lightly on the open door.

Andy was right behind her, and Anne was struck by the contrast: slender, blond, live-wire Cynthia against huge, bearded, bearlike Andy.

"Hey, partner," Cynthia said. "What's up? You look upset."

"What? Oh, a little girl I saw at the clinic yesterday. She's missing from her foster home. But that's not what I want to talk to you about. Come on in."

Peggy followed the two of them into the office. Anne came over to sit on one end of the small sofa, leaving the rest for Andy. Cynthia and Peggy took the wing-backed chairs.

"I've taken on an unusual case," Anne told them.

She explained what it was about, that even though it was a homicide case she certainly didn't expect any of the dangerous complications that had arisen the last time she worked with the police.

The look on Peggy's face said she wasn't buying Anne's reassurances, but voices in the outer area announced the beginning of patient arrivals, so she left without comment.

"Probably mine," Andy said, adding before he lumbered off. "Listen, Anne, I know this sounds like it shouldn't be risky, but you be careful anyway."

Andy was by nature sweet and gentle, but through his family therapy practice he was well acquainted with how quickly and senselessly violence could erupt.

Cynthia stood up, too, but hesitated, something clearly on her mind.

"What?" Anne said. "You're worried, too?"

"About your safety?" Cynthia asked. "Yes, but I don't think any of our concerns are going to affect your decision to do this. Not that they should. I guess what I'm wondering is if you're really ready to take on this kind of case. I'm not going to pry," she said quickly, holding up both hands. "I never have. If you wanted to share the details, I figured you would've told me by now. I just know that until recently you've had a very hard time dealing with abuse cases."

Cynthia was right, of course. There were reasons Anne had resisted involvement in cases of child abuse, resisted to the point of structuring her practice to minimize her chances of becoming drawn into one.

"I'm trying to change that," Anne said, knowing she sounded defensive. "That's why I'm volunteering at the abuse clinic."

"I know," Cynthia said. "I hope you didn't think I was criticizing you. I just meant it's tough for any of us, on the best of days, and for you—if it's a problem—oh, go ahead and tell me to mind my own business. I've got no right to butt in."

"Friends always have a right to express their concern," Anne said and, saying it, realized that although she often bemoaned the fact that she had little time for a social life, her interaction with Cynthia and Andy was much more than a business relationship. "Thanks for caring."

"Hey, it's what I do," Cynthia said with a grin, "and, speaking of which, I better go do it. Just don't forget I'm here if you need me."

"I won't," Anne promised.

Alone, hurrying through the rest of her paperwork so she could go meet Bern and Kathleen, she wondered if Cynthia had a point. Was she really up to facing all the grim realities she might encounter when she started digging into little Rachel Graley's life?

Stop it, she told herself firmly.

Self-doubt creeps in insidiously—a trickle of fear here, one or two avoidance tactics there—and pretty soon you find it has shaped your life. She knew this only too well.

In college she had had a part-time job in an after-school program in Phoenix for latchkey kids, one of them shy ten-year-old Nicki Craig. Anne worked with her all summer, confident of the wonderful rapport she had with the child. Six months later she was to learn how little she knew about Nicki. When the girl slashed her wrists with her father's straight-edged razor, the ugly truth came out. Not only had her father been abusing her for years, he had begun passing her around to his friends. Anne had never once suspected any of it.

She had been so badly shaken that, if it hadn't been for Rosemary, she might have dropped out of school. Even with Rosemary's help, she had not dealt with the problem completely. Guilt is like an infection. You get treatment, and it appears to clear up. Only time and escalating symptoms make you realize the poisons are still there, deep inside, generating a devastating lack of confidence and undermining self-esteem.

Well, she had come to accept that facing her guilt and dealing with it was a painful, ongoing process. Given that reality, there were bound to be times when she would doubt her capabilities and second-guess her decisions.

As Rosemary liked to say, "So you're a human with human reactions and failings. What's wrong with that? If you ask me, most therapists could stand a reminder once in a while that they are not God."

Outside, brilliant sunshine was taking the chill off the brisk early-morning air, but the beautiful day was wasted on Anne. In her car, driving downtown to police headquarters, her thoughts kept circling back to Christina.

Knowing she was grasping at straws, she called Joyce back on her cellular phone.

"This is a long shot," Anne said, "but what if Chrissie's mother came back to their campsite and discovered Chrissie was gone?"

"You mean maybe *she* took the child from the Trent house?" Joyce asked, making the intuitive leap.

"Is it possible?"

"Anything's possible, I suppose. But she didn't go to the police—"

"Too scared, maybe," Anne put in.

"All right. Assume that's an accurate guess. Also assume she figures Christina would end up in protective custody. How does she get to the foster family? CPS would notify the police if she showed up asking for information, and I doubt they would have just handed her the Trents' name and address."

"I'm sure you're right," Anne said. "The idea's pretty remote."

"Yes, it is," Joyce said. "Still, I think I'll run it by the police and CPS anyway."

"And you'll let me know if you hear anything?"

Joyce promised she would.

After she ended the call, Anne told herself she must stop worrying about Chrissie and focus on Rachel. Of course, it was understandable that her feelings were much more immediate for the live little girl she had held in her arms and comforted. But if she was going to complete the job she had agreed to do, it was time to make some decisions about how to proceed and whom she should interview.

Rachel's grandmother was the obvious choice to head the list. She should also speak to the neighbors here although they might not know the Graleys well, the family having been in Arizona for only a short time. Neighbors and friends back in California ought to be a better source of information. Anne would have a better idea about that after she talked to Kathleen.

Of course, the housekeeper who died with Rachel—
Rufina?—would have seen the latest interactions between
the child and her father. Had she passed those observations
on to family or friends?

Through Anne's thoughts and planning ran a single,
dreadful question: Was there any secret in the Graley
household so ugly that it required the terrible power of fire
to obliterate it?

She parked the car near the corner of Sixth and Washington with Andy Braemer's warning to be careful echoing
in her head.

Even the big, square Police and Public Safety Building
looked gracious and inviting in the splendid sunlight.
Scrubby olive trees growing in the cement planter on the
side of the building played host to dozens of twittering
birds. An old bag lady sat on the low planter wall, one
hand on a shopping cart piled with her possessions, the
other holding an opened red umbrella as though she didn't
trust the perfect weather. Another half-dozen homeless
people were sitting slumped against the wall or lying on
top of it. Two men sat on the sidewalk and played check-
ers.

For years the city had authorized police sweeps to chase
these people from the area. Today, there seemed to be a
truce. Several uniformed officers stood outside the front
entrance, taking a break in the fresh air, trying to unob-
trusively enjoy a smoke. One of them walked over to observe the checker game and kibitz.

As Anne locked her car and crossed the street, she found
herself scanning the faces of the homeless. There was little
chance that Chrissie's mother could be here, outside police
headquarters, even less that Anne would recognize her;
still, Anne looked. But there was only one other woman
in the group besides the old lady with the umbrella, this
person so gaunt, gray, and hopeless it was impossible to
estimate her age. And she looked so withdrawn, Anne

could not imagine her as the woman who lovingly braided her little girl's hair.

Anne went inside to check in at the front desk. Upstairs, in the squad room of the homicide department, Kathleen was already on hand, sitting with Bern.

Today she wore olive-green cotton pants, a beige jacket over a black T-shirt, and black leather flats. Her knapsack purse hung on the back of the chair. Tendrils of red-blond hair escaped an elasticized circlet of black fabric to curl around her face where freckles stood out like a scattering of tiny gold coins against the pale skin. Whatever sleep the pills had provided, it had not been enough to erase the shadows that looked like old bruises beneath her eyes.

As for Bern, his fatigue was plainly visible, too. He looked distant and reserved; when he said, ''Anne, hello,'' he might as well have been welcoming a stranger.

''Mrs. Graley just arrived,'' he went on. ''Shall we find a place to talk?''

Anne agreed and said hello to Kathleen, matching her even tone to Bern's, all the time trying desperately to decide if this was just Bern the cop being his cold, detached self or if something precious between them really had been slowly slipping away.

ten

ANNE TRIED TO CORRAL HER STAMPEDING THOUGHTS AS Bern held open the door to a small interrogation room. Time enough for personal problems later, and she was grateful to be able to put off thinking about them.

The dingy, windowless room was empty except for a metal table and four thinly padded chairs, and it smelled of stale cigarette smoke. Bern offered Kathleen coffee, which she gratefully accepted.

"Sugar?" he asked. "Cream?"

"Just black."

"Anne?"

She shook her head.

"I'll be right back," he said and left the room.

Kathleen sank down in one of the chairs; Anne sat beside her.

"How are you doing?" Anne asked. "Did you get any rest?"

"Some," Kathleen said.

"How about breakfast?"

"Toast and orange juice." She gave Anne a small, rare smile. "Because I knew you'd ask."

"Well, I'm glad my nagging paid off."

Bern came back in bearing a mug of steaming coffee,

the rich fragrant odor a bonus, covering the stink of old misery that lingered in the room. He put the coffee in front of Kathleen and took a chair across from them.

"About last night," Kathleen said. "I didn't mean to make a scene. No, that's not true. I wanted to make a damn *big* scene. The thought that somebody deliberately set that fire—that maybe *Randy* set it—Sharon came by this morning, woke me up."

"What did she want?" Anne asked.

"To tell you the truth I was so groggy I really don't remember."

"Kathleen, I know you told Anne that your husband kidnapped Rachel—"

"I bet he denied it."

"Let's say he had his own version of the story. Right now I want to hear yours. Pretend I don't know anything." The coolness in Bern's voice was replaced with kindness. But Anne had seen him question witnesses before and knew how skillful he was. And make no mistake, this was an interrogation, albeit a friendly one.

He added, "I'd like to record this. It helps keep my records straight. Okay?"

Kathleen nodded. Bern set up the recorder and started the tape, then established who was present and got Kathleen's official consent.

Kathleen hadn't touched her coffee. Now she sipped it as the tape turned, set down the mug, said, "This is so hard." She turned to Anne. "I don't know where to start."

"Anywhere is fine," Anne said.

"I guess I have to go back to the beginning, when I met Randy."

As Kathleen began to speak, Anne remembered what she had said the night before about chaos theory. Kathleen's own stupid, life-transforming act happened seven years ago when she had just turned eighteen, a freshman at Kansas State back in Wichita where she lived at home with her family.

It had been a week before spring break, although Kathleen said you'd never have known by the weather, which was cold and miserable; a fine mist of rain was turning to sleet as she drove home with a girlfriend, who suddenly said, "I'm so goddamn sick of this weather. Know what, Kath? Let's do something crazy. Find some sunshine. Boys. Parties."

"I'd never done one impulsive thing in my life," Kathleen told Anne and Bern. "I knew I'd have a big fight with my folks, that I might lose my part-time job, but I didn't even hesitate."

A coin toss had decided their destination: Palm Springs over Fort Lauderdale. Two other girls joined in, sharing expenses, and the four drove straight through to California. Kathleen met Randy Graley an hour after checking in at the hotel, practically jumping into his arms in the hotel's overcrowded swimming pool.

She paused to drink some coffee. Anne and Bern just sat quietly and listened.

"He wasn't exactly a hunk," Kathleen went on, "but he had a killer smile and this way of focusing on you that made you feel like the only person in the world."

She didn't find out until later that Randy wasn't a student, that he'd dropped out two years before but still liked to come to Palm Springs during spring break to troll for college chicks.

Kathleen said, "He reeled me in quick enough. *Now* I think I might have fallen for just anybody. That's a terrible thought, isn't it? For a long time I wouldn't allow myself to face the fact that what I called love was just plain old lust."

For an overprotected girl whose only sexual encounters had been quick and guilt-laden, the experience was a heady, hormonal rush that swept aside all rational thought.

"Randy begged me to stay, and I almost did," Kathleen said. "When I got home, he called me twice a day. We talked for hours. He'd describe exactly what he'd be doing to me if we were together. These days people get paid for that kind of phone sex." Her lips twisted in a bitter parody of a smile. "I think if I'd stayed in California with him, the whole thing would've burned out. Being apart, well, it was like I had a romantic movie soundtrack always playing in my head. My friends were as caught up in it as I was. When he proposed, I swear it was as though I was saying yes for every starry-eyed woman in Wichita."

Her family had their own template of how life was supposed to happen; a whirlwind romance was not a part of the plan. Randy's mother didn't approve, either. At that point Kathleen hadn't met Sharon Graley, but from things Randy told her, she suspected Sharon would disapprove of anybody her son wanted to marry.

"So I withdrew the money I'd saved for college and met Randy in Las Vegas," Kathleen said. "We got married in one of those tacky wedding chapels—canned music and strangers. I think I got pregnant with Rachel that night."

Randy had told her that he and his mother had their own real estate business. Kathleen was soon to learn this was a very loose description. Pressed for specifics, both Randy and Sharon turned vague. Kathleen only knew that their "deals" provided a wildly unstable existence: luxury condos in Newport Beach and leased Beemers one day; cheesy apartments in Garden Grove and used Hyundais the next.

"I'd lived my entire life in the same house with my folks in Wichita. Now I was a gypsy. I can't tell you how much I hated it."

Worse, their independence didn't last long. Randy had lived with his mother before the wedding; six months afterward, a "down cycle"—one of Randy's euphemisms that Kathleen grew to despise—forced them to move in with Sharon. And neither reason, threat, nor outright begging could persuade him to change that arrangement.

"At first Sharon acted as though I was just a lapse in

judgment by Randy that she was forced to tolerate. I got the feeling she was sure she could whip me into line. When she couldn't, she went out of her way to make my life as miserable as possible. Randy didn't see that, of course. He never saw anything bad about his mother." Kathleen shook her head ruefully. "Money and mothers-in-law—God, it's all so mundane, such ordinary stuff."

"Most family problems are," Anne said, noting that Bern was asking no questions, just letting Kathleen run with it.

"For a long time I kept thinking there had to be something I could do to fix the situation," Kathleen went on. "I tried—God, it makes me sick now to think of how I tried, how I—*abased* myself trying. Then one day I looked in the mirror and saw a woman with a cranky baby on her hip who looked miserably unhappy and ten years older than she really was."

It was a terrible moment. She had had to do something, but her options were limited. She considered leaving, taking Rachel back to Wichita, but couldn't bring herself to go back and admit her grand romantic gesture was such an awful mistake. And since her parents firmly believed in lying in the bed you made for yourself, she knew they wouldn't welcome her home.

A job? Her meager experience included working as a retail clerk and flipping hamburgers. She'd never find employment that paid enough to keep her and Rachel. And forget child support. Knowing Randy, he would squirm out of that obligation.

She decided the only way out was to finish her education. To accomplish this in a reasonable amount of time meant she had to stay in the marriage and pretend commitment, all the while planning her escape.

"It wasn't honest of me," Kathleen said, "but I didn't care. I was drowning, and that was the only lifeline I could find."

Randy might not have put up much of a fuss when she

announced her intention to go back to school, but Sharon made no bones about her feelings. All that trying to please had turned Kathleen into their house slave, and Sharon wasn't at all happy with the prospect of doing her own laundry, cooking, and cleaning—not to mention the fact that she and Randy might have to take some responsibility for Rachel. They both adored the baby—when she was clean, fed, and quiet. As far as changing diapers and feeding the kid, well, that was Kathleen's job.

"But you managed," Anne said.

Kathleen nodded. "Part-time jobs and day care on campus for Rachel. Worked my butt off to get my bachelor of science, but I found out damn quick you can't get a decent job in my field without an advanced degree. When I was offered a fellowship at UCLA, I had to take it. Rachel was already in school. I didn't want to move her—that's why I tried to commute—a hundred miles round-trip in the worst traffic you can imagine. When I realized I couldn't take the driving, I was ready to make the break, take Rachel and go, get by somehow.

"I didn't come right out and tell Randy I was leaving him." That bitter smile again. "No guts. Maybe he knew. Anyway, he was upset, very hurt, suddenly willing to hire somebody to be there after school, promised he'd take care of Rachel. I thought he was finally acting like a parent, shocked into it by the prospect of losing his daughter. Now, when I think what the real reason might be. . . ."

She paused to stare into the coffee that Anne was sure must be cold now.

Bern asked, "Was there anything specific that made you suspect your husband might be molesting your daughter?"

"At the time? I never even *dreamed* of such a thing."

"Any physical signs?" Bern persisted. "Bruises? Infections?"

"*No.* My God, I would never have allowed him *near* Rachel if I thought something like that was going on. It was just the way she acted at Christmas when I left for school. That was the first flag. I already told Anne."

"Tell me," Bern said. "For the record."

She related the heart-wrenching scene with Rachel and told him about the nagging worry that the scene had planted in her mind. "School wasn't even in session yet, but I needed to put in some time on my research project. It seemed so important, more important than listening to Rachel. . . ."

She trailed off as tears began to run from the corners of her eyes. She dashed them away with the backs of her hands, whispering, "Dammit."

Anne handed her tissue and said, "That's all right. You're doing fine."

Kathleen made a visible effort for control as she dabbed at her cheeks. "That next week I called every day, sometimes several times a day, because I wanted to reassure her."

But Kathleen spoke to her daughter only twice. She was always told that Rachel was asleep or outside playing. It really began to bother her, and she told Sharon so.

"We argued over the phone," Kathleen said, wadding up the damp tissue and leaving it in a little white ball on the table. "Well, *I* argued. I yelled at her. She never argues, she just—denigrates. If anybody can make you feel like pond scum, it's Sharon."

By then, Kathleen had made up her mind. She was going down on Saturday, and if Rachel was still upset, Kathleen intended to take her away. But when she called on Friday, the Graleys' phone had been disconnected.

"I tried to tell myself it was the same old routine, that Randy would call me later that night, or the next morning for sure. But all the time I had this terrible feeling. . . ."

She looked very pale, and the bleakness in her eyes suddenly reminded Anne of little Christina when her foster mother had carried her out of the abuse clinic.

Dear God, Anne thought. *How do any of us stand such loss?*

"Do you want to stop?" Anne asked. "Take a break? We'll get you some fresh coffee—"

But Kathleen was shaking her head. "No, I want to get it over with."

"Your husband didn't call to tell you where he'd gone." Bern made it more of a statement than a question.

"No. I hoped maybe they just hadn't paid the phone bill, so I drove down to Costa Mesa—that's where he and Sharon were living with Rachel—but they were gone. I looked; I called anybody I could think of. Finally I went to the police—for all the good it did."

"They took a report?" Bern asked.

"Oh, yes, but I could tell it was just routine. And the way they looked at me when they heard I was going off and leaving her—well, it was like I was the one at fault and she was damned lucky her dad took her away."

"Did you tell them you suspected Rachel might be abused?"

"No, because I didn't suspect it then. It was only afterward, all that time remembering what she said when I left her, the desperation on that little face, and wondering why. I didn't believe it when I first thought of an answer; I'm not even sure I believe it now. What's killing me is the not knowing and thinking about her—*seeing* her in that fire—hearing her calling for me, and I wasn't there, I wasn't there."

She crossed her arms, hunching forward and hugging herself tightly as though she were physically holding herself together, that she might fly into pieces if she let go.

"Bern," Anne said urgently.

Bern stopped the tape. He leaned across the table and looked directly into Kathleen's pain-filled eyes. "Kathleen, listen to me. I know what you're going through. I do. Not firsthand, but I see people all the time, suffering like you are. I see so many of them that, hard as I try to be objective, I think maybe I share a little of their pain. So I hurt for them and I'm angry for them and I try damn hard to find them some justice. Not because it will make them stop hurting, but because it's all I can do.''

He reached out and laid his hand against her cheek. Seeing his tenderness, Anne felt her breath catch in her throat. She always suspected what lay beneath that armor of detachment, but this was the first time she'd ever heard him articulate it.

''I can't make any of this go away,'' Bern said, removing his hand from Kathleen's cheek, speaking only to her. ''But I promise you I'll do my best to find out what happened to Rachel, and I'll personally see to it that the son of a bitch who killed her gets what's coming to him.''

Kathleen reached out blindly and clasped his hand in both of hers, like a drowning person reaching for a lifeline. Watching the two of them, Anne felt an uneasy stirring of something close to jealousy.

And she knew in some strange way that at that moment Bern's connection to this woman was deeper and stronger than it had ever been to her.

eleven

ANNE'S CHEST ACHED. SHE REALIZED SHE'D BEEN HOLD-
ing her breath, and let it out in a chuffing sound that was
loud enough so that Bern glanced at her. She hoped he
couldn't read her face; God only knew the jumble of emotions he might see there.

But if Bern was aware of Anne's reaction, he didn't
show it. His attention was still on Kathleen.

"Can you go on?" he asked.

She nodded.

"Okay." He withdrew his hand from hers and turned
the tape back on. "Sharon told me they carried insurance
on their belongings, but none on Rachel. Is that true?"

"Yes. I have a small policy on Rachel," she volun-
teered. "I got it through school. Whatever's left after the—
the funeral, I'll use to pay Anne's fee."

"I'm curious about Randy and Sharon's business,"
Bern said. "Can you tell me more about that?"

She shook her head. "Not really. Like I said before,
they were always so vague about everything, like it was
on a need-to-know basis and I was the last one who was
going to be told. I blamed Sharon for being possessive of
Randy, but now I don't know. I mean, they were just making real estate deals, so why was it a big secret?"

Maybe because they were doing something illegal, Anne thought. She knew Bern must be thinking this, too.

If he did, he kept it to himself, saying instead, "What companies did they work for?"

"They never worked for other people. Sharon had her license. And from the little I picked up, it wasn't like she and Randy were just selling houses, I mean like you usually think real estate agents do. Sometimes I'd hear them talking about rental and investment property, limited partnerships."

"Did they have a company name?"

"Names," Kathleen corrected. "Sunshine Properties, Westco, Pacific—something. They all kind of run together. Is it important?"

"Could be. Think about it. See what you come up with. Were there ever any lawsuits? Disgruntled customers?"

"Not that I remember."

"Well, if anything comes to mind, write it down. Also all the places you lived. Friends, neighbors—especially those you socialized with. I know this could turn into a long list, but Anne's going to need those names, too."

"The list of friends might be shorter than you think," Kathleen said. "We never lived in one place for very long. Anyway, people in Southern California are friendly enough, but it's all on the surface, you know? There's always a wall—around their yards, around *them*. Well, *most* of them."

Anne didn't say anything, although having grown up in San Diego she knew Kathleen's observations were very generalized. There were good people everywhere. Unfortunately, Kathleen just hadn't encountered many on the West Coast.

"Try to give us as complete a list as you can," Bern said.

"Should I do it right now?"

"Why don't you go back to your motel," Bern said. "Give it some thought. In the meantime, Anne and I need to discuss a few things. But you have to do something for me, Kathleen. Stay away from Randy. And Sharon. Let me handle them. Okay?''

She nodded reluctantly, stood up as Bern switched off the recorder, and turned to Anne. "Will you call and let me know what happens next?"

"I will," Anne promised. "And you have my card. If I'm not in the office, my secretary or the service can page me."

"You can call me, too, anytime," Bern said. He got up and opened the door for her.

She paused there, looking up at him, and said a soft, "Thank you," before she went out.

As soon as Anne and Bern were alone, he seemed to sag as though invisible weights were dragging at his shoulders. He looked downright gaunt, as thin as he had been when he got out of the hospital. Her worries for him came back in a rush.

"Bern, I'm glad you set aside some time, because we need to talk."

"Yeah, we do," he said. "But not here. How about an early lunch?"

She wasn't the least bit hungry, but she knew he never ate breakfast, and she had her doubts that he'd eaten any dinner the night before.

"Sure," she said. "Good idea."

Anne offered to drive, and he seemed glad to let her. During the short ride to a nearby coffee shop, he put on his sunglasses, leaned back against the headrest, and gave her a brief accounting of his meeting with Sharon Graley the night before, after she left.

"She's every bit as warm and wonderful as Kathleen said," he observed wryly as Anne parked the car outside the restaurant.

She couldn't help thinking that he'd timed his story perfectly so there was no chance of getting into any of their own personal problems. She was trying to decide what to say, how to ask him all the difficult questions, as they entered the restaurant and went through the routine of getting a table and ordering: a small salad for her, soup for Bern.

When the waitress brought coffee and finally left them alone for a minute, they just sat there, silence building between them, until Bern finally spoke.

"Are you still mad?"

"Mad?" She was astonished at how far off the mark he was.

"About the dog. I know I promised Duke would be my responsibility, and I've been neglecting him the past few days. I've been really busy, but that's no excuse, and I promise you—"

"Bern," Anne burst out. "Forget the damn dog. It's you I'm worried about. You're not sleeping or eating—*just soup?* No wonder you're losing weight."

"But it's split pea, babe." He flashed her a grin. "I'll have extra crackers." Then he sobered, seeing the look on her face. "Ah, Annie, you really are worried."

"Of course I am. You've got to have a checkup, Bern. If you won't make an appointment—"

"I already did. Four o'clock. *Today.*"

Relief flooded in. She'd experienced so many emotions in the past hour that she felt the way she had when she was little, riding the roller coaster down at Mission Beach with her dad.

"Well—good," she said, at a loss for words because she'd been prepared for a fight.

As if on cue, the waitress arrived with the food. Anne really didn't want the salad, but she ate it, hoping to set a good example. Bern's soup bowl was oversized, and he made a show of eating with gusto—for her benefit, she was sure. All that worrying—a stupid waste of time. Bern was worn out, run-down, and now he was acknowledging that. The way he had been acting had nothing to do with their relationship.

While they ate, Bern filled her in on what was happening in the rest of the case. The housekeeper who had died in the fire with Rachel had a husband, Stuart, and a son, Darrel. Bern hadn't been able to reach either of them yet.

"Will and I are going to talk to the arson investigator at two."

He paused as the waitress stopped to clear some of the dishes, and Anne got the distinct feeling that the other shoe was about to drop.

"Anne, you know I didn't like the idea of your being involved in this case."

"Bern, please," she said. "Don't start."

"Let me finish. Knowing you, you're going to do what you want whether I like it or not. So," he said as he gave her a wry smile, "I give up."

She eyed him warily. "You expect me to believe that."

"I can prove it by offering you your old job back. I ran it by Jane this morning, and she agrees. We'd like you to consult on the case."

"I'm already consulting on the case. I have a client."

"You really don't think Kathleen will object, do you?" he asked. "You saw yourself she's eager to cooperate with us."

With you, Anne thought, remembering that special connection between Bern and Kathleen.

"Think of the advantage to her from this arrangement," Bern urged. "You'll have access to everything we know. And if we help defray your expenses, Kathleen can keep some of the insurance money for school."

"I get the feeling she's pretty broke," Anne agreed.

"Well, then . . ." Bern picked up his coffee cup and regarded her over the rim. "Is it a deal? I could really use your help, babe."

"I think you're right. You really do need my help, but this is still a crock," Anne said tartly. "You want to keep an eye on me, don't you?"

"Okay," Bern said. "I admit it. Is that so bad?"

"No, but you could be up front about it, Bern. You could tell me how you feel. When we stop talking, that's when small things turn into big problems."

Now she wasn't referring to their conflict over the case. She thought he knew it, too. She might have said more, but just then her pager went off.

She recognized the number on the display—the abuse clinic. Taking out her cell phone, she said, "I need to return this call."

Bern nodded, waved to the waitress, and gestured to his cup for a refill as she punched in the clinic's number and asked for Joyce.

"The police found Chrissie," Joyce said immediately. "I knew you'd want to know."

"Thank goodness," Anne said. "Is she all right?"

"Tired," Joyce said. "And hungry. That's one determined little girl. She'd walked a good five miles. Rena put her down for a nap, but she told me that Chrissie was asking for you, Anne. Is there any chance you could see her later today?"

"Well—" Anne considered. "I suppose I can if Rena will bring her to my office. Tell her to call Peggy and figure out a time."

After they said goodbye and Anne ended the call, Bern said, "Everything okay?"

"For now." She told him about Christina's plight.

"Poor little kid. I could find out who's looking for the mother. Maybe nudge them a little."

"Would you?" Anne hated to add another task to Bern's already overloaded work schedule, but she had to ask for Chrissie's sake.

"Of course. The guy she mentioned, the wino—"

"Harlan," Anne supplied.

"Frank's already going to be checking out street people for another case. I'll ask him to keep an eye open." Bern glanced at his watch. "What time do you have to be back?"

"My first appointment's at two-thirty."

"Looks like we both have a couple of free hours. I was thinking about taking a ride out to Stuart Vaughn's place. See if he's there and just not answering the phone. Do you want to come along?"

Anne hesitated, weighing her options. Going with Bern, officially part of the investigation, could cut both ways. Some people would be instantly leery; she might never get them to open up about Rachel.

On the other hand, she'd already been entangled in one murder investigation, and she wasn't sure she wanted to be off snooping around on her own, at least not here. Neighbors and acquaintances back in California were one thing; people who might be considered suspects were quite another.

"Okay," she said. "Let's go."

Bern wanted to retrieve his car from the parking lot across the street from the station, but Anne said, "Don't be silly. We can't spare the time."

She was hoping he would rest, maybe even take a nap, but he was on his cellular phone as soon as they got into the car, checking in with Will.

As they headed west on I-10, South Mountain loomed off to the left, crowned with a bristle of TV antennas. She was reminded as always of that neighborhood of small, grim houses over near the base of the mountain, and one house in particular where she had sat on hot, bare earth one terrible night and tried to talk a madwoman out of shooting Bern in the head.

If Bern was remembering it, too, he did not let on—except she noticed he never looked at her or past her, toward the south. He was filling Will in on the interview with Kathleen and speculating just as Anne had about what kind of business dealings Randy and Sharon must have been into—assuming the worst, of course. That pessimism was one of the things she liked least about Bern's personality, but in this case she thought he might be right.

He had recalled the general area where the Vaughns lived. Now, he asked Will for specifics, jotting down details in a small notebook.

After he completed the call, he paged through Anne's Thomas guide. While he located their destination, he mulled over the necessity of a trip to the L.A. area.

"I'm sure you're going to want to talk to people over there," he said. "How about I tag along?"

"You're assuming you won't make a quick arrest?"

"I guess I am. Maybe we'll get lucky, but somehow I doubt it. We could fly over this weekend."

"You don't have to watch over me every minute, Bern. I can't imagine I'd be in any danger just talking to a few of the Graleys' neighbors."

"You can't know that. All these years of police work have taught me to be cautious—"

"And a little paranoid."

"That, too."

"You'd have to find a kennel for Duke," she reminded him.

"I'll ask the vet," he said in that tone that told her she might as well stop wasting her breath.

They were way out on the fringes of town now, an area as remote as Cave Creek but with a very different look. Plowed cotton fields had given way to stretches of scrubby creosote bush and grama grass dotted with paloverde—mostly flat and desolate with a few saguaros raising their arms skyward. Low barren mountains made jagged silhouettes off to the southwest.

They passed Perryville State Prison on the right. A sign warned: *Do not pick up hitchhikers.* On the left was an abandoned stadium, derelict ever since Anne could remember, meant for horse races, huge crowds, money.

Bern directed her to take the next exit, Jackrabbit Trail, and turn south. Buckeye was off in the distance. The road followed the contours of the land, dipping into arroyos where a damp sandy residue reminded them that the channels had been cut by water.

Here and there a narrow, rutted drive wandered off to a mean-looking dwelling: trailers mostly, interspersed with a few small cinder-block houses and sagging wood shacks.

"Slow down," Bern said. "I think we turn up there."

He rolled down the window, looked at names on mailboxes, and finally said, "Wait—I think that was it."

Anne stopped. There was nobody on the road, so she backed up about a hundred feet, then turned in and bumped her way up the dirt track toward a shiny trailer. An old Airstream, all rounded aluminum, it sat in a circle of rough, hummocky earth, fronted by a porch of corrugated sheet metal set atop wooden posts.

All around this porch was a dense growth of huge castor bean plants and enormous sunflowers. Frost had browned the sunflowers and left dry plate-sized blossoms to droop unharvested on the stalks; however, the castor beans looked untouched, the big leaves still a dark, evil green.

From where Anne braked to a stop about twenty feet away, this unruly crop turned the porch into a dark cave of shadow. The shade must have been precious in the scorching summer, but Anne wasn't so sure how nice it was today. Out of the winter sun, it could be downright chilly.

An old dark-blue Bronco was parked next to the trailer. Anne said, "Looks like somebody's home," shut off the ignition, and reached for the door handle.

Bern was getting out, too. When she thought about it later, she was sure she hadn't noticed anything peculiar in the way he was acting. This was understandable because as she came around the front of the car to join him, she was still sizing up the place. Beyond the utility vehicle she could see one end of a propane tank, some kind of storage shed, and a brightly flowered sheet flapping on a wire clothesline strung between two more wooden posts.

It was then that she glanced back at Bern and saw that

he was out of the car, but he was standing behind the door, staring at the porch, pale as a ghost.

"Bern? What is it?"

Her puzzlement rapidly turned to alarm as he stood, mute and unresponsive.

"Bern?"

She hurried around, intending to grab him, shake him, look at his ashen face up close to determine what was wrong. Perhaps her movement across his field of view got his attention.

He said, "What?" His voice had a thick, displaced tone.

"Are you okay? What's the matter?"

"Nothing—just—nothing."

Moving slowly, still staring at the trailer, he got out from behind the door and shut it while Anne's worry and speculation came tumbling back. With her attention fixed on Bern, she only got a peripheral glimpse of movement on the shadowy porch.

But she heard the sounds, shockingly loud in the bright stillness. The unmistakable slide and the distinct thump of a shotgun being cocked.

twelve

A GREAT MANY THINGS WENT THROUGH BERN'S HEAD IN the time it took for the slide action of the shotgun to chamber a round. Chief among these was the thought that Florence Mosk must be laughing down in hell. Although she'd botched up the job of killing him, she was still messing with his head, giving somebody else the chance to finish what she had started.

The porch looked very little like the one in front of Florence's house, but something about it had triggered the memory, whole and fresh, a vivid snare that caught and held Bern while he should have been assessing the situation, searching the shadows for movement, and getting the intuitive warning cops usually receive.

What had he said to Anne about police work teaching you to be cautious, even paranoid? He had been neither, and that slipup had left them horribly exposed.

Shaky and sick but charged now with adrenaline, he grabbed Anne, thrusting her behind him. Not an ideal move—a shotgun blast could easily pass through his body and into hers—but all he could do.

"Hold it right there."

The bellow from the dark porch overlapped Bern's own shout.

"Stuart Vaughn? Detective Bern Pagett, Phoenix police."

"My ass," the man yelled back. "Since when do the Phoenix cops ride around in Camaros? Now, get those hands where I can see 'em."

Bern had options, moves he could make, none of them a possibility with Anne there. So he complied, holding his arms out, saying, "Okay, no problem. Just take it easy."

The man stepped from under the shadow of the porch cover, through an opening in the overgrown foliage. Past sixty, Bern guessed, but still lanky and fit and perfectly capable of using the ugly but efficient gun in his hands. A worn blue flannel shirt was tucked into faded jeans, the jeans tucked into run-over boots. Exposure to the fierce Arizona sun had turned his skin to leather and left vertical cracks in his cheeks, giving his neck the look of being layered with red scar tissue.

He walked toward them, halving the distance, close enough so Bern could see a violent gleam in the light-colored eyes. The left one wandered around in the socket; however, the other was locked on them as solidly as the gun was.

Bern heard a car out on the asphalt highway, something with a noisy engine, the sound reminding him how little traffic there was and how there was not a chance in hell of attracting any attention.

"You, lady," Stuart said. "Step away from your friend there so I can see you."

"No, don't—" Bern began in a fierce whisper to Anne, but she was already doing what Vaughn said, moving away from the nominal shelter of Bern's body.

"Mr. Vaughn." Anne's voice was clear and calm. "I'm Anne Menlo. Detective Pagett and I really are from the Phoenix police. You're right about the car. It's not an official vehicle. It's mine. We're here to talk to you about your wife."

Bern often wore his badge clipped to his belt, easily

displayed, but now it was in his inside coat pocket.

"I can show you some ID," Bern said. "Just let me—"

"No, sir," Stuart said, jabbing the shotgun barrel forward for emphasis. "I don't care who you say you are. You ain't gonna show me nothin' 'less I say so."

"Mr. Vaughn," Bern said sternly, "this has gone far enough. Put that piece down right now, and I'll consider this all a misunderstanding. If you don't, you're going to be in a whole lot of trouble."

The noisy engine was getting louder. Not a car. From the corner of his eye Bern saw it was a pickup that had turned off the road and was bouncing toward them on the narrow dirt driveway, a white Nissan streaked with reddish dust.

Anne, seeing it, too, whispered, "Somebody's coming."

Bern's hope that the approaching pickup would distract Stuart Vaughn was quickly dashed as Stuart took another step toward them, the shotgun leveled, finger on the trigger, his attention not wavering.

"Stay where you are," he ordered as the pickup braked to a stop next to the Bronco, and called, "Darrel," as the driver got out.

Darrel Vaughn had inherited his father's build but not much else. Under a Cardinals baseball cap, he had longish black hair and a complexion that was several shades darker than his dad's even after the sun had worked on Stuart's skin. Bern hadn't given Rufina Vaughn's ethnic background much thought, but now he realized she must have been Mexican, and, looking at her son, that there was probably a good percentage of Indian in the mix—Apache, maybe, judging by the cheekbones.

A black tank top displayed the ropy muscles in his shoulders and arms and the tattoo of a rattlesnake winding around his left biceps. A jailhouse tattoo?

Old cami pants were further mottled with streaks of paint, and Bern saw commercial-sized paint cans in the back of the truck along with a couple of aluminum ladders.

"Yo, Pop," Darrel said, coming over to join his father, an insolent grin licking at his mouth. "Whatcha got here?"

As the younger man got closer, Bern could see he'd also inherited his father's pale eyes. They shone with a merry, wolfish glint, although they seemed to track well enough, moving quickly over Bern, narrowing and lingering on Anne. The rattlesnake tattooed on his arm was definitely not crude jailhouse work.

"These two claim they're cops," Stuart Vaughn said. "Say they're here about your mama."

"I'm a homicide detective with the Phoenix police," Bern said to Darrel. "I'm investigating your mother's death."

Darrel gave Bern his full attention, and his amusement vanished as the import of Bern's words sunk in.

"Put down the gun, Dad," he said.

"What?" Stuart sputtered. "He can *say* anything he wants. That don't mean—"

"Put down the fucking gun," Darrel snapped and stepped directly in front of him.

Stuart had no choice unless he wanted to shoot his own son in the stomach. As he slowly lowered the shotgun, Anne expelled a shaky sigh of relief. Bern's instinct was to rush over, grab the older man, cuff him, and call the Maricopa County sheriff.

But the son turned back to Bern to make a plea. "Sorry. The old man spends too much time out here by himself. With my mother dying and all—well, Officer, I sure wish you'd cut him some slack."

Bern could have Stuart arrested, but would the charges stick? In Arizona it wasn't against the law to have a gun or for a man to defend his property. Hell, until recently it hadn't even been illegal for kids to take guns to school. Bern could just hear some attorney making the case that there were lots of weirdos wandering around, and here was this poor man, half out of his mind with grief—how was he to know some guy in civilian clothes arriving in a civilian vehicle was really the police?

"All right," Bern said. "But I want the gun. He can have it back when I leave."

"Just give me a minute."

Stuart kept shaking his head as Darrel talked to him. Bern couldn't hear what the younger man was saying, but he'd bet Darrel was spelling out things in no uncertain terms to his father.

"Are you okay?" Bern asked Anne quietly.

"Fine," she whispered back. "I've seen Darrel Vaughn before, Bern. When I met Kathleen yesterday at the burned house, he was there talking to somebody. A neighbor, I think."

"Interesting," Bern said. And something he would definitely keep in mind when he took an official statement from Darrel.

After several minutes of listening to his son's argument, Stuart finally gave up the shotgun. Darrel unloaded it and brought the gun to Bern while Stuart stood where he was, scowling grimly.

"Sorry about all this," Darrel said.

He handed over the weapon. It felt heavy in Bern's hands; the stock was polished with use, and it smelled faintly of cleaning oil.

"Listen," Darrel said. "Why don't we all go inside. I'll make us some coffee."

"I don't want strangers in my house," Stuart said belligerently.

"Jesus, Dad—okay, we can sit on the porch."

The last thing Bern wanted to do was sit in that shadowy cave. He might have steeled himself to do it, but this confrontation had used up the time. The next time he faced Stuart Vaughn, he'd just as soon it was in an official interrogation room.

"Thanks for the invitation," Bern said, "but I think

we'll have to continue this downtown. I came out here in the first place because I couldn't reach you on the phone."

"He probably unplugged it," Darrel said. "He does that. And I was at work. You sure we can't just talk right now? You said you're from homicide, but my mom died in a fire, so this is just some kind of routine stuff, right?"

"Not exactly. Somebody deliberately set the fire. That makes it murder."

Stuart made a strange, choking sound.

Darrel, looking visibly shaken by the news, said, "Oh, man—are you sure?"

"I'm sure."

"But how? What happened?"

"I can't tell you that right now."

"It's just—it's crazy. Who'd do a thing like that? Mama—that little girl. I was there, you know, earlier. My mom asked me to get her some things for lunch. She never liked what they had in the house. I was in a hurry 'cause I was going down to Nogales. If I'd stuck around, if I hadn't been in such a damned rush—"

He broke off, looking grief-stricken.

"It's natural to blame ourselves in a situation like this," Anne said. "That doesn't mean that what happened was your fault."

"It does make it very important that we talk to you," Bern said. "Your dad, too. How about tomorrow morning? Ten o'clock."

"I'm supposed to work. Could we make it later today?"

Bern considered. The only way he could work in the interview was to cancel out with the clinic.

As though reading his mind, Anne said quietly, "Don't forget your appointment."

"How about this evening?" Bern asked Darrel. "Say eight-thirty?"

"We'll be there."

"Good." Bern handed back the shotgun and gave him a card. "See you then."

In Anne's car, driving back to the station, something about that last part of the scene kept bothering Bern, and then he knew what it was. Stuart Vaughn had been vocal and animated enough until he heard that the fire had been deliberately set. After that, he had stood stone-still, his face gone ashen under his dark tan, staring at them like a man whose worst nightmare had just come true.

thirteen

ANNE TURNED IN TO HER OFFICE COMPLEX PARKING LOT with ten minutes to spare before her first afternoon appointment. Although she had downplayed her reaction to Bern, to be honest she was still a little shaky as she got out of her car and locked the door, almost an hour after they had stood helpless in front of Stuart Vaughn's shotgun.

During the drive back to police headquarters, she had fended off Bern's renewed objections to her involvement, telling him firmly that she intended to remain on the case, either as a part of the official police team or as a private consultant. Feeling guilty for once again putting her at risk, he didn't like it, but he'd backed off and agreed reluctantly to let her sit in later when he questioned the Vaughns.

Now, hurrying into her office, she knew it was time to rechannel her energies. She had other priorities, patients who needed her undivided attention.

Her two-thirty appointment had not arrived yet. In the reception area, a harried young woman waited with an infant on her lap. A preschool boy sat at her feet, sullenly shredding a magazine—Cynthia's patient, Anne assumed.

Next to them sat Sharon Graley, elegant with her silver hair and a tailored navy suit.

Anne noted that she left as much space between herself and the mother as possible and that she bore a look of thinly disguised distaste. She stood up as Anne stopped at the reception desk.

"Mrs. Graley," Peggy murmured. "But I'd guess her first name isn't Kathleen. Right?"

"Yes," Anne said, repressing a sigh. "It's Kathleen's mother-in-law. Did she call for an appointment?"

"Yes. I told her you were pretty well booked, but since she just said she was Mrs. Graley and I was thinking she was Kathleen, I told her if she came over, you could probably fit her in. Sorry if that's a problem."

"No, it's fine," Anne began as Sharon approached, saying, "Dr. Menlo? I'm sure you remember me."

"Yes, Mrs. Graley, of course. I'm afraid I only have a few minutes before my first patient—"

"I don't plan to take much of your time," Sharon said, pleasant enough although her eyes were devoid of any warmth.

"All right." Anne gestured toward her office. "Go on in." Anne lingered at the reception desk long enough to ask Peggy if Rena Trent had called.

"Twice," Peggy said. "I had figured out a slot for her to bring in the little girl—Christina?—but Mrs. Trent just called back to say she's got car problems. She'd like to come tomorrow morning."

"Okay. Buzz me when my two-thirty arrives."

Anne went into her office and closed the door behind her. Sharon stood with a hand on the back of one of the wing-backed chairs, looking around.

"Very—" She searched for an word to describe the homey furniture and the toy-filled play area and settled on: "Appropriate."

"Thank you," Anne said dryly. "Sit down, won't you?"

Sharon came around to take the chair. Anne sat across from her on the sofa.

Sharon's skirt stopped well short of her knees, revealing legs that even a young woman might envy. Beneath the navy jacket she wore a white silk tank top. There were thin silver hoops in her ears, plus a single diamond earring in an extra piercing on her left lobe.

"Last night I distinctly got the impression you were with the police department, Dr. Menlo," Sharon said.

"I'm consulting for them."

"So Kathleen said. This morning I went by that miserable place she's staying at to try and talk some sense into her. I know it's an awful time for her—for all of us—but I just can't imagine she really believes Randy had something to do with the fire."

She propped an elbow on the arm of the chair and rested a cheek against her hand. Her nails were perfectly shaped—ceramics, Anne guessed—and polished with a clear, glossy shine.

"Frankly," Sharon went on, "I think Kathleen's on something. She looked all drugged out, and she made even less sense than she did at the hotel."

Anne recalled Kathleen reporting Sharon's visit to her and Bern. "She's barely slept, Mrs. Graley. I urged her to take a prescription sleeping pill last night."

"I see. Good. If she gets some sleep, maybe she'll be more reasonable. At any rate, she said you were a psychologist and that you were helping her. I was surprised, of course, but glad to hear it because naturally I assumed you were counseling her about handling her grief. Then I discovered you were a *child* psychologist."

To discover that, Sharon must have been checking up on her, Anne decided.

"So I confess I'm at a loss," Sharon said. "What exactly are you doing for my son's wife?"

Anne could easily have claimed client privilege and politely refused to say anything at all. But Sharon and Randy were going to find out sooner or later why Kathleen had hired her. When they did, one could assume they would not be happy—or cooperative—people. If Anne expected to glean any information from them, she would have to do it quickly.

So she said, "Of course, Kathleen's distraught over Rachel's death, but she's particularly upset because she wasn't with her those last few weeks before she died. She's asked me to help fill in the gaps."

Sharon shook her head, puzzled. "I don't understand. Fill in with what?"

"Whether Rachel was happy. If she understood that Kathleen's absence was only temporary, that her mother hadn't abandoned her."

Anne thought these were important things for Kathleen to know, but of course they were only minor points compared to the answers to the ugly questions Kathleen really needed answered.

"Well, I'm sure you're good at your job," Sharon said, although her tone suggested otherwise, "but why on earth didn't she just come and talk to us about it?"

"That seems self-evident, Mrs. Graley, all things considered."

"You mean this silly business that we kidnapped Rachel? I still don't understand why she jumped to such a bizarre conclusion. She knows we move a lot."

"Why is that?" Anne asked. "I can't stand moving myself."

Sharon shrugged. "I guess Randy and I don't have the same attachment to places as some people. Anyway, most of the time our moves are just business. We buy a property at a really good price, hang on to it for a few months, and sell it at a profit. We just feel it's better to live in the place, rather than pay rent."

"Is that what you did here in Phoenix?"

"No, that was different. We'd been thinking about relocating for a while. Real estate isn't what it used to be in Orange County since the county went bankrupt.''

"How did Rachel take the move?'' Anne asked. ''Was she upset?''

"Oh, no. Just a little—'' Once again she consulted her own private thesaurus and came up with: ''Unsettled. Of course she missed her mother. Kathleen spoiled her rotten.''

"How did Rachel get along with Mrs. Vaughn?''

"Who? Oh, *Rufina*. Fine, I guess. Why shouldn't she?'' If there was a trace of defensiveness in her tone, she covered it up immediately by declaring, ''Believe me, Rachel was basically a happy, well-adjusted child, Dr. Menlo.''

The stock description and the veiled look in the woman's eyes told Anne she was wasting her time. Rachel may very well have been experiencing a normal childhood. But if she wasn't, Anne was not going to hear about it from Rachel's grandmother.

For one thing, people usually saw what they wanted to see. Often they were hanging on by their fingernails, furious at circumstances that were going to loosen that precarious grip, furious at the child for being the cause of impending catastrophe. Some people were simply in denial. In either case, they could look you straight in the eye and refuse to admit, refuse to *believe*, what must have been impossible to overlook.

Or sometimes, Anne reminded herself grimly, what they told you was an out-and-out lie because they themselves were the abusers.

The phone rang on Anne's desk. She excused herself and went to answer it.

"Your two-thirty's here,'' Peggy said.

"I'll be right out.''

When Anne hung up, Sharon got to her feet, saying, ''That must be your patient.''

"Yes, it is,'' Anne said, adding with no hope that Sharon would take her up on the offer: ''I know you've been through a terrible ordeal, Mrs. Graley. If you ever need to talk some more, I'd be happy to listen.''

"Oh, I doubt that will be necessary. But thanks for your time, Dr. Menlo. When you speak to Detective Pagett, I hope you'll pass along what I've told you."

"I certainly will," Anne promised.

She met Sharon at the door and held it open. Sharon hesitated in the doorway, looking down at Anne, and for a moment that polished facade slipped just enough so Anne glimpsed the tortured and devastated woman hidden there.

"Whatever Kathleen's told you," Sharon said, "whatever comes out of all this, I really did love my granddaughter, Dr. Menlo."

Then she walked away quickly toward the front door, leaving Anne to wonder if she'd misjudged Sharon Graley after all.

STEVE GAINEY WAS ALREADY AT THE BURNED HOUSE ON Carolton when Bern arrived. Steve was a tall, muscular man, Bern could easily imagine him running up a ladder with a heavy coil of water hose over his shoulder. Steve had done just that, having begun in the ranks of the fire department as a foot soldier in the fight of what he called "the red demon." He continued the battle now, using his brain instead of his brawn, and was uncanny at reading an arson scene.

Since he would be going on to the clinic from here, Bern had driven his own vehicle. Will pulled in behind him just as Bern got out of the Jeep.

The odor assailed Bern as soon as he opened the door, something harsh—metallic and chemical—mixed with the underlying smell of old wood ashes. He joined Will to duck under the yellow protective tape surrounding the house. Cinders crunched under his feet as the two of them walked through the rubble.

Steve wore jeans and a faded blue rugby shirt, his clothes already soiled by his work. Unruly brown hair curled around prominent ears. A strong chin dominated his tanned face. He was wearing latex gloves, so he gave them an absent nod instead of a handshake and said without preamble, "Come and look at something."

They were standing in what was left of the kitchen, what would have been a small room with a table and chairs taking up a portion of the floor space. There was still an impression in the charred debris of Rufina Vaughn's body—or rather what had remained of it—the spot marked with yellow tape.

"Back here."

Steve stepped over the threshold to a small utility room. Bern recognized a dented water heater tank and a rectangular metal box he thought must have been the furnace. Steve gestured to the box.

"Plenum chamber," Steve explained, confirming Bern's guess. "Used to be gas heat, but they went to an air pump a couple of years ago. Water heater was still natural gas."

He went down on his heels next to the ruptured tank. "Stop me if I tell you stuff you already know."

"Run with it," Bern said.

"Okay. To start with, we know it was a low-order explosion because there was a pushing effect instead of shattering. That causes a twisting and tearing—everything scattered erratically, the roof falling in."

He pointed to the blackened copper tubing that was still attached. "There was a crack here." He tapped the fitting where the line went into the heater. "So, it happens. Enough gas leaks out, you get a spark, and—boom! At least that was our original theory. But somehow it just didn't look right. Anyway, I started thinking, and—" He began to unscrew the copper tubing from a check valve located about eighteen inches in back of the fitting. "What if somebody wanted it to *look* like a natural gas explosion, but didn't want to depend on it? This person wants a good hot fire when and where he wants it. So he cracks loose the fitting to fool us, then blocks the line back here at the check valve—''

He held out the tubing for their scrutiny. Bern could see a heavy deposit of black soot inside, along with a few shards of burned wood.

''He figures nobody'll check,'' Steve went on. ''Or if they do, the wood plug will've burned. He was damn near right, too.''

''Okay,'' Will said, ''so what did he use for the explosive?''

''Exactly the question.'' Steve carefully screwed the check valve back in place, got up, and went back into what had been the kitchen area. ''There were some sliding glass doors here out to the patio.'' He stepped over what had been the sill to a concrete slab covered in debris and gestured. ''Barbecue grill.''

The grill lay upended with its legs twisted, but the round metal bowl was intact. A closer look told Bern the unit was not meant to burn charcoal.

''Propane,'' Bern said. ''Where's the tank?''

Steve grinned and led them to it, just outside the house, lodged under some bricks. ''Now, of course, if the grill was right up against the doors, maybe the explosion could've ripped apart the connection. Then again, maybe somebody took the tank off and left it in the kitchen.''

''Is the tank empty?'' Will asked.

''Yep. And Mr. Swale says he put in a new one just before the Graleys moved in.''

''How'd our bomber set off his device?'' Bern asked.

''Nothing fancy,'' Steve said. ''Over here.''

Back in the kitchen he pointed to the boxy hulk of a refrigerator. The appliance lay on its side. Steve indicated the top. ''See this?''

Looking closer, Bern saw a waxy smear. ''A candle?''

Steve nodded. ''Picture it this way. He puts the propane tank down low, the candle up high on the fridge. Cracks open the tank. Gas fills the room like water. When it reaches the candle flame, the place blows up."

"Thought he was being real cute," Will said. "Just didn't know who he was messing with."

"Yeah, well—" Steve shrugged off the compliment with a smile, then quickly sobered. "Something else I wanted to show you."

He led them back to a corner of the house where Rachel Graley's body had been found: the child's bedroom, where she had probably been taking a nap.

"I found enough of the door to know it was closed," Steve said.

Had she been awakened by the fearful roars of the red demon? Had she huddled on her bed, terrified? Or had she gotten up and opened the door to the beast?

Steve picked up a couple of shards of wood with some hardware still attached, and Bern saw that the little girl could not have let the fire in or tried to escape. What Steve held in his hands were pieces of a door and a jamb that bore a six-inch barrel bolt of heavy steel, the bolt still in the strike and locked down.

There was no doubt in Bern's mind that Rachel had been locked in her room when the door and the casing burned.

fourteen

BERN LEFT WILL WITH STEVE TO GATHER THE EVIDENCE and drove to the clinic for his checkup. He was not looking forward to the medical exam but was more than happy to depart the crime scene. And he was glad he was lead on this one and didn't have to deal with the physical collection.

As he drove through early rush-hour traffic, he was haunted by the thought of Rachel trapped in her room. He knew it was more likely the explosion had shattered the door, but the image in his mind was of her beating on it and crying for somebody to let her out.

Even if she had not been locked inside, even if there had not been an explosion, chances were good that if she had left the room she would have run out into an inferno. Still, he couldn't keep from speculating about the sliding lock. Was it installed before the Graleys arrived, or had they put it in?

After he finished at the house on Carolton, Will would track down the Graleys and tell them to come in tomorrow for a second interview.

Bern couldn't wait to ask Randy about the bolt; he only thought he would have to be careful when he popped the question, have Will around to make sure he didn't smash in Randy's boyishly good-looking face. Come to think of it, from Will's sickened look when he saw the lock, he just might want to beat on Randy, too.

Inching along in the traffic, Bern put the time to good use and kept the promise he'd made at lunchtime to Anne. He called and tracked down the person who was trying to find the mother of the abandoned child, Christina.

The investigator was Doug Brickel. The name dimly rang a bell, although Bern couldn't put a face to the voice. Brickel didn't even remember enough about the case to talk about it without digging out the file. Bern wasn't sure whether his request would move the case any higher on Brickel's priority list, but at least he had asked.

And the call had served another purpose. It kept him from dwelling on his health concerns for at least ten minutes. As soon as he hung up, the dread settled back in, and he found himself remembering what had been his father's most often repeated advice: *Stay out of jails and hospitals.* Well, Bern had managed to avoid the first, but he hadn't been doing so well on the second.

At the clinic, after a nurse had weighed him and taken his blood pressure, he was left to cool his heels and worry some more until Dr. Carrey arrived.

"You've lost eight pounds," Carrey noted from the chart. "Lean and mean is good; skinny's something else again."

Bern felt a flash of annoyance; Carrey could've stood to lose some of the flab he was carrying around. Not much older than Bern, the doctor was acquiring jowls and a bay window as rapidly as he was losing his hair.

"So what's the problem?" Carrey asked.

"Working too much, I guess," Bern said. "I've missed a few meals, that's all."

"Uh-huh." He studied Bern over the tops of half glasses with the cynicism of somebody long accustomed to patients who censor their stories.

"The main thing," Bern said, "the reason I'm here, is that I'm having problems sleeping."

"You can't fall asleep? Or you fall asleep and then wake up?"

"Both."

"How's the chest? Any pain?"

Bern shook his head.

"Headaches? Dizziness?"

Bern shook his head again.

"Well, take off your shirt," Carrey said. "Let's have a listen."

He began a routine tapping and probing, with that unreadable look on his face that always made Bern babble.

"Since I can't sleep, I wake up exhausted," he said, "and then I feel lousy all day. Go around biting people's heads off—"

"Deep breath," Carrey commanded, cutting off Bern's outpouring.

He might have said something at that point about the nightmares, but he couldn't talk while the doctor was listening to his lungs.

Then Carrey was finished with the exam, making a few notes while he said, "Well, everything seems okay. You change your schedule? Working a different shift?"

"No," Bern said, slipping his shirt on.

"Up your intake of alcohol, maybe?"

"No," Bern said emphatically.

"How about caffeine?"

Bern stopped in the middle of buttoning his shirt and stared at the doctor, stunned by the simplicity of the explanation. How many cups of coffee had he drunk today, most of it Frank Trusey's high-test kind?

"Caffeine," Bern said. "Oh, yeah, now that you mention it. Being so tired, well, I keep drinking the stuff to stay awake."

"That could do it," Carrey said. "Vicious cycle." He tapped his pen on the chart, staring at it meditatively.

"I'm going to give you a couple of sleeping pills. Sometimes that helps to break the routine. Meantime, cut back on the coffee. Don't go cold turkey; believe me, you don't want that. Just restrict your intake, especially after three o'clock. But if you don't see any improvement in a week or so, I want you back here, understand?"

Bern promised he would follow instructions.

Out in the parking lot, walking to the Jeep, he felt light-headed with relief. Talk about overreacting. Just showed how fatigue could mess with your mind.

Right on cue, his dad's voice popped into his head. *Damned witch doctors. What do they know?*

This one time, however, Bern refused to remember how often his father's opinion had been right.

ANNE HURRIED HOME AFTER HER LAST PATIENT TO LET the dog out, then rummaged in the freezer, determined to have a decent meal ready when Bern arrived. Leftover spaghetti sauce, made the week before, defrosted in the microwave while she broke up romaine and sliced a green pepper for a salad. Duke retreated under the table to watch her make garlic toast, uncork some Chianti, and start a pot of water simmering. She knew the preparation was busy work. Too bad she couldn't distract her mind so easily.

Preoccupied with things at the office, she'd shelved her worries about Bern. Now she tried to sidetrack them again by focusing on that visit from Sharon Graley.

The woman had been sending out feelers, that much was obvious. She was also putting her own spin on Kathleen's story. One thing was for certain: Beneath that cool, polished exterior Sharon was running scared. The question was: What was she afraid of?

Duke began his low, rumbling growl. He came out from under the table to stand at the gate with his ears pricked forward. Within seconds Anne heard the Jeep coming up the driveway.

Duke kept on growling as Bern came in the house, although Anne could have sworn she saw one tentative wag of his tail.

"Hey, babe," Bern said. "Something smells good."

He stepped over the expandable gate and reached down to pet the dog, but Duke backed away, his lips peeling back over his teeth. Bern cheerfully ignored the rebuff, came to put his arms around Anne, and kissed the top of her head. He looked so happy and at ease, Anne immediately suspected he'd skipped the clinic appointment and was now all set to jolly her out of being upset.

She pulled away and looked up at him, prepared to really give him what for, but he said, "Annie, before you get pissed, I went to the doctor."

"And?"

"And," he said, "I'm fine."

She remembered the look on his face out there today at Stuart Vaughn's, the way he had stood, paralyzed and unresponsive. "Dr. Carrey said you're okay?"

Bern nodded. "Good as gold. Right as rain." He sniffed the spaghetti sauce, took a green pepper strip from the salad bowl. "Or I will be if I lay off the caffeine."

He popped the pepper strip in his mouth and crunched it.

"Caffeine?" she said, her disbelief mingling with rising hope. Could it really be something so simple?

"Yep. I'm supposed to cut back on coffee, eat once in a while, and walk old Duke here twice a day. Well," he said with a grin, "I threw in that last part. It'll have to be a short one tonight, because of the interview with the Vaughns. Should I take him now? Or do you need some help here?"

"No, go," Anne said. "But be back in twenty minutes."

After he left with the dog, Anne set the table, put on the noodles, and tossed the salad. She felt as though an enormous weight had been lifted from her shoulders. As for Bern, from what she saw he wasn't just happy, he was euphoric, the way you might be if you suspected you needed surgery for stomach cancer and the doctor prescribed an antacid instead. Until this moment, Anne hadn't realized just how worried Bern must have been.

She still found it hard to believe his behavior was caused by too much coffee, but she also realized her training had taught her to be skeptical, to question easy answers. Then again, hadn't she also been taught that we all tend to complicate things? Maybe she had simply jumped to conclusions. For now she would accept the possibility. Beyond that all she could do was wait and see.

ANNE DECREED THAT THEY WERE NOT GOING TO DISCUSS business over dinner, either hers, his, or theirs. So Bern waited until they were in the Jeep driving downtown to tell her about the findings at the Graleys' house.

Hearing about the lock on Rachel's door, Anne felt sick, especially when she thought about telling Kathleen.

"How can parents do something like that?" Bern asked, a rhetorical question since he knew as well as Anne did that parents were capable of a lot of much worse things.

"I wonder if that's what's bothering Sharon," Anne said, then told Bern about Sharon's visit, concluding, "Although I don't know why she'd feel guilty about the lock since she wasn't home when the fire started. *Assuming* she wasn't home."

"Remember that's just an assumption," Bern said grimly. "But say she's not responsible for the fire. Still, she might know that the housekeeper locked Rachel up. Hell, maybe Grandma said it was okay."

"Do you think the Vaughns can tell us about that?"

"Yeah," Bern said. "That and maybe a whole lot more."

fifteen

AT EIGHT-THIRTY P.M. THE SQUAD ROOM FOR THE HOMI-
cide detail was practically empty. Anne knew there were
usually detectives on night duty—covering all crimes, not
just homicide—but she saw only two and didn't recognize
either of them.

One was tapping out a report on a computer with two
fingers and didn't look up. The other was on the telephone.
When he saw Bern, he clamped his hand over the mouthpiece and said, "Your two guys are back there. You gonna
need some help?"

"No," Bern said. "Just keep an eye open. I'll talk to
them separately, and I don't want the one who's waiting
to decide to take a hike."

The detective nodded his understanding and returned to
his phone conversation.

Bern went to his desk to take out an Advil bottle, saying, "Headache," as he shook out some pills.

"Withdrawal," Anne told him.

"Jesus," Bern groaned. "Glad I'm not kicking heroin."

He detoured to the water cooler to take the pills, then
led the way to one of the interrogation rooms and knocked
twice before he opened the door. Both the Vaughns were

there, Darrel pacing around, his father sitting, hunched over a foam cup filled with coffee.

Stuart acknowledged their presence with a quick glance, then went back to staring into the cup that he held with hands that had a faint line of black grease under the nails.

Darrel gave them a quick, anxious smile. "Detective Pagett, ma'am. Thanks again for letting us come in tonight. You know how it is, missing work."

"Sure," Bern said, standing in the doorway. "Listen, Darrel, we're going to leave your dad here to finish his coffee while we go talk in another room."

"Oh. Couldn't we just do it all at once? I mean, with the both of us—"

"No," Bern said. "We couldn't."

He waited politely for Darrel to go through the door before he said to Stuart, "Just wait here, Mr. Vaughn. I'll get back to you in a while."

Darrel had changed from his paint-stained work clothes to jeans, a white T-shirt under a purple Suns warm-up jacket, and high-topped combat boots. His black hair was combed straight back, shiny and sleek, held in place with mousse or gel. He shrugged the jacket off as soon as he sat down at the table in the interrogation room, letting it drape back across his chair.

As Anne took a seat next to Bern on the other side of the table, she got a closer view of Darrel's rattlesnake tattoo. The diamondback pattern was so realistically done, a quick glance might give you the impression that a real serpent was curled around his upper arm, the tail sporting a half-dozen rattles and coming around Darrel's elbow, the head out of sight up under the sleeve of his T-shirt.

Noticing her interest, Darrel said, "My hobby," and put his elbow on the table to present his arm for a better look.

"Tattoos?" Anne asked.

"Snakes," he said with a sly gleam in his peculiar light-blue eyes.

"Everybody to his own tastes," Bern said with a grimace, then launched into the preliminaries required to tape the interview.

Darrel acknowledged that he knew he was being recorded, stated that his name was Darrel Stuart Vaughn, and gave his address as the trailer out near Buckeye. He said he was a contract house painter, that he worked mostly for developers at a variety of locations.

Bern also established that Darrel's mother was Rufina Vaughn, who had been employed as a housekeeper by Randy and Sharon Graley and was one of the victims of the fire.

"You told me earlier that you were at the Graleys' house the day of the fire."

"That's right," Darrel said. "I was."

"Had you ever been there before?"

"Oh, sure. My mom and me—we were close. Sometimes Dad took her to work or picked her up, but mostly I did. Once in a while I'd drop by to see how she was doing, if she needed something."

"What were you doing there yesterday?" Bern asked, a harder note in his voice.

"What? Oh—" Darrel looked at Anne. "I thought I'd seen you before. You were at the house with another woman." He looked away, focusing on a point between them, somewhere in the middle distance. "I don't know. I was down in Mexico when—when it happened. My dad couldn't get in touch with me right away. After I got back, well, I just had to go there and see the place."

Anne could understand his reaction. Sudden, unexpected death is hard to process. Those who are left behind often want to see for themselves where their loved ones died, to know the most gruesome details. There could be no comfort in the knowing, but somehow it helped them accept the unacceptable.

"Let's go back to the day of the fire," Bern said. "Why did you go that day?"

"Like I told you yesterday, I stopped by to check on

my mom. She wanted me to get her something for lunch. You wouldn't believe how little food they had in that house. I mean, considering there was a kid around. And Mama said the stuff they had was tasteless. So I went out and brought her back a couple of burritos from Taco Bell.''

"What time did you leave?"

"Pretty close to two. I was going down to Nogales to visit some friends. I was running late. I didn't even really say goodbye. . . .'' He ducked his head and stared down at the imitation wood grain of the table. A muscle worked in his jaw.

"Did your mother mention seeing anything unusual going on in the neighborhood?'' Bern asked. "Strange people? Cars?''

Darrel shook his head.

"Were the Graleys having trouble with anybody? Did they warn your mom about answering the phone or the door?''

"Not that Mama told me.'' He leaned forward, appealing to Anne. "I keep going over and over it. The people who did this, they musta figured the house was empty, don't you think?''

"It's possible,'' Anne said.

But she'd didn't think it probable. Rachel had been in her bedroom in the back of the house, perhaps asleep. But Rufina Vaughn had been in the kitchen when she died— right where the explosion had taken place.

"What did your mother tell you about the Graleys?'' Bern asked.

"Not much. She only worked for them for about a month.''

"How did she get the job?''

"I think the Swales recommended her. That's the old couple who own the house. Mama used to clean for them every other week.''

"Tell me about your mother," Bern said. "Has she had any run-ins with anybody?"

"Mama?" Darrel said, incredulous. "God, no. You don't think this fire had anything to do with my mom? Man, that's crazy."

"How about you, Darrel? Anybody got it in for you bad enough to kill one of your family?"

"*Me?*" His shock sounded real enough. "*Jesus.* No way."

"Your father?"

"Oh, *man,*" Darrel said, shaking his head, "you are totally on the wrong track."

"How about your mother's friends?" Anne asked. "There may have been things in her life she couldn't tell you about."

Anger flashed in his eyes. "My mama worked long hard days cleaning up other people's shit and taking care of their nasty little brats. Then she'd go home and take care of me and my dad. So she didn't have time for a whole lot of social life. She had friends, but they weren't Anglo and they weren't here."

"She spent a lot of time in Mexico?" Bern asked.

"As much as she could. When Dad took his Social Security early, she wanted to move back. They could've lived real well down there. She could've retired, too. But Dad wouldn't go. He hates the place. Hates Mexicans." There was bitterness in his voice. "I never have figured out how he and Mama got together."

Lord, Anne thought. *What an awful way for a little boy to grow up.*

Anne agreed entirely with William Wordsworth when he wrote: *The child is father of the man.* So she wondered about the forces that had shaped Darrel Vaughn, but mostly she wondered about something he had just said.

She asked, "Darrel, did your mother describe Rachel Graley as a brat?"

He hesitated, weighing his words, then said, "Well, I

hate to say mean things with the kid dead and all, but yeah. She was all the time following Mama around, whining. Her dad and her grandma—they never told Mama that she'd have to baby-sit when she took the job. Mrs. Graley just started going like, oh, we'll be out for an hour. Or two. Or all day. They weren't even going to pay Mama extra until she raised a stink.

"Don't get the wrong idea," he added quickly. "It isn't—I mean, it wasn't that Mama didn't like kids. She was always going, Darrel, you don't hurry up, I'm never gonna have no *nietos*. I know Mama was real nice to that little girl. But she was just getting older, and it was too much, all that work."

"You were around Rachel, too," Anne said. "What was your impression?"

"I didn't see that much of her," Darrel said. "She kind of hid out when I came. Guess she didn't like strangers."

Bern shot Anne a glance, and she knew what he was thinking: *Or maybe Mama locked Rachel up.*

Anne had to agree. For the older woman, tired and resentful, it may have been a great temptation to simply put an unruly child in her room and bolt the door, especially when Rufina wanted an uninterrupted visit with her son.

"Did your mom ever tell you how she thought Rachel was being treated by her father and grandmother?" Anne asked.

Darrel immediately grew wary. "What do you mean?"

"Was Rufina there every day?"

"Yeah."

"Then she saw a lot of Rachel. Children say things. Sometimes their clothes need changing. I'm wondering what Rachel said—or what your mother observed."

He shrugged. "Nothing much. I mean, when Mama got home, work was the last thing she wanted to talk about, you know?"

"How about the lock on the outside of Rachel's door?" Bern asked, his voice growing raspy. "She mention that?"

"Oh." Clearly the lock was no surprise to Darrel. "Yeah, I do remember Mama talking about that. It bothered her, but the grandma said they had to put the lock on because the kid walked in her sleep."

"How did your mother get along with the Graleys?" Bern definitely sounded hoarse, and he had slumped a little in his seat. "Did she like them? Did they treat her well?"

"I guess so."

"Do you know them?"

"No, never met 'em."

Bern's earlier euphoria had leaked away, like air from a balloon. He looked tired again, deflated. He rubbed his temple and paused, as though he was trying to decide on his next question.

Darrel was studying Bern, too. He said, "Listen, it's getting late, so if that's all, maybe we could wrap this up and—"

"How much insurance did your mother have?" Bern asked abruptly.

"Insurance?"

"How big a policy, and who was the carrier?"

Darrel recoiled as though he'd been slapped. "Jesus, how can you think—? She didn't have any insurance. Wait, I take it back. I think my dad's getting something from Social Security to bury her—if you people ever give her back to us. I don't know how much. Some whopping big amount." He stood up, his face stormy with anger. "That's it. I come in here on my own. I drag my old man in. I answer your dumb questions. But if this's where you're going—accusing me of something so—so *sick*— I'm not saying another word, and—"

"Sit down, Darrel," Bern said.

"—and neither is my dad, not without a lawyer."

"*Sit,*" Bern thundered.

Darrel might have thought he detected some weakness in Bern a minute before. If so, there was none now. Bern was all granite authority, and Darrel did what he was told.

"Get something straight," Bern said. "There are questions I may not like to ask, but I have to ask them anyway. And I haven't charged you with anything. So far, we're just having a simple conversation. If a lawyer comes in, it'll get messy. I guarantee it. But—your choice. You want to call one, we have pay phones just for that purpose. Need a quarter?"

Darrel hesitated, then shook his head. "I didn't mean to lose it, but you gotta understand. It's painful, man, hearing stuff like that."

"Yeah," Bern said wearily. "I'm sure it is. Okay, that'll do for now. You wait here, and we'll go talk to your father."

"Listen," Darrel said. "Detective? My dad can be a little—weird. You two saw how he was this afternoon."

"Oh, yeah, we did," Bern said.

"He's been a lot worse since Mama died. Almost like he's going senile or something. So if he starts saying things, acting peculiar. . . ."

"We'll keep it in mind," Bern said.

Outside, in between interrogation rooms, Anne said, "You don't really think Darrel had anything to do with the fire, do you?"

"I don't know, babe. You're the shrink. What do you think?"

"He seems to be trying very hard to be open and honest."

"Yeah. Maybe too hard."

Anne sighed. "I guess there's only one thing I feel strongly about. I really believe Darrel loved his mother."

"You're probably right," Bern said. "But then everybody who burns, stabs, shoots, drowns, or suffocates their old lady says the same thing. They all loved her dearly."

A powerful smell of cigarette smoke greeted them as they entered the second interrogation room. Stuart Vaughn still sat where they'd left him. As a matter of fact, the only thing that suggested he had moved was his foam cup, now empty of coffee and filled with butts, with a crumpled pack of Camels lying next to it.

Anne thought he barely looked like the same man who had glared at them over a barrel of a shotgun earlier today. He seemed shrunken, diminished, almost fragile. He wore the same blue flannel shirt and jeans, but they hung loosely on his body as though he'd lost weight in these few hours.

"Mr. Vaughn," Bern said as he dropped into a chair across from the older man.

Bern sounded gruff and clipped, but Anne thought this had to be from fatigue. Stuart's bluff and bravado were long gone. There was no need for intimidation.

"Darrel—" Stuart said. "Is he in trouble? Did you lock him up?"

"Should he be locked up, Mr. Vaughn?"

"He loved his mother." This anguished declaration was addressed to Anne. "You can see that, can't you?"

The whites of Stuart's eyes were inflamed. The left one wandered off course, as though looking for answers on its own. What was the condition called? Amblyopia? A lazy eye, in common terms.

"Yes, Mr. Vaughn," Anne said. "I can."

Her own eyes were going to be red and irritated, too. She could feel them burning from the secondhand smoke in the room.

"So he wouldn't hurt her," Stuart said. "It wouldn't make sense. Had to be somebody else. Had to be."

"Stuart, where were you that afternoon when your wife died?" Bern asked.

"Fixin' the Bronco. Changin' a gasket on the oil pan. A deputy came out. I heard him comin' a long ways away. Lyin' under the car, the sound just drummin' in my head. Knew it was something terrible. Just didn't expect it to be 'Fina."

"Do you know anybody who would want to harm your wife?" Bern asked.

"There are people," Stuart said darkly.

"Who are they?"

"People."

"Can you give me some names?"

Stuart shook his head so violently that strands of his white hair flopped down to string in his face. Hands shaking, he grabbed up the pack of Camels and began to try to dig out the one remaining cigarette. No wonder Darrel worried about senility.

Bern muttered, "Jesus," under his breath. Aloud, he said with weary kindness, "Tell you what, Stuart, it's late. Why don't we talk about this another time?" Bern got to his feet. "I'll go get your son, have him take you home."

"Home." He seemed to savor the word. "Yeah, I'd like that. Thank you."

He managed to fumble out the cigarette and stick it in his mouth. On her way to the door, Anne smelled the match he struck with a thumbnail, then the first, almost fragrant odor of burning tobacco.

"Officers," Stuart said just as Anne and Bern stepped outside. "I never woulda shot you today. Maybe I'da shot the car, shot in the dirt, but I wouldn'a hurt you."

"I'd like to think that's true, Mr. Vaughn," Bern said.

"It is," Stuart insisted. "I ain't crazy. I just know what I know. There's bad things and bad people."

"Yes, sir," Bern said. "You got that right."

sixteen

ANNE INSISTED ON DRIVING THE JEEP HOME. BERN DIDN'T argue. He tilted the seat, leaned back, and closed his eyes. The night was cold enough that the warmth from the heater felt welcome. A breeze picked fitfully at the tops of the trees and sent leaves skittering in the gutters.

In the light of the instrument panel and the streetlamps, filtered into the car through the tinted windshield, Bern's skin was the color of putty.

"How long before I get rid of this headache?" he asked.

"I don't know. A few days."

"Great," he muttered, then, "What do you think? Is the old guy totally loony-tunes or just your normal, functioning paranoid personality?"

"It's hard to judge. He's scared of something, but I couldn't tell you if his fears have any basis in reality."

"Then you have Darrel. Does anybody grow up in a normal family anymore? Except you, I mean."

"Listen to us," Anne said. "I understand more and more how this job skews our outlooks."

"And speaking of dysfunction," Bern said dryly, "you picking up any vibes that say Rachel was anything but a very unhappy little girl?"

"Not really," Anne said. "Poor Kathleen. I know she's

anxious for something, but I don't want to give her a report in bits and pieces. I think it would be better to wait until I can put everything together in a clear picture.''

''I think so, too. She's so mad at Randy and Sharon already. God knows what she'd do if she heard about the lock. . . .''

His words trailed off. Anne glanced over and saw that he had fallen asleep in midsentence.

They were leaving the city now, far enough from the streetlights so she could see the sky. Stars winked off and on through a filigree of high, thin, fast-moving clouds, as though they were sending a secret code, maybe even the secrets of the universe, if only she were smart enough to decipher the signal.

The only sounds in the Jeep were the muffled thrum of the engine, a hiss of tires on asphalt, and, if she strained to listen, Bern's heavy, even breathing. At least he'd get some rest tonight. The sleeping pills would see to that, even though they were a temporary fix.

Bern was so convinced that excessive caffeine was the cause of his insomnia. Anne wanted to believe it, too, but she knew that part of the medical protocol was to try the simple, obvious treatment first. This didn't guarantee anything. All it did was tell you that if the first course of treatment failed, you should move on to a second.

At least the fear that Bern was drifting away from her could be put to rest. Interesting how this possibility was almost the first thing that had leaped into her mind. Something to take to Rosemary, a basic insecurity that needed to be explored.

Meanwhile, she still had a small bur of worry lodged in her mind. All along she had been seeing avoidance in Bern's behavior. There were things he wasn't telling her. Maybe he had kept them from the doctor, too.

But what things?

On the outskirts of Cave Creek, a car pulled out of a side street, and she had to brake sharply to avoid it. Bern stirred, opened his eyes, and said groggily, "Are we home yet?"

"Almost."

He closed his eyes again. "Did I tell you I called the investigator who's looking for your homeless woman? And Frank's got the word out about the wino. Hope it helps."

Anne started to say thank you, but he was dozing again. Even in the middle of a hectic day, even exhausted, he'd remembered to call about Chrissie's mother.

How could I doubt his love for me? Anne wondered.

At home he stumbled straight to the bedroom. When Anne reminded him about the sleeping pill, he said, "Don't think I need it," but took it anyway when Anne insisted.

Anne went to let Duke out, leaving the back door open while she waited to clear some of the doggy smell. She returned to the bedroom to find Bern sprawled face down, dead to the world, and that night, for the first time in weeks, she didn't hear him up prowling the house at three in the morning.

AT SIX A.M. ANNE SLIPPED OUT OF BED AND PUT ON HER sweats. The room was lit with a pale gray light, enough light to dress by, so she didn't turn on the lamp, and she tiptoed out, although such precautions probably weren't necessary. Bern was still sound asleep, in almost the same position he had been in when he went to bed. At this point it would probably take a bomb blast to wake him up.

Through the kitchen windows Anne could see the sky, suffused with a pearly pink glow from the sun, which was still below the mountains to the east. She shivered out on the deck, waiting for the dog to relieve himself, and noted a dusting of frost on the cholla and wild grasses on the hillside. The landscape had a remote, otherworldly quality this early on a winter morning. She saw nothing stirring and wondered again if the wild things had decided it was wiser to move on.

Back inside, she tied the hood of her sweatshirt close around her face and put on a down vest. Duke stood on the other side of the gate in the kitchen and whined as he watched her belt on a fanny pack and put on gloves.

"Sorry, boy," she said. "I know you were promised a walk this morning, but I wouldn't count on it."

Outside, she took her mountain bike from the storage unit in the carport and rode off down the drive. The cold air stung her cheeks and filled her head with earthy, pungent smells that seemed edged with ice. Despite the frost, the hillsides were coming alive with new growth as the plants recovered from the searing summer heat.

The high clouds from the night before were gone, the weather system probably sliding north as was often the case in this part of Arizona. The sky was clear, the flush of dawn pink already changing to a pale luminous blue. A morning like this reminded her of why she put up with Bern's complaints and the inconvenience of a long commute to live out here.

She had just turned out of the driveway when she caught a flash of movement behind her, something large following her into the street. She thought *coyote* but immediately saw she was wrong. It was Duke running in a wild, free gallop with what she could swear was pure joy on his ugly face.

"Duke!" She skidded to a stop. "How in the world—"

With visions of broken windows and shattered door frames, she pedaled back to the house. Duke followed, lagging farther and farther behind as he realized what was happening. When she opened the front door and called to him, he sat down on the driveway beside the bike and refused to budge. She would have to get the leash.

A draft from the kitchen led her to the dog's escape route. The back door was open. Probably hadn't closed properly when she came in from the deck. How could she blame him for bolting?

Back outside, after a few growls of protest, Duke submitted to the leash, but he resisted every step back to the house; at the front door he sat down and looked at her with the biggest, saddest eyes she'd ever seen.

Anne sighed and said, "I'm probably going to regret this, but—okay. Come on."

She had to experiment with the correct way to hold the leash and where to position the bike in relationship to the dog. She knew she'd better keep him on the asphalt. The bike had tires designed to resist cactus barbs, but the pads on Duke's paws had no such protection.

It was amazing how quickly they struck a balance. Duke ran alongside as though he'd been practicing. It helped that they pretty much had the narrow street to themselves. Still, reminding herself how recently the dog had recovered from wounds that had nearly killed him, she cut the ride short. He was limping a little as they went back inside, but seemed content enough as he lapped water and retreated under the kitchen table.

"Don't think it's going to be a daily routine," Anne warned him.

It took some doing to get Bern up and moving, but once in motion Anne thought he did look more rested, even if he was bleary-eyed and just as surly as ever. She mixed regular coffee half-and-half with decaf and allowed him one cup.

And if she saw shadows in his eyes that remained after almost nine hours of sleep, she had plenty of time in the car on the long drive to work to convince herself she was just looking for something to worry about.

AT WORK, BERN DESPERATELY NEEDED A FULL HIT OF coffee but poured only half a mug, diluted it with water, then zapped the weak stuff in the microwave. The damned pill had worked all right, but the induced sleep was far from restful. The Seconal had dimmed the nightmares, but what the dreams lacked in vividness they made up in persistence, and he had lain there paralyzed, helpless, unable to escape.

Neither the pathetically weak stuff in his mug nor the Advil he'd taken was doing a damn thing for his headache. He set himself to endure the throbbing pain and went to join the small group gathered around Will's desk. The way they all eyed him told him he looked like hell, but nobody said anything. They just took off, pleading work, and left him with Will and Frank Trusey.

Bern slouched in a chair next to Will's desk and sipped his nasty coffee while the two filled him in on what they'd accomplished the day before.

Frank had talked to the owners of the Graleys' house. "Nice old couple," Frank said. The Swales carried only the bare minimum of fire insurance, maybe not even enough to cover rebuilding costs. There was some liability coverage, and Randy and Sharon had already been making noises about suing. Even though arson was a terrible thing, it let the Swales off the hook, so they couldn't help but be a little relieved. And no, they told Frank, they couldn't think of anybody who would want to burn down their house.

The rest of Frank's time had been spent in alleys, soup kitchens, and other haunts of the down-and-out segment of the population. He hadn't found either the wino named Bunny who was supposed to have witnessed the knifing of the John Doe by Bill Moultry or the other one, Harlan, who was connected to Anne's little homeless girl.

As for Will, he had succeeded in digging up some good stuff on the Vaughns. "I put the files on your desk when I left yesterday," Will said and left it at that, but his meaning was clear enough. It was Bern's fault if he had interviewed Darrel and Stuart Vaughn before reading the reports.

Listening to Will's summary, Bern told himself he could

have avoided a lot of aggravation and frustration, not to mention a close encounter with a crazy man wielding a shotgun, if he'd just done things the old-fashioned way—working the phones and using up shoe leather.

Will had turned up no outstanding wants or warrants on either of the Vaughns. Credit checks revealed that neither was in serious debt or had other financial trouble.

From various sources Will had learned that Stuart Vaughn was originally from Santa Fe, New Mexico, and had spent twenty years in the army. He'd met Rufina while he was stationed down on the border at Fort Huachuca. They had settled in Phoenix when Stuart mustered out. Darrel was eleven at the time, so he'd gone to school here.

After Stuart got out of the service, he went to work for Arizona Power Service doing janitorial work. His last five working years had been spent out at Palo Verde, the atomic energy facility located fifty miles outside of the metropolitan area that seemed to generate as much controversy as it did electrical power.

"Maybe the guy got a little too close to the reactor," Will said dryly.

During the last two years of his employment, he began making reports to Security that were met with more and more skepticism: cars following him to work, strangers lurking in the bathrooms, men out on cactus-covered knolls with what might very well be high-powered rifles.

Finally Personnel had a talk with Stuart about two things: early retirement and psychological counseling. They'd succeeded in convincing him to agree to the first but had no idea if he'd followed through on the second—and claimed total lack of responsibility if the man had failed to listen to their advice.

With a military pension and Social Security, Stuart should have had adequate income. There had been term life policies on both him and his wife while he was working at APS, but these had lapsed.

As for Darrel, he had no service record, lived at home, and seemed to be keeping his nose clean after a couple of juvey arrests: one for joy riding, the other for disorderly conduct at a party raid. His only recent brush with the law occurred when a misdemeanor complaint was filed by a local environmental activist who happened upon Darrel and a friend conducting a rattlesnake roundup. Since diamondbacks were not protected, the complaint had been dismissed. Darrel worked for himself and had left so few credit tracks that Will suspected the guy had to be part of the underground cash economy.

So far, Will had uncovered nothing in the background of either man to suggest they were familiar with rigging a house to blow up.

"Of course," Will pointed out modestly, "I only worked on this for a day."

"You're doing such a bang-up job," Bern said, "I sure as hell hope you can keep it coming." He gestured toward three people who had just entered the squad room.

Randy and Sharon Graley had arrived for their formal interviews with a portly old geezer in a two-thousand-dollar suit named Louis Zeigler, who had the reputation of turning open-and-shut cases into revolving doors—if the price was right. Bern figured the only things he was going to learn about the Graleys from now on was what he and Will could dig up on their own.

During the next hour Zeigler earned his money and proved Bern right. He refused to let his clients answer any but the most innocuous questions and pompously warned that since the insurance company was now holding up payment to these poor people, he was instituting suit against the police department forthwith. Bern's only small success was the look of sick culpability in Randy's eyes when Bern told them Rachel was locked in her room when she died.

"You're a cruel man," Sharon hissed, shutting up immediately when Zeigler laid a fat, ringed hand on her arm.

The thing was, Bern thought that Sharon's observation was probably right. He also thought that he really didn't give a damn.

seventeen

RENA TRENT ARRIVED AT ANNE'S OFFICE WITH CHRIS-
tina for a nine-thirty appointment looking tired and worried. Anne had come out to greet them, paying special
attention to Chrissie, and was rewarded with a brief, shy
smile from the little girl.

At least Chrissie didn't look any the worse for her escape attempt. Today she wore yellow leggings under an
oversized T-shirt, white with pink tulips and yellow daf-
fodils. Her hair was neatly braided with the grubby pink
ribbons tied in place.

"Can we talk for a minute?" Rena asked.

"Of course. Come on in."

Anne noted that Rena had a firm grip on Christina's
wrist and didn't let go until they were inside the office
with the door shut behind them.

"Please." Anne gestured to the sofa. "Sit down."

Usually children were drawn like a magnet to the play
table, the brightly colored floor pillows, and the shelves
bearing a wide assortment of toys. But Chrissie stood still
on the spot where Rena had released her, staring at the
play area with wonder.

"Would you like to look at the toys while I talk to
Rena?" Anne asked.

Chrissie nodded, then she walked over slowly and did exactly what Anne had suggested: She *looked*, her little hands closing into fists and pressing against her sides.

Anne realized that this was a child who had learned to control her natural instincts to touch and explore, one who had no playthings of her own and had not had the common experience of going to toy stores or visiting other children's toy-strewn rooms.

Anne went over and said, "You're allowed to play with anything that's here, Chrissie. Okay?"

Christina nodded but remained where she was. Since she seemed to have homed in on a blue plastic basket full of hand puppets, Anne took the container down, placed it on the floor, and suggested, "Maybe you'd like to start with these first."

She left Christina to begin a hesitant exploration and went back to join Rena.

"Just breaks your heart, doesn't it?" Rena said, sinking down heavily on the sofa while Anne took one of the chairs.

"Have the police come up with anything about the mother?"

Rena shook her head. "Joyce said they've checked the hospitals and the morgue, and police records to see if she's been arrested, of course. That happens a lot with the homeless."

"Is Chrissie settling in at all at your place?"

"No. That's the problem. She didn't get far, but she's tried to run away twice since her big jailbreak yesterday. I didn't tell CPS yet. I will," Rena added quickly. "I'm not trying to hide anything. But when they hear, I'm afraid they'll feel I'm not being responsible and want to move her. You'd think I might not mind." She gave Anne a rueful smile. "I mean, the child is wearing us out. I have to watch her every minute—my kids and I do. Of course, you always have to pay attention to little ones her age. But take your eyes off her for a *second*, and she's gone."

Rena sighed and looked across the room at Christina, who was carefully picking up each toy on the shelves, studying it, and putting it back in place.

"She can be the sweetest little thing," Rena said. "And I really do think it's better for her not to be moved around."

"I agree," Anne said. "Christina needs some stability right now, and she's lucky to be with you, Rena. I'll tell CPS so."

"Thank you, Dr. Menlo," Rena said gratefully. "It sure would help if you could talk Chrissie out of trying to run away again."

Anne promised she would try, and Rena left to wait in the reception area, where Anne could hear Peggy offering to get her some coffee.

Chrissie had found a box of washable markers and was drawing on a big pad of paper. The pad was attached to an easel that stood next to the play table. She froze as Anne came to sit on the floor pillows.

"I like your picture," Anne said. "Is it okay if I watch you draw?"

"Uh-huh," Christina said and went back to her work.

Curving lines in electric blue and sunshine yellow radiated out on either side of a brown stick figure that looked insectile. The drawing could be a butterfly, but Anne knew better than to place her own interpretation on Chrissie's concept.

A final blue arc and Chrissie backed away, sat down beside Anne, and looked soberly at the image.

"Mama draws," Chrissie said in her twangy drawl. "She can draw real good."

"You miss her, don't you?"

Chrissie nodded. Her face mirrored dejection and loss.

"Where were you going when you ran away yesterday?"

"Back to our place," Chrissie said, confirming Anne's suspicions. "I walked and walked, but I couldn't find it."

"It's a long way from Rena's house, sweetie," Anne said. "And your mama isn't there."

"But maybe she'll come back, and I won't be there, and she won't find me, and I'll be lost forever."

Huge tears formed on Chrissie's lashes and rolled down her cheeks as she scrambled into Anne's lap. Anne held her silently for a minute, breathing in her soapy, salty smell. There was simply no use trying to maintain an objective distance with this one. Anne acknowledged a linkage here, heart to heart.

"Oh, Chrissie, I understand why you want to go back to the place where you and your mom were staying. But trying to do that on your own is a very dangerous thing. Rena worries about you; I worry; everybody does."

Chrissie didn't say anything, but Anne felt her bony little shoulders stiffen and saw her tear-streaked face set with stubbornness.

"Tell you what," Anne said. "Maybe you and I can do something to help you find your mom or to help her find you." *If she ever comes looking.* "Do you want to hear my idea?"

"Wh-what is it?" Chrissie asked.

"We'll make some posters," Anne said. "And we'll take them to where you lived and put them up."

"B-but I—can't—" Her chin trembled, and more tears fell. "I can't make ABCs," Chrissie wailed.

"I'll write all the letters," Anne promised. "You can make some special drawings for your mom. But first, let's wipe those tears." Anne reached for a box of tissues beneath the play table, took a few, and blotted the wet little face. "Now, come and help me find some poster board."

With Chrissie "helping," Anne took the board and a fat black indelible marker from her supply closet and carried them to the low play table. Anne sat back down on the pillows, but Chrissie hovered tensely.

"What do we write?" she asked.

"Well," Anne said, "if you could remember your

mom's name we could put that on the poster—but we don't have to," she added hastily as Chrissie's face pinched with anxiety. "We could just say—"

"Sue Lynn Bowes," Chrissie burst out. "I heard Harlan. He said Sue Lynn Bowes. That's my mama's *name*, Anne. Now we can write it on the poster."

Better than that, the police would now have something to work with. As a result, Anne hoped the chances of finding Christina's mother had just improved dramatically.

After a consultation with Chrissie on the wording, Anne began to print in big, bold letters: SUE LYNN BOWES—CHRISSIE MISSES YOU—PLEASE CALL. . . .

SINCE ANNE HAD NO OTHER SESSIONS PLANNED FOR THE morning, she and Rena were able to take Chrissie out right away to the area where the child had been found. Rena drove. Chrissie sat in the van's built-in car seat with the posters—decorated with the little girl's bright abstract drawings—right beside her.

Before they left the office, Anne took a minute to call Joyce Levy and ask her to pass on the information about Chrissie's mother to the police. Joyce was not optimistic. Sue Lynn Bowes was not a woman whose name would be in the system—unless she'd landed in jail somewhere, and even then who was to say she wouldn't use an alias?

Joyce clearly thought Anne's effort with the posters wouldn't bring a call from Sue Lynn, but if the ploy kept Christina safe at the Trent house, it was worth the effort.

Rena was game to try anything at this point.

Chrissie had chattered for a few minutes, then fell silent. She wasn't asleep, however; she stared out the window and rubbed a frayed pink ribbon on the end of one braid back and forth between her fingers.

Rena was nervous and talkative. Anne led her into conversation about her own two children as Rena headed south. It might have been faster to take a freeway route, but Seventh Avenue was a straight shot, and the traffic wasn't too bad this time of the morning.

As they passed police headquarters, Anne found herself wondering about Bern, how he was holding up, if he really was only suffering from an overdose of caffeine—and quickly squelched that line of thought. But Rena had sensed her lack of attention and fallen silent.

Just past I-17 they crossed over the Salt River. Dams and the white man's agriculture had long since transformed the river valleys of the Gila and the Salt. Once, enough water had flowed here to irrigate the crops grown by the Pima Indians and to allow willow, cattails, and devil's claw to flourish, providing raw materials for the beautiful baskets that were so well made they could even be used for cooking. Now all that was left was a wide, rocky scar, barren except for scant pockets of stunted cottonwood and paloverde.

Today sunlight flashed silver on a quiet streamlet winding along the sandy bottom, a residual trickle from the rainstorms that had lashed the area just after New Year's Day. But at times the river still raged between the broad banks, powerful enough to wash away roads and bridges, a reminder of what used to be.

Rena turned onto Broadway, and the neighborhood rapidly deteriorated. They passed a junkyard with chain link fences topped by razor wire. Even the poorest of the small houses were fenced and had bars on the windows. Spiky graffiti covered all available walls. No water was spared for landscaping here. Both yards and vacant lots grew prickly pear, stunted fan palms, and weeds.

On the street outside a run-down Mexican restaurant, a desperately thin, dirty man held up a cardboard sign with the crudely lettered plea: *Will work for food.*

In the backseat, Chrissie began straining to look out the windows and trying to undo the seat belt restraints.

"Not yet, honey," Rena cautioned. "Leave that belt alone."

She left Broadway to drive slowly down a side street nearest the river. She said Joyce had given her a good idea of where the homeless camp was. Still, she had to double back once before she decided this must be the right place. She parked at the end of a short dead-end street behind an old VW minibus, leprous with rust spots.

There were no buildings, just a weedy, trash-filled vacant lot and a thicket of creosote, paloverde, and bunchgrasses with giant sprays of seed tassels. After taking a closer look, Anne could see a faint path through the lot into the trees.

Chrissie knew where she was. She had unfastened her seat belt and was trying to get the sliding door open, saying, "Anne, Rena, come *on.*"

"Just a second," Rena said.

She dug in her purse, came up with a canister of pepper spray, and clipped it to her purse strap. When she opened the door for Chrissie, she grabbed the little girl's hand.

They followed the path with Chrissie pulling at Rena, leading the way. On the river side of the thicket, the small trees thinned out quickly. Anne smelled the camp before she saw it: an odor of garbage and no sanitation. Within the small grove, tarps were strung between trees, and there were shelters made of cardboard and plywood.

Wary eyes watched them—mostly men, but a few women and children. Anne estimated twenty or twenty-five of them. They sat quietly on the dusty ground, a few small groups, many alone, all isolated. In this desolate place, even the sunlight seemed dimmed.

Rena stopped and said uneasily, "I don't know if this is such a good idea."

Just then an impatient Chrissie jerked free and took off through the trees with Rena following at a trot, yelling for her to slow down. Quicker on her feet, Anne got to Chrissie just as the little girl came to a stop out on the edge of the camp in front of one of the cardboard shelters.

This one had been simply constructed by shoving a

large box up under some bushes. Black plastic garbage bags lay on top, pushed back and tucked under the branches. Fading lettering announced that the carton had once held a 22-cubic-foot refrigerator. The box lay lengthwise, the outward-facing side cut away, forming a snug, low-ceilinged little cave. A tattered old blanket served as a privacy flap and fluttered in the breeze, revealing a sleeping bag spread inside.

A scrawny, middle-aged woman sat on the ground just outside the shelter, legs splayed out. She wore layers of clothing: a green plaid shirt over a blue T-shirt, a broomstick skirt in tropical reds and oranges over black sweatpants. Knobby ankles protruded over a pair of old, unlaced high-tops. Her hair was pushed up under a bright-pink knit hat with a puffy yarn ball on top. The few messy strands that escaped were a mixture of dull brown and iron gray. Next to her sat a child's wagon, holding a pile of belongings that were lashed in place with a length of new nylon rope.

She stared up at Anne and Chrissie, frozen in the act of peeling an orange with long fingernails that looked like grimy yellow horn. Bits of peel lay in her lap, and the tangy citrus scent filled the air, overriding the smell of garbage.

Anne had dropped her hands down on Chrissie's shoulders. She could feel the little girl tensing with indignation.

"That's *our* place," Chrissie said. "You get away. You get away right now."

The woman, taking in the way Anne was dressed, looked incredulous. "You ain't staying here?"

"No, the child and her mother did."

"Where's all our things?" Chrissie tried to wriggle free from Anne's grip. "What'd you do with them?"

"This's *Audrey's* stuff," the woman declared in a combative tone. She scrambled to her feet, crouching and glaring at them and at Rena, who had just arrived, puffing a little. "This's Audrey's place, and don't you be thinkin' you can take it."

"It's all right, ma'am," Anne said soothingly. "Nobody's going to take anything from you."

"Chrissie lives with me now," Rena said, stepping up beside Anne and turning so the pepper-spray canister was visible, attached to her purse strap. "She's upset because we don't know where her mother is. Dr. Menlo and I are just trying to help get them back together."

"Well, she ain't *here*. So you and *Doctor* Menlo just get the hell away and go bother somebody else."

"Sure," Rena said. "We'll do that. Come on, Chrissie."

"But, Anne—" Chrissie's eyes were full of frantic pleading. "I want to show you something. Inside. Please."

Anne sighed and said to the woman, "Ma'am? Audrey—would you mind very much if we look inside?"

The woman gave her a crafty look. "Some people ain't so damn pushy. *Some* people don't expect things for free."

"All right," Anne said. She opened her purse and took out a five-dollar bill. "Just give us a few minutes, okay?"

Audrey snatched the money from her hand. "Two minutes. I ain't got no watch, but I can count." She backed off a few feet, dragging the wagon with her. "*One* one thousand, *two*—"

Without hesitation, Chrissie crawled into the cardboard box. Anne lifted the blanket flap gingerly and put it on top of the carton, then sat down on the ground in front of the opening. Rena gave her a look that said, "Better you than me."

"Anne," Chrissie said insistently.

Anne leaned into the box, trying not to think of what might infest the filthy bedroll.

Drawings decorated the ceiling and part of the back of the carton. Some were clearly abstract crayon scrawls done by Chrissie; the rest were the work of somebody older and with some talent.

Anne thought of the time represented here, hours of being cooped up in this tiny space by foul weather, poverty, fear. And she thought of a mother doing what she could to entertain and delight her child. There was love here. Anne was certain of that.

Birds, flowers, a teddy bear, a Santa, a Christmas tree with ornaments and garlands. Although the plastic garbage bags had kept the cardboard from disintegrating, enough water had seeped in to smear many of the images. But one picture had not suffered water damage. It was clear and bright, done in markers that stood out vividly against the brown background.

And now there was no mistaking what Christina had been drawing in Anne's office. Chrissie reached up to touch it.

Feathery light-blue wings spread out from the angel's body, which was clothed in a white robe. A gold halo crowned a sweetly smiling face with dark curls and dark eyes. A pale yellow glow surrounded the entire figure, bleeding off into the cardboard.

"Isn't it pretty?" Chrissie whispered.

"It's beautiful," Anne said.

"—*One hundred twenty* one thousand," the woman chanted. "That's it. Get outta Audrey's place now."

"Come on, sweetie," Anne said to Chrissie. "Let's go put up the posters."

Chrissie obeyed, but slowly, head down. Her cheeks were wet, and she clung to Anne's hand as they walked away. A few people showed interest in the posters, but either none of them knew Sue Lynn or the man named Harlan, or they were too wary of strangers asking questions to supply any answers. Chrissie had retreated into silence and didn't appear to recognize anybody.

Back at the van, Anne said to Rena, "I think I'll sit with her," and climbed in beside Chrissie's car seat.

As they drove back down Broadway, Chrissie had turned her head away and sat so still that Anne thought she'd gone to sleep until she finally whispered something. Anne caught only, "The angel lady."

"What, honey?"

She turned to look at Anne, tears trembling on her lashes. "I think maybe Mama went to the angel lady."

Anne might have translated the words in other ways, except for the anguish on Chrissie's face. Regardless of what protective parents like to think, five-year-olds might not understand the mechanisms of death, but they understand the abandonment very well.

"Oh, no, Chrissie," Anne said. "We don't know that, not for sure."

"She did," the little girl declared miserably. "I know she did, just like before. Only this time she didn't come back."

eighteen

BY THE TIME ANNE GOT BACK TO THE OFFICE, PEGGY HAD a stack of pink message slips waiting for her. Bern, Kathleen, a junior-high-school counselor calling about one of Anne's patients, Anne's accountant—she put these aside to return what was probably the least urgent message, the one from Rosemary.

"You sound a little depressed," Rosemary said. "I prescribe lunch on my patio. Norman's made minestrone soup."

"It sounds wonderful," Anne said wistfully.

"We could say it's business. I saw Kathleen Graley yesterday. We can talk about that. Oh, and I spoke to my friend at UCLA. *And*—" Rosemary added the one thing she knew Anne couldn't resist. "The cattleyas are blooming."

THE ONLY CATTLEYA ORCHIDS ANNE HAD EVER SEEN, like most people, were those extravagant corsages worn at weddings, the blooms gorgeous but usually cold from the refrigerator and always odorless. The orchids that bloomed naturally were like a totally different plant.

Norman grew a half-dozen different specimens. At the Beidermans' house in Paradise Valley, they were all in flower. The foliage was downright unattractive; just a few long leaves, folded at the base, growing out of what looked like brown tubers set in bark. Norman kept them in his small greenhouse about ten months out of the year, bringing them out when the buds appeared. Now the blossoms had opened, as many as three or four on a spike, velvety white with purple or yellow throats that could last a month.

Anne just stood for a second in the sliding door that opened to the patio, contrasting this place with the homeless encampment down on the other side of the Salt River.

In summer the covered patio was an oasis in the heat, cooled by misting devices and crowded with barrels of ferns and ivy, and hanging baskets of fuchsias. In winter, sliding Plexiglas panels kept out chilly winds or were opened to welcome the sunny warmth. And now, in addition to the cattleyas, there were banks of cymbidiums with spikes of blooms ranging from creamy white and pale yellow to a rich chocolate brown. Bright-pink sweet peas spilled over the ivy that grew in the barrels.

Rosemary sat on an upholstered lounge chair amid the flowers, looking right at home in her deep ruby-red pants and a pullover top made of quilted silk. A wheelchair was parked behind the lounge.

She said, "Well, dear, was it worth the drive?"

"Oh, yes," Anne said. "Absolutely."

She detoured past the cattleyas to breathe in the heavenly scent, surprised all over again by the fragrance, which was roselike but also beautifully unique. Norman had once explained he used no special growing techniques. The fact was that cattleyas had no odor when they first opened; the perfume developed slowly, and growers cut the flowers that were destined for florist shops immediately to guarantee the longest life.

Anne went to brush a kiss on Rosemary's forehead. The ravages of illness had only refined the bone structure of Rosemary's face and made her brown eyes seem larger and more luminous. But Anne noted with a twinge of sadness that new white strands threaded the short black hair, already winged with white at the temples.

"Norman's bringing the food," Anne said.

"Good. I told him you were on a tight schedule. Ah— here he is."

Norman bore a covered enameled pot, which he brought to a glass-topped wrought-iron table. He placed the pot on a trivet and announced cheerfully, "Soup's on."

"Very original, darling," Rosemary said dryly, but there was a world of love in her eyes for this bearish man with grizzled hair and beard, tan and fit in a dark-green polo shirt and tan cotton slacks.

Norman came to pick Rosemary up and put her in a chair at the table, somehow making the transfer as normal as passing Anne a basket of breadsticks and filling all their glasses from a pitcher of iced tea.

Several years ago he had resigned a federal judgeship to take care of his wife when her multiple sclerosis had progressed to the point where she had to retire from teaching. One of the best and most selfless people Anne knew, Norman was always truly surprised and embarrassed if anybody pointed out his goodness.

He lifted the lid off the soup pot, and momentarily the hearty aroma of tomato, vegetables, and pasta, seasoned with herbs and Parmesan, overpowered the perfume of the garden. The soup tasted as good as it smelled, and Anne ate hungrily.

While Norman cleared the bowls away, stacking them on a cart, and brought over a tray of sliced melons, Rosemary asked, "Anne, have you spoken to Kathleen today?"

"No," Anne said with a touch of guilt. "She tried to reach me, but I was out and I haven't returned the call."

"She plans to go back to California as soon as the coroner releases Rachel's body. I think I've persuaded her to get therapy when she goes home. A child's death is so hard to deal with in the best of circumstances. In a case like this. . . ." Rosemary shook her head sadly. "Are you making any progress with your profile?"

"Some." Anne told her how Rachel had been locked in her room at the time of the fire, and that there was certainly the suggestion that the child had been routinely locked in. "I'd call that a form of physical abuse, wouldn't you?"

Rosemary, who had definite beliefs about how children should be treated, said crisply, "I certainly would."

Norman said nothing. After his years in law, first as a prosecutor and then on the bench, he had witnessed enough human cruelty to know that people were capable of anything; however, he rarely rendered an opinion unless asked.

"That's really the only concrete thing I've come up with so far," Anne said, suddenly realizing how much more she had to investigate. "The father drinks. The grandmother is not your milk-and-cookies type. Of course, to hear her tell it, her son adored Rachel, and Kathleen was a neglectful mother."

"How about the housekeeper who died in the fire?" Norman asked. "Does she have family? She may have talked to them about the child."

"I spoke to the son. He was actually there at the house just hours before the explosion. His mother wasn't at all happy to have to take care of Rachel, and you know Rachel must have gotten a dose of the woman's resentment. But he claims his mother never told him that she saw any sign of abuse. I haven't talked to Mrs. Vaughn's husband yet—well, not in what you could call a coherent manner.

"I think my best bet is to go to California. I want to interview neighbors, teachers, her doctor—although the laws are so stringent these days, you'd think any sign of abuse would have been reported."

Anne helped herself to pale-green honeydew and cut it into bite-sized chunks. "I don't plan to tell Kathleen any of this until I have a complete picture for her—or as complete as I can make it.''

''I think that's wise,'' Rosemary said. ''As for Daniel, I'm afraid I overstated the importance of our conversation a bit to get you out here. He first met Kathleen in the fall when the school year began and has only good things to say about her.''

Anne nodded absently and ate a piece of sweet melon. She hadn't expected much input from Kathleen's professor. And to tell the truth, her thoughts had left the case to circle back to more personal matters.

She was aware of a look that passed between Rosemary and Norman, then Norman got up, said, ''I think I'll put the leftovers in the refrigerator,'' and went off to the kitchen with the soup pot.

Anne felt a wave of envy. The Beidermans could practically read each other's minds. Would she and Bern ever be that close? Considering how things were going, she had serious doubts.

''Do you want to discuss it?'' Rosemary asked.

''It's Bern. I'm worried about him, and he won't talk to me. That's the worst part.''

She told Rosemary about Bern's insomnia, his strange moods, her suspicion that he might be suffering from impotence, and his visit to the clinic.

''Well, any diagnosis is only as good as the information the doctor has for a basis,'' Rosemary observed.

''Yes, so all I can hope is that Bern was honest.''

''The incident last summer,'' Rosemary said. ''Did he work through that?''

''I thought he did,'' Anne said. ''The department psychologist released him. Oh, I don't know. Maybe the doctor's right and it's just some ordinary physical problem. But I can't shake the feeling that there's something else going on.''

''Well, you have good instincts, Anne, so you may be right to worry. On the other hand, we both know how hard it is to be objective about somebody we love.''

"So what do I do? And please don't make me answer my own question. I've gone round and round about this in my head. I really need your opinion.''

Rosemary's dark eyes twinkled. "Big challenge to treat somebody in the profession who knows all the techniques.'' In a more serious tone, she added, "All you can do is give it a little time. If caffeine's the problem, there should be some sign of improvement soon. Meanwhile, just be observant—and supportive.'' She looked past Anne and smiled ruefully. "Uh-oh, my gatekeeper cometh.''

Norman stepped out onto the patio with a look on his face that said, "Time's up, so don't waste your breath arguing.''

He was right, of course. Rosemary looked frail and tired, more than ready for a rest.

"I have to go anyway.'' Anne stood up and began picking up her dishes.

"No, no, just leave those,'' Norman said. "I'll have plenty of time to clean up after I lay down the law to this one about a nap.''

"It's hell being married to an ex-judge.'' Rosemary's smile belied the words. "Call me, Anne. Let me know how things are going.''

Anne promised she would, gave Rosemary a kiss and Norman a hug, and said she'd let herself out. Leaving the patio to step back though the sliding door, she took one last look to fix the beauty of this special place in her memory.

Suddenly she thought of the homeless camp again. That river bank had once been a beautiful place, too, home to a whole civilization, to a whole ecology of wild birds and animals. The Pima must have thought their world would go on forever. But they had learned what we all know: The future comes, and things change—not always for the best.

Suddenly Anne saw how fragile this perfect little corner

of paradise was, as fragile as Rosemary herself. It was a construct, impermanent as a soap bubble. And like that floating bit of whimsy, it could so easily be whisked away on a breeze to burst against the cruel reality of the hillside beyond, where every plant, every tree, was covered in thorns.

nineteen

BERN ALLOWED HIMSELF A FULL MUG OF JAMAICA BLUE Mountain with the sandwich he ate at his desk. After a morning of watered-down coffee, his headache was a dull knife blade just behind his eyes. The high-test stuff gave him some relief, but it also left him wired and irritable.

Earlier, while he and Will had played out that exercise in futility with the Graleys and their attorney, the final autopsy report had arrived. Bern had not seen the remains of these victims, but he had seen others, and it amazed him that so many conclusions could be drawn from observing such charred corpses.

From the descriptions in the report, he learned that Rufina Vaughn's body had suffered the most damage, being nearer the flash point of the fire. There was little left except a skull, a torso, and stubs of limbs. The medical examiner expressed surprise that the head was still intact. Often in such intense heat the brain literally boils, and the pressure becomes so great that the skull can shatter.

Rachel had been found in the pugilistic stance typical of burned bodies, a condition caused by muscles contracted from the heat.

Enough blood and tissue had survived to show that neither victim had drugs or poison in her system. Their lungs showed signs of inhaled smoke, so both had been alive when the fire started. Both also had broken bones, not unusual given the amount of fallen debris from the brick walls, furniture, and roof. Specifically, both had skull fractures and broken ribs; one of Rachel's legs was shattered.

The report also told him what had *not* happened. There appeared to be no gunshot injuries; X rays had turned up no bullets lodged inside. While the skin and flesh showed a lot of cracks and fissures, the medical examiner believed that these were caused by intense heat and were not knife wounds. In his opinion, both Rachel Graley and Rufina Vaughn had died of trauma as a result of the fire.

Rachel's body was being released today. Medical and dental records had arrived from California, establishing identity. The coroner's office was still awaiting records on Mrs. Vaughn, temporary identification having been made by general size and sex as well as various articles of jewelry found on the body.

So the Graleys would get to bury their child. Maybe they would put aside their differences long enough to hold a funeral. Nice thought, but in Bern's experience this was often not the case. Like as not, there would be more conflict and more pain for Kathleen to endure.

He caught movement at the door of the squad room and looked up to see Kathleen coming in, as though he'd summoned her with his thoughts. He closed the autopsy file, shoved it beneath a stack of reports, and stood up as she made her way through the desks toward him.

She wore jeans and a black cotton sweater, the long sleeves pushed up to her elbows. She was not a small woman, nothing at all like his petite Anne, but grief had given her a look of frailty and vulnerability. There was not even the usual female defense of makeup, not even lipstick on the pale mouth, and she had simply scraped her hair off her face with a black plastic headband.

"Detective Pagett," she said. "I took a chance you'd be here. Is it okay? Are you busy?"

"No, no. You caught me at a good time. Please, have a seat. Can I get you something? Coffee?"

"No, thanks." She took the chair beside his desk and began fumbling in her bag, one of those things that looked like a knapsack. "I brought the list you asked me to write." She extracted two sheets of yellow lined paper torn from a legal pad. On them she had written a neatly printed list. "Neighbors—I put our old addresses as a reference, or at least as close as I could remember. Those are all the company names I could think of. I'm sure Randy and Sharon used more."

"I'll check out everything," Bern said, accepting the list. "How are you holding up otherwise?"

"I don't know. What do they say? As well as can be expected." She gave him a ghost of a smile, just enough so he could appreciate how much a smile could light up her face under normal circumstances. "I made a copy of the list for Dr. Menlo. I'll take it to her. Meanwhile, I need to ask you—as soon as the coroner releases Rachel's body, I want to finish up here. So is it okay if I go home? Back to California, I mean."

By all rights, Bern the cop should be keeping her name on his list of suspects, and caution would dictate the wisdom of keeping her in town. But caution be damned. He did not believe for one second this woman had lit the fire that had killed her only child.

"It's absolutely okay," he said. "And you may be able to leave soon. I have the medical examiner's report. You should give the office a call."

"I will, thank you." She got to her feet and slung her bag over one shoulder. "It's amazing how I managed to find such good people to see me through this nightmare— you, Dr. Menlo, Dr. Beiderman." She held out her hand. "You won't forget the promise you made me?"

"No," Bern said, taking her hand and gripping it briefly. "I won't forget."

• • •

USING ALL OF HIS WILLPOWER TO STAY AWAY FROM THE coffee machine, Bern spent the next two hours butting his head against various stone walls.

Nothing had turned up on NCIC on Randy and Sharon Graley. The next step was to call the Orange County Sheriff's Department in California. An obliging investigator there said that all arrests were cross-referenced in the Department of Records computer, and that he would be happy to check for Bern; however, individual cities in the county didn't always share data except for drugs and vice arrests. Those would have to be called individually.

He also referred Bern to the state real estate board for complaints that hadn't resulted in charges being filed.

Bern worked his way through several of the cities where the Graleys had lived. *Nada.* The Orange County investigator called back with the same: zip. Bern finally gave up on the real estate board and the Better Business Bureau, sick of voice mail and busy signals.

So much for good old-fashioned police work.

Will, however, was still on a winning streak. Earlier he'd tracked down the property manager of the apartment complex in Apache Junction, who verified that Sharon and Randy Graley had indeed been there the afternoon of the fire—one of the few pieces of information Louis Zeigler had allowed his clients to pass along. The manager was, however, a little vague on times.

Now Will came over, wearing a triumphant grin, and plopped down in a chair next to Bern's desk. Good timing, because Bern was ready to suggest that they recanvass the neighborhood where the house burned down or help Frank Trusey look for winos—anything to get away from his desk and, hopefully, out of the squad room.

"Know that other guy named on the complaint with Darrel?" Will asked.

Darrel Vaughn, the complaint filed by the environmental activist about the rattlesnakes—it took Bern a second to switch gears. He nodded.

"I finally got hold of his mother. She said he left for Vegas a week ago to look for work. She hasn't heard from him. *But,* she tells me, there was a third guy out there that day who never got named on the complaint. One Ralph Waldo Beaumont, Bo for short. I've been beating the bushes for him since lunch."

"You found him." Bern tried to keep the sour note out of his voice without much success.

Will's grin widened. "Yep. Just a couple of blocks away, as a matter of fact. He couldn't make bail, so he's over in the Madison Street jail waiting trial on aggravated assault. I'm having his record pulled, and he's on his way over."

Well, Bern thought, *at least I'll get as far as the interrogation room.*

BO BEAUMONT WAS SHORT AND WIRY WITH A NARROW skull, sandy hair that at age thirty already showed the horseshoe-shaped inroads of pattern balding, and a thin, mean mouth. Some yellowing bruises on his left jaw and cheekbone indicated that somebody had gotten in a few good licks during the fight that had landed him in jail.

He was wearing the standard jail uniform: blue cotton shirt and pants, both stenciled MCSD for Maricopa County Sheriff's Department. A week in the cooler had done nothing to damper the flames of the reckless temper that burned in his hazel eyes.

According to his jacket, Bo had run into his ex-girlfriend, Sheila, in a bar. He said he'd dumped her a couple of weeks earlier, although there was some heated dispute about this because Sheila claimed she had dumped *him.* There was also some dispute about whether Bo was just making conversation and trying to be nice or whether he was annoying her. In any case, she proceeded to pick up another man—"just to push my buttons," was the way Bo described it.

If button pushing was what Sheila set out to do, she

definitely succeeded. Bo left the bar, waited in the parking lot, and, when the two came out, assaulted them with a forked metal stick he kept in his truck to pin down unlucky rattlesnakes. Well, as Bo said in his statement, the guy outweighed him by fifty pounds. Naturally an equalizer was called for.

Now, in the interrogation room after the deputy removed the handcuffs and withdrew, Bo rubbed his wrists and eyed Bern and Will with surly wariness as Will sat on the edge of the table and offered him a cigarette and his choice of coffee or a soft drink.

"I don't know you guys," Bo said sullenly. "Whaddaya want? My P.D. said I ain't supposed to say nothin' if he ain't here."

"You can call him if you like." Bern picked up a chair, turned it around, and straddled it. Friendly and relaxed, that's what he and Will were aiming for. "But this has nothing to do with your case. This is something else we're really hoping you can help us with."

"Yeah? Why would I do that?"

"Because this is the second time you beat up on somebody," Will said. "Couldn't hurt if it comes to the D.A.'s attention that you're being cooperative."

Bo considered the option. This took some doing; thinking about something rather than just reacting was an unusual process for him, Bern was sure. Will had left his cigarette pack on the table. Bo reached for it and shook one out. Will lit it for him with a lighter.

"So," Bo said after taking in a lungful of smoke and blowing it out. "Who I gotta fuck over to get all this cooperation?"

"You got it wrong," Will began, but Bo cut him off.

"Yeah, sure. Who is it?"

"Darrel Vaughn," Bern said.

"Darrel? Oh, man." Bo shook his head at the prospect of ratting on his friend. "What'd he do? Jesus, his mother just died. Why are you hassling the guy?"

"He's not charged with anything," Bern said. "His name came up in one of our investigations. We're just trying to get some background on him, that's all."

"Oh, right. Whaddaya think I am, stupid?"

"I don't know, Bo. Are you? We want some standard information about the guy which is easy enough to come by. Asking you saves us some time, that's all. Seems to me as though you'd want to help us out, that when you come to trial you'd want all the kind words you could get. But, hey, it's your call."

Bern got up, replaced the chair, and headed for the door.

"Wait," Bo said. "Wait a second. You said just standard stuff, right?"

"Right," Will said. "Come on, Bern. Let's give Bo here a chance."

This time Bern positioned himself on the other side of the table. The distance was deliberate. It allowed Will to be on Bo's side, encouraging him to overcome Bern's skepticism. Will fired up his own cigarette, reinforcing the relationship. Bern hoped to God Beaumont would talk fast. Bern's eyes were starting to itch from the secondhand smoke.

By the time they finished, his head was pounding, too. But the information they obtained had saved them hours of legwork.

Bo and Darrel had been high school buddies and had maintained an off-and-on friendship ever since. Choosing each word with care, Bo told them Darrel had mostly lived with his folks, except for a couple of tries at sharing an apartment with some other guys—Bo went vague on names—and the year he spent out in Sacramento.

When asked what Darrel was doing out there, Bo took his time lighting up another cigarette and inspected his fingernails while he recalled that Darrel never said much about that period in his life.

Bo reported that Darrel seemed to making good money as a house painter—Bern thought he detected a touch of envy there—and worked as steadily as suited a laid-back lifestyle. Hobbies? None Bo knew about except trying to exterminate the local rattlesnake population. Darrel had friends and distant relatives in Nogales and went down there a lot, and so did his mother.

"He sure did love his mom," Bo declared, the only statement that Bern would bet was spontaneous and un-edited.

After Bo was taken back to jail, Bern swallowed some Advil and sat at his desk, rubbing his temples and staring at the case file spread out in front of him. Sharon and Randy Graley had an alibi. Darrel had waved to a neighbor as he left the house after visiting his mother—hardly the action of somebody leaving a crime scene. And Stuart? The Maricopa County patrol officer verified he did indeed have the oil pan down on his Bronco when he was notified of his wife's death.

Of course, there were alternate spins Bern could put on these stories. The Graleys' alibi was far from ironclad, and either Sharon or Randy could have hired somebody to set the fire. Darrel's actions were those of an arrogant idiot, and he was certainly the last one of the suspects on the scene. Stuart might have just returned to the trailer in Buckeye and quickly disassembled the oil pan before the patrol car arrived.

Still, the thing that was missing from all of this was motive. And so far, aside from Kathleen's unproven allegations against her husband, nobody had one. That didn't mean there wasn't a motive, just that the reason for committing the crime was something dark and buried and would require more digging to bring it to light.

What Bern couldn't rule out altogether, however, was the remote possibility of a wildcard, a firebug, a nut. Crazy people were out there. . . .

Leaving you broken and helpless, flat on your face on the hot earth, with pain arcing through your head and tuning up your senses so you can smell the spilled wine, the rank, bitter weeds, the dog feces, see Florence up there on the dark porch, hear her swallowing from the new bottle, and feel, oh yes really feel every fragment of broken bone and razored nerve ending. . . .

The episode came in a flash and lasted only a heartbeat, an eyeblink, leaving Bern flooded with adrenaline. His heart beat wildly, and he had to clench his hands to still their trembling.

He had done what the doctor said, and yet here the memory was again, coming out of nowhere to blindside him. But, Christ, what had it been? Less than a day since he'd been to the clinic. And the memory had come and gone quickly. Surely that was a good sign. He had to be realistic. Give it some time.

He almost convinced himself, but he was, after all, his father's son, and the thought kept running through his head: *Nine times out of ten things are just as bad as you think they are.*

Words to live by, courtesy of dear old Dad.

twenty

WHEN ANNE FINISHED HER LAST SESSION OF THE DAY, she found Kathleen Graley waiting in the reception area. Kathleen's skin was very pale against a black, long-sleeved cotton sweater she wore over jeans. By contrast, the dusting of freckles stood out more than ever.

"Do you have a minute?" Kathleen asked. "I really need to talk to you."

"Of course. Come on in." Anne held the door open for Kathleen, then closed it behind her. "I'm sorry we kept missing each other today. Let's sit."

Kathleen sank down on the sofa, letting her knapsack bag slide off her shoulder to rest on her lap. Even her strawberry blond hair, pushed back by a black headband, looked dull and leached of color.

Something has changed, Anne thought as she sat beside her. The fires of indignation were banked; Kathleen was calm and subdued.

"Rachel's body was released this morning," she said. "Not to me. Randy and Sharon had her cremated. If she'd died a different way, it's what I would've wanted, but somehow—now—it's just not right."

"I'm sorry," Anne said, feeling a surge of guilt that she had gone off to lunch at Rosemary's and delayed returning Kathleen's call. "I know it's very painful for you."

Kathleen jerked her head in a nod. "Well, it was typical of them not to consider what I wanted. But—it's done. I spoke to Randy on the phone. He said they didn't want a service. It would just hurt everybody too much. I agreed. Not with his excuse, but because the three of us—we ought to be able to put aside our differences for Rachel's sake. I ought to be able to do that, but I can't. . . . Sorry," she finished in a choked whisper.

"It's all right," Anne said. "Take your time."

Kathleen removed a tissue from her purse, then just held it. Her eyes were dry, but they burned with a feverish glow. "I asked for her ashes. Randy didn't argue. So I'm taking them home with me. Daniel—Professor Dees—has a boat. He said he'd take me out when I'm ready. Rachel loved the ocean, going to the beach. I remember how she used to laugh at the sandpipers. 'Funny birds,' she'd say and clap her hands. 'Mommy, let's go see the funny little birds.' I'd take her whenever I could. Not much lately, though. Too self-absorbed."

She fumbled in her purse again, put back the tissue, and took out two sheets of paper. "This is a copy of the list you and Detective Pagett asked me to make. I dropped off the original at his office." She handed Anne the pages. "I don't mean to push you, but have you found out anything at all?"

"Some things, yes, but I'd prefer to wait until I can give you a complete report. I know you're anxious, Kathleen, but I really think that's best."

Kathleen obviously didn't like it, but she nodded her agreement.

"I had lunch with Dr. Beiderman today," Anne said. "She told me you planned to go home soon. Have you decided when you'll leave?"

"I'm leaving from here."

"Does Bern know?"

She nodded. "I was going to wait till morning. I even paid for the motel, but I can't stay in that place another minute." She stood up abruptly and picked up her bag. "Call me if you need any more information, or you have anything you can tell me. I don't know what else to say. Just thank you."

Anne promised she would stay in touch, walked Kathleen to the office door, and squeezed her hand briefly in goodbye.

Lingering a moment to watch her cross the empty reception area and go out into the rapidly approaching darkness, Anne was reminded of little Christina Bowes. The two cases had bracketed Anne's day: a child grieving for her mother, and now a mother mourning her child.

In a perfect world, perhaps these two who had suffered so much loss could come together. But little girls were not interchangeable, and neither were mothers. And the world was far, far from perfect.

"Anne?"

Since Peggy wasn't at her desk, Anne had assumed she must have gone home. But she had come out of the storage room and stood staring at Anne with a worried look on her square, kind face.

"Everything okay?" she asked.

"Not really," Anne said, "but nothing I can do about it, Peggy."

"Well, just remember that," Peggy said. "Go home. You have nobody scheduled tomorrow, so enjoy your weekend."

"I'll try."

But the truth was, Anne didn't expect much of a respite. Whether she went to California or stayed in town, she would be interviewing people about Rachel. And she would be following Rosemary's advice about Bern, being observant and supportive—not as easy as it sounded when she was worried. So she didn't expect to have a good weekend.

She just didn't have any idea at that point how bad it was going to be.

ANNE MULLED OVER THE LOGISTICS OF A TRIP TO CALIfornia as she drove home. The most expeditious thing to do was to fly into John Wayne Airport in Orange County and stay someplace nearby while she tried to track down the people on Kathleen's list. On the other hand, if she flew into Lindbergh Field in San Diego, she'd be more likely to find some time to visit her folks.

As appealing as this last option was, it could mean hours on Interstate 5, depending on the traffic. When she was a little girl, her family had often headed up the coast on weekends, a relaxing drive with frequent views of the ocean that might end with lunch and a stroll through Laguna Beach, or the more exciting destinations of Disneyland and Knott's BerryFarm. Nowadays her parents rarely ventured north, even on weekdays.

"Too damn many cars," her dad declared, convinced that Los Angeles and San Diego exchanged populations every Saturday and Sunday. "Not worth the hassle."

Anne was pulling into the driveway of her house in Cave Creek when she realized she hadn't even thought about dinner. But Bern's Jeep was in the carport, and she knew he'd solved the problem of what they were going to eat when she walked in the front door and was greeted by the smell of pizza.

Bern was standing at the counter in the kitchen wolfing down a slice. "Starving," he explained, looking little-boy-guilty as he wiped his hands on a paper towel. "Sorry, babe."

"That's okay." She joined him, lifted her face for a kiss that tasted of tomato sauce and basil.

Under the table, Duke actually left the sanctuary of the far corner and came to stand with his nose sticking out from under the edge.

"Should we finish the pizza off with our bare hands?"

Anne asked. "Or be civilized and eat off plates at the table?"

"You sit," he said. "This will taste better if I zap it in the microwave."

While he busied himself heating the food and getting some beer from the refrigerator, Anne sat at the table and spoke to the dog, who had retreated a couple of steps. His tongue was lolled out, and he was breathing heavily.

"Hey, boy, what's with the panting? Did you have a walk?"

"He did for a fact," Bern said.

He had changed into gray sweats and running shoes, Anne noted. If the cheerfulness in his voice sounded a little forced, well, maybe it was because of the nagging headache he admitted he had suffered all day.

"It'll get better," Anne assured him, and told herself he must be on the mend if he'd regained his appetite.

"God, I hope so," Bern said.

He brought over plates and silverware, then the warmed pizza. Sausage, pepperoni, mushrooms, green peppers, black olives, loads of melted, stringy cheese—a real meal, and never mind the fat count. She even drank half a bottle of beer, not her favorite beverage; she only had it with pizza.

The smell of the food proved too much for Duke. He crept out from under the table and sat several feet away, licking his chops, a longing look in his yellow eyes. Taking pity on him, Anne broke off a piece of crust with a smear of cheese and laid it on the floor by her chair. The dog stared at the scrap and whined.

"You'll have to come and get it," Anne said.

He made a sudden dash to grab the morsel, then quickly retreated to chew it a couple of times and gulp it down.

"Well, well," Bern said. "Progress."

She hadn't told him about the bike ride with Duke that morning, and now she thought maybe she should keep it to herself and not give him any ideas. Better for all concerned if Bern exercised the dog.

After they finished eating, Anne made some decaf while Bern cleaned up the table. Then they took their coffee cups to the living room and sat on the couch next to each other, feet up on the coffee table, bodies touching shoulder to thigh.

"Should I light a fire?" Bern asked.

"No, stay here," Anne said, not wanting to break the connection. "But glance over—*casually*—toward the kitchen."

He did and said, "More progress."

They hadn't put the gate up. They never did in the evening until it was time to go to bed. For the first time, Duke had left his refuge under the table to come and lie on his belly on the tiled floor with just his front legs on the carpet.

Anne leaned her head against Bern's shoulder, for now perfectly content and thinking how moments like this always come so unexpectedly and how they are doomed by their perfection not to last.

"Did Kathleen come to see you today?" Bern asked, and the moment was gone.

"Yes, to say goodbye. She went home."

"I thought she might." He put their cups on the table and slipped his arm around Anne.

"I'm debating about going to California tomorrow," she said. "Do you think I'd have any luck just contacting people cold?"

"Hard to say. I'd like to come with you if you decide to go."

That didn't surprise her. Maybe it would even be nice for the two of them to get away. A little enforced togetherness.

"What about Duke?" she asked, snuggling up against Bern, her head in the hollow of his collarbone, her hand against the hard musculature of his chest.

"I lined up somebody." He ran his fingers along her spine. "Patrol officer who lives in Carefree. Used to be with K-9, so Duke doesn't scare him. He'll come by twice a day. All I have to do is give him a call."

Bern must have perspired a little, while walking the dog. She didn't care. She liked the way he smelled, slightly salty, distinctly Bern. Odors were powerful attractants, proved by lots of research. She could certainly verify that. How long since they had made love? One week and six days, but who was counting?

He said, "If we're going, I ought to make some reservations," but she could tell from his breathing that his mind wasn't really on airline flights.

"Tomorrow," she said as she laid a line of kisses up his neck and along his jaw.

"Good thinking," he murmured as her mouth found his.

EVEN THOUGH SHE'D GROWN UP A FEW BLOCKS FROM THE Pacific, Anne was not a surfer. But her brother Kevin was, and he'd talked her into going out a few times, often enough so she could compare making love to Bern to those waves offshore—sometimes wild and unpredictable, sometimes just powerful and satisfying.

Tonight it quickly became apparent that it would be low tide and flat seas.

Abruptly Bern moved away, rolling over to lie on his back, leaving her feeling very much alone.

"Sorry," he said.

"It doesn't matter." But of course it did, and she was sure he heard the disappointment in her voice. She tried again. "Put it in perspective. One time out of a thousand. It happens, darling."

"I guess. Just tired—the caffeine and all."

And all, she thought. Dear God, what kind of things lay behind that phrase? She turned to him, lying close and putting her arm across his chest.

"Bern? You'd tell me, wouldn't you—if there was something really wrong?"

"More than this, you mean?"

She hesitated. Observant and supportive, Rosemary had advised. But how could she not also try to help?

"Sometimes we repress things," she said. "Or we downplay what we're feeling because we can't believe our emotions have such a powerful effect."

"Oh, Christ, Anne. Please spare me the shrink talk." He pulled away, sat up, and swung his legs over the side of the bed. "Having a few rough days doesn't mean you're heading for a meltdown."

"No, of course not. But, Bern, we really need to talk about this."

"No," he said emphatically. "We don't."

She recognized that implacable tone. *Stonewalling* was a term that might have been coined just to describe Bern when he spoke like that. Her anger at his pigheadedness mixed with a sad tenderness as he walked, naked, to the closet to pull out a terrycloth robe.

He had a good body, if not a perfect one, leaner now than she'd ever seen it. Flat stomach, defined muscles in his upper arms and shoulders. But there was also that pale ridge of scar on his chest where the surgeon had to go in last summer to repair his punctured lung and stop the internal bleeding.

That sign of his vulnerability always frightened her, and now it kept her silent as well, as he slipped on the robe and said, "I'm going to watch TV for a while."

She wanted to remind him to take another of the sleeping pills the doctor had prescribed, but he had made it clear he didn't want her company or her advice. He flipped off the light as he went out and closed the door. She lay in the darkness, overwhelmed by a welter of emotions, not the least of which was sexual frustration.

From the living room came the muted sound of voices. She couldn't make out what they were saying, but could tell from the tones of outrage and righteous indignation that he was watching some newsmagazine.

Ah, Anne. Always the shrink, always analyzing. Well, how could she help it?

She got up and fumbled in the darkness for flannel pajamas in the drawer of her chest, somehow loath to turn on the lamp as she dressed. The blinds at the window had not been closed, but no light leaked in. Kathleen would have a black, moonless drive across the desert, alone with the ashes of her only child.

With this grim image for company, Anne thought she'd never be able to go to sleep, but she did. She remembered rousing once and still hearing the television, wondering if Bern had fallen asleep on the couch, then later knew without really waking that he had gotten into bed beside her.

After that she dreamed of being endlessly pursued, echoes of an old childhood nightmare. She ran down endless corridors, down narrow paths where trees bent down and reached for her with clawlike branches . . . and awoke to the very real sound of Duke barking furiously, loud thuds that she knew instantly were the dog hurling his body against the gate that barred the entrance to the kitchen, and a smell that was sickeningly familiar.

She reached for Bern, urgently saying his name, but he was already coming groggily awake as the gate crashed free. Then Duke's barks increased in volume as he ran down the hall and charged into the bedroom.

Bern acted on instinct, reaching for the drawer on the bedside table where he kept a loaded .38 revolver.

Although Anne was terrified by being awakened in the total darkness by an animal she had every reason to believe might have gone mad, she saw that Duke had stopped a few feet from the bed. She also recognized panic, not menace, in his bark at the same moment she realized that she could see Duke because the room was lit by an eerie orange glow from outside the window, and that what she smelled was smoke.

twenty-one

ANNE GRABBED BERN'S ARM AS HIS HAND DIPPED INTO the drawer for the gun, yelling, "No, stop!"

But he was already hesitating, staring beyond the dog and out the window, saying, "Jesus *Christ!*"

Anne switched on a lamp and grabbed the phone as he jumped out of bed, reached for his sweats piled on a chair nearby, and began pulling them on and jamming his feet into running shoes.

He said, "Good boy. Very good boy," to the frantic dog, who was still barking his warning while Anne got the 911 operator and reported the fire.

"It's outside," she said to the operator. "No, I don't know if the house is burning, but it will be if you don't hurry."

Meanwhile, Bern snatched some clothes for her out of the closet, saying, "Come on, get a move on."

Hanging up the phone, Anne asked, "Can we do anything?"

"I'll take a look, but not without you."

"I'm right behind you," Anne said. "*Go.*"

Duke ran after Bern, stopped at the door, and came back to her, alternating his barks with yips and whines as expressive as language.

No time to change. Anyway, Bern had pulled out an expensive pantsuit for her from the closet. Flannel pajamas would do fine. She shoved her feet into plush-lined booties, and went out into the hallway and down to the front door with Duke right behind her.

She got a look through the kitchen windows of flames leaping, consuming her back deck with fiery glee. She could hear the hiss and crackle, too, and smell the burning wood, the odor overlaid with the stench of the varnish she'd applied last fall as waterproofing.

The front door was open. Bern must have gone out that way. Cold air swirled in, making her realize she'd need more than the pajamas. She grabbed coats from the hall closet—both hers and Bern's, she hoped—seized her purse from the hall table, and ran outside.

The wind, calm during the evening, was now blowing fitfully, fanning the flames. All the shrubs at the base of the hill were ablaze, lighting up the dark night with a fierce red glow. She raced around toward the back, with the rocky ground hurting her feet through the scant padding of her booties, pulling on a coat as she ran and calling for Bern. He was silhouetted against the flames running up the wooden supports of the deck cover and licking at the roof above the kitchen.

"Stay back," he yelled.

He had a garden hose going and was spraying water on the back wall and the roof. Above the snap and roar of the fire and Duke's frenzied, hoarse barking, she thought she could hear sirens in the distance.

"What can I do?" she cried, unwilling to stand there while her house burned.

Just then the wind shifted, and a long runner of fire found a path through the rocky yard around the back of the house toward the carport, jumping from one clump of dry grass to another.

"I'll get another hose going," Anne said.

"*No*—" Bern began coughing and choking as the wind

gusted and blew smoke and cinders around him.

She caught something about low water pressure. The smoke had started to burn her lungs, too, so she turned back, leaving him to stamp out burning embers deposited by the wind, and ran back to the front.

Later she would think she was crazy, but at that moment she knew she had to do *something,* so she headed for the carport, determined to save at least one of the cars. The Cherokee was the logical choice, parked on the side opposite the burning wall. She had keys to both vehicles in her purse.

Duke was at her heels as she went into the carport. She could feel the heat of the fire as she unlocked the door. The whimpering dog jumped in ahead of her. It took two tries to start the engine; she backed out just as flame engulfed the roof.

Looking through the rear window, she steered the Jeep down the driveway and off into the gravel, leaving the way clear for the two fire trucks, fast approaching, lights flashing. The sweetest sound she'd ever heard was the screaming of the sirens as the trucks came roaring up.

The men worked fast and efficiently, quickly subduing the fire. At one point she left Duke in the Jeep and went to speak to one of the firemen, but he just urged her to stay in the car and out of the way.

Awakened by the sirens, a couple of neighbors arrived, leaving when Anne assured them she was okay and there was nothing they could do.

She glimpsed Bern over by one of the trucks and knew he was safe. She also saw a fireman up on the roof of her kitchen swinging an ax, and the charred, water-soaked timbers of the carport falling on her Camaro.

At first Duke sat behind her, but he had crowded up into the space between the front seats right next to her, and she realized now she'd had her arm around him the whole time. She laid her head against the rough fur of his shoulder, fully aware that he had probably saved their lives. How long since she had checked the batteries in her smoke alarm? For whatever reason, the thing hadn't worked. If not for Duke, the smoke might have overcome her and Bern while they slept.

She began shivering, not only from shock and the cold but from her reaction to the narrowness of their escape. As she started the engine to warm up the Jeep, she also remembered the blackened rubble of the house where Rachel and Rufina Vaughn had died; the hair rose on the back of her neck at the memory.

Was it possible there was some connection?

The dash clock read 4:05, still more than an hour before dawn. Still too dark to perceive a pattern in the fire. She knew only that it had started outside. Something in the carport? No, she remembered the fire coming around the house from the other side. More likely the cause was a cigarette or a match carelessly tossed by somebody driving past. An accident. It had to be.

But the suspicion of foul play, once it had surfaced, could not be repressed, and neither the toasty air flowing from the heater nor Duke's comforting presence did much to help the chill that had settled deep in her bones.

BERN SAT ON THE RUNNING BOARD OF ONE OF THE RURAL Metro fire trucks and gratefully accepted a hit of oxygen from the man who introduced himself as Captain Hodge. Bern could feel an ominous pain in his chest when he coughed. Was it possible he had retorn the lung? He sure as hell hoped not.

"Better?" Hodge asked, offering a heavy yellow coat that he helped Bern drape across his shoulders. Bern got the impression of a seamed, weathered face below the headgear, and eyes that had learned calmness by looking at a great many conflagrations much worse than this one.

"Thanks," Bern croaked and wiped a hand across his forehead, where sweat was fast cooling in the chill pre-dawn air. The headlamps of the trucks lit the scene. Still, with the flames out, the firemen were bulky silhouettes in the darkness as they mopped up.

"I'm Bern Pagett, homicide detective, Phoenix PD." Bern's throat was raw, and his voice sounded hoarse. He'd never worked a case with Rural Metro and didn't know their protocol. He'd also heard from people in the Phoenix Fire Department that the guys out here were not particularly cooperative, although he had no idea how much stock to put in this rumor. Whatever the politics, he didn't have the luxury of playing games—or the time.

He said, "Captain, I really think you ought to get an investigator out here."

"You have reason to think this wasn't an accident, Detective Pagett?"

"I'm working a double homicide—arson related."

"Coincidence?" Hodge offered.

"Could be," Bern conceded.

After all, how likely was it that the arsonist had found him? Police officers' addresses and phone numbers are never released or published. Anne had an unlisted number. Still, Bern knew that true privacy was a thing of the past. Today we all reside just a couple of mouse clicks away, down the information highway.

"I'd just like to play it safe," Bern said.

"Understood," Hodge said. "Don't worry. I'll get somebody on it soon as it's light. I'm going to leave one of the trucks, have the men stand a watch. Wouldn't want a flare-up. Any idea where you and your lady will be?"

"Is it safe to go back inside?"

"In the front of the house—yeah. Of course, it'll stink like an old campfire. We shut off your power. Leave it like that until we get a chance to check it out. And, listen—I know you might be tempted to go poking around, but hold off till the investigator gets here, okay?"

When Bern promised reluctantly that he would, Hodge stuck out a hand. It felt all bone and calluses as Bern shook it, thanked him again, then gave him back the coat and went down the driveway to find Anne.

He was happy to see the Jeep parked unscathed on the gravel; however, by the time he walked to it, he was furious, too, thinking about the chance Anne had taken by going into the carport, risking her life for a stupid vehicle that was fully insured and easily replaced.

Duke started barking, deep and ferocious, as Bern approached, but Anne had a grip on his collar and was telling him it was okay as Bern opened the door on the passenger side. The dog broke off in midbark and gave Bern a sheepish look as he slid in.

Anne crawled across the middle console and into his lap, hugging him fiercely, and his anger vanished. Even Duke gave him a swipe on the cheek with a warm tongue before retreating to jump up on the backseat.

"Are you all right?" Anne asked. "You're not hurt? I'm sorry, I wasn't thinking. . . ."

She started to pull away, but he held her close.

"No," he said. "Stay right here."

The engine wasn't on now, but it must have been running earlier because it was definitely warmer in the car. Anne was even warmer in his arms. Outside the firemen were packing up their gear.

"I think your car's totaled," Bern said. "The back deck is gone, and I'm sure the kitchen's a disaster."

"But the rest of the house is okay," Anne countered. "And so is the Jeep."

Bern smiled wearily, thinking how perfectly the exchange illustrated the way they looked at life.

"The most important thing," Anne went on, "is we're both alive and well."

"Yes," Bern said. "When it gets right down to it, that's really all that matters."

They sat silently for a few minutes just holding each other and watched one of the fire trucks roll away. The men left behind on watch had climbed into the remaining truck to rest. It was still very dark outside, the darkness hiding the worst of the damage as well as any clues to the fire's origin. No sense alarming Anne at this point about his suspicions; morning would be soon enough.

But, as usual, there was no keeping things from Anne. She said quietly, "It crossed my mind that the fire might have been set deliberately, Bern."

He sighed. "Yeah. Me, too. There'll be an arson investigator first thing. We'll check it out."

The air in the car was rapidly cooling off. He shivered, and Anne said, "I have your coat—in the back." She got up and leaned over the seat to get it, crowded with the two of them in the same small space, but crowded in a very nice way.

He shrugged the jacket around him and said, "We need to decide what to do. Go to a hotel or call somebody—"

"At this time of night? Anyway, what would we do with Duke?"

"Well, it wouldn't be all that comfortable, but we could stay here in the Jeep. Or we can go inside."

She thought about it for a moment, then said softly, "I'd rather be home."

He had a couple of halogen flashlights in the Jeep. The powerful beams lit their way and illuminated more of the damage than Bern felt they needed to see just then. Tomorrow was soon enough.

The front of the house looked perfectly normal, but the place did indeed smell like an old campfire. The odor permeated the clothes in the closets, too. There was enough hot water left in the water heater for Bern to quickly shower off the soot. Then there was nothing to do but to dress in a flannel shirt and pants that reeked of smoke. Only the coat that had been taken out to the Jeep didn't stink.

Anne put on corduroy slacks and a sweater. She insisted she'd never be able to sleep, but she dozed on the couch next to Bern under a shared blanket, curled up with her feet flat against his thigh.

Duke lay on the floor next to the couch—nearest to Anne, Bern noted. Occasionally he heard the firemen moving around outside. He hated the waiting, wanted to go and start looking for things to prove—or disprove—his suspicions. But he knew Hodge was right. Better to wait until daylight.

Even better, he ought to get some rest. But he couldn't sleep. Duke stayed awake, too, standing guard. Bern's watch was somewhere in the bedroom; he'd forgotten to look for it, so he lost track of time. All he knew was that it seemed to take forever for the sun to come up.

twenty-two

THE MEN WHO HAD REMAINED ON FIRE WATCH PRO-
nounced the area safe and left just after dawn, promising
that a fire marshal would return to make an inspection of
the house.

Although Anne kept telling herself the damage could
have been so much worse, the sight revealed in the early-
morning light was devastating. She could see daylight
through the hole the firemen had chopped in the roof just
above the kitchen sink. The fallout from that messy, albeit
necessary, exercise littered the counters and the floor with
chunks of wood, insulation, and shingles. There were burn
marks in the tile. Water and soot streaked the whitewashed
cabinets and the wallpaper border with its print of bright
sunflowers.

Although the worst of the destruction had been in the
kitchen, water from the fire hoses had flowed toward the
living room to soak into the carpet. Anne was sure every
surface and all the blinds and drapes in the house would
have to be cleaned to eliminate the smoky odor. In addition, their clothes would have to be either washed or taken
to the cleaners.

Outside, the deck had been reduced to charred timbers
and ashes, and the whole back of the house had been

blackened. Part of the carport had collapsed. She thought Bern was right about her car; she'd have to write it off. The storage unit in the front section of the carport looked undamaged, so her bike was probably all right—one small comfort.

As for the rest of the property, Anne had an acre and a half of yard and hillside that was all rocks and sandy earth. Except for two big paloverde trees that had been planted for shade near the front of the house, nature had designed the landscaping. There was mostly cactus—cholla and prickly pear—but last summer's monsoonal rains had brought a bounty of seasonal plants: desert marigold, buckwheat, and clumpy grasses.

Anne thanked God the paloverde had survived. Everything else that lay in the fire's path was gone, the small plants now ashy powder being stirred by a dawn breeze, the cactus like charcoal sticks stuck in the ground. At least the fire had been stopped about halfway up to the natural water basin in the outcropping of boulders. The blaze could have easily engulfed the whole hillside, perhaps ravaging even more of the wild lands beyond.

Bern, grim and silent, walked with her to make the survey; Duke trailed along behind. They ended up on the driveway in a spot that provided an overall view. Standing there with the bright early-morning light showing the destruction with such crisp clarity, Anne felt a welter of emotions ballooning in her chest: disbelief, fear, sadness, rage. She backed up, pressing her body against Bern's, fighting tears.

Bern wrapped his arms around her. "We can have the house fixed. You can get a new car."

He was right. She had to keep that firmly in mind and ignore the nagging voice that said, *After you fix it, what's to keep somebody from burning it down again?*

Best to concentrate on the positive steps she could take; even Bern, who was usually so negative, was doing that.

But, so many things to do. She'd just have to take them one at a time.

First, breakfast. They would both feel better with some food in their stomachs.

With the electricity and gas shut off, cooking was not an option. As a matter of fact, Anne didn't even want to think about opening up the refrigerator yet. She figured she would have to throw almost everything away, although for once it seemed her hectic schedule of the past few days might be a blessing. With no time to market, the refrigerator—as well as the pantry—was almost bare.

She went into town for orange juice, muffins, and coffee. When she returned, Bern had all the windows open, so the odor of smoke wasn't quite so bad in the living room as they sat on the couch to eat. Bern had made some calls while she was gone but had left it to her to call the insurance company.

Suddenly the enormity of what lay ahead hit her—from digging out copies of her policies to the protracted aggravation of the repairs. Her appetite gone, Anne gave Duke the other half of her oversized blueberry muffin.

Just as he finished wolfing down the food, the dog's ears pricked up. A growl rumbling in his chest, he stood, stiff-legged, looking toward the front door. A few seconds later, Anne heard the sound of a car coming down the street, slowing, turning into her drive.

"It's probably the arson investigator," Bern said; then to the dog, whose growls turned to loud barks as the car approached the house, he said, "Shh, Duke, it's okay."

Regardless of his remarks and the lack of concern in his voice, when Bern got up and went to the door, Anne noticed that he unzipped his jacket, giving him quick access to the holstered gun which he had clipped to his belt—just in case.

THE ARSON INVESTIGATOR WAS PETER HAVELCHEK, a slender man, five inches shorter and ten years older than

Bern, with thick iron-gray hair cropped short and a modest mustache. He wore jeans, boots, and a gray T-shirt under an old brown-leather aviator's jacket.

After Bern provided a rundown on what had happened the night before and reiterated his suspicions, Havelchek took a camera from his car, and they did a slow walk around the yard. Unlike Steve Gainey, who did his scene inspections in a silence so profound Bern could swear he could hear Steve's brain clicking away, Havelchek gabbed incessantly.

He talked about the weather, the Suns' latest basketball game, his plans to go skiing up at Sunrise next weekend; a constant flow of chatter that required little or no response from Bern. Havelchek made frequent stops to snap photos, but he offered no explanations of what he was preserving on film. Bern, unimpressed, was already planning to call Steve as soon as Havelchek left—the politics of the situation be damned.

Then, after the circuit was completed, Havelchek said, "Over here," and led the way, skirting the burned area to a location a good fifty feet in from the street. "Way I read it, the fire was set in two places. Take a look at this."

He hunkered down and pointed to an irregular mound where tufts of grass grew, seared to a crisp paper-bag brown by the late summer heat.

Bern, who dropped down on his heels beside him, shook his head. "Sorry, I don't get it."

"Some of the grass has been pulled up," Havelchek said patiently.

Then Bern saw what he meant. There were shallow holes in the sandy soil, and a closer inspection revealed faint marks along the tops of the holes that were consistent with the dry grass brushing the dirt as it was twisted and removed.

"Our arsonist used the grass for extra tinder," Havelchek explained. "Not enough ground cover, so he couldn't be sure a fire would spread in from the street. So what he

did was start his number-one blaze nearer the house, then
he goes back to the street and lights up number two.''

Damn, Bern thought, *the guy does know what he's doing, after all.*

Havelchek leaned over and sniffed like a bloodhound.
''Used a little accelerant for insurance—smells like benzene to me.'' Havelchek stood up and snapped a few pictures. ''He—or she, not to get too gender-specific—hopes
we'll miss the benzene, that everybody will assume it's
just a careless cigarette. He also probably figures we won't
notice there's two points of origin.'' Havelchek hesitated,
and Bern knew there was more.

''What else?'' Bern prompted, slowly getting to his feet.

Havelchek headed back to street. No small talk now. He
stopped, gestured toward the house, and said, ''Think
about our firebug out here surveying the place. What does
he see?''

''Damn dark at three in the morning,'' Bern said. ''So
not much.''

''Yeah, but suppose he drives by earlier, maybe more
than once. So he makes his observations in daylight and
again with the lights on. Whole lot you can tell about a
house, looking at it like that.''

Bern felt the hair bristle on the back of his neck because
he understood exactly what Havelchek was driving at. Put
yourself in the arsonist's shoes and what do you see? An
older structure with a typical layout, so probably the
kitchen is in back. A picture window marks the living
room. Lights go out there and on in another room. Bingo,
you've marked the bedroom.

And he and Anne had gone to the bedroom early. The
guy could've been out here during the time Bern had tried
to make love to Anne and failed so miserably. Wouldn't
the asshole have loved knowing that?

The fire had been set on the side of the house where
their bedroom was located. Only chance and wind patterns
had sent it veering toward the back to do its damage there,

then caused it to circle around to the carport.

"He meant to fry us," Bern said.

Havelchek nodded soberly. "You got two things here, Detective Pagett: a mean son of a bitch, and one who likes to play with fire. That's a hell of a bad combination. You got to ask yourself if he means to try again."

"What do you think?"

"I'd say it was a damn good possibility. So if it was me, I'd be thinking about either hiring some security or moving out for a while."

"There is a third solution."

"What's that?" Havelchek asked.

"I nail the bastard and put his ass in jail," Bern said.

twenty-three

WILL HANSON, SUMMONED BY BERN WHILE ANNE WENT for breakfast, arrived in time for a second walk-through with Bern and Peter Havelchek. Except for a soil sample containing traces of benzene, the three men combed the area for physical evidence without success.

The rocky ground yielded no shoe prints; they found no matches, cigarette butts, or anything else that could have been used to start the fire; and there were no tire impressions within a quarter of a mile in either direction from Anne's driveway.

Bern, once again functioning on a few hours of sleep, was irritable, edgy, and feeling as though he'd been mainlining adrenaline as he and Will stood in front of the house and watched Havelchek drive away.

"This guy didn't leave anything," Bern said. "Maybe he took something away." Desert plants are tenacious and hardy. They come with thorns and barbs that stick to anything they touch. "What are our chances of getting a warrant to do some checking?"

"Zero to none," Will said gloomily. "Face it, we got nothing."

"Yeah," Bern said, "but our firebug doesn't know that."

He paused, quickly assessing the danger to Anne if he left her here. He didn't expect daylight to be a deterrent to the arsonist; he'd done his work at the Graley house in midafternoon. But Duke was standing guard, and the fire marshal should be arriving soon. So should somebody from the insurance company. And if Anne could arrange it, a work crew would soon follow. In addition, Bern had put the county sheriff on alert, so a patrol car would come by regularly.

Bern turned to Will. "Mind if we take your car?"

"And go where?"

"To shake up the overconfident," Bern said, relishing the manic, reckless tone in his own voice. "And maybe, if we do it right, strike terror in the heart of an asshole who burns down houses and kills hardworking housekeepers and innocent children."

Will shook his head. "Do the words *Internal Affairs* mean anything to you right now?"

"Not much," Bern said. "You coming or not?"

"I guess I'd better," Will said.

ANNE SPENT THE MORNING DEALING WITH THE REALITIES that come hard on the heels of tragedy. A fire marshal arrived to give an official okay and turn the utilities back on. He was followed by an adjuster from the insurance company, who estimated the cost to repair the damages and gave Anne the names of companies that could supply emergency work crews. She was fortunate to find people who would come right away to put a temporary cover over the hole in the roof and begin cleaning up the inside.

Duke barked furiously at each new arrival and made such a fuss when Anne attempted to shut him in the bedroom, she put him on a leash and kept him close beside her. The people coming and going would have much preferred having the animal behind a good solid wall, but the move reassured Anne; any unwelcome visitor had good reason to be leery of the big, ugly dog who looked as if he ought to be guarding a junkyard.

Even in the midst of all the activity, Anne kept remembering Bern and Will's abrupt departure. It had been Bern the cop who strode out the door with that cold, flat look on his face and only a noncommittal answer when she wanted to know where he was going and when he would be back.

Had he found something out there during that slow, careful search? She didn't know, but she'd seen him this way before—cloaked in rigid resolve and fueled with righteous anger, going forth like some warrior of old to meet the enemy.

She did her best not to think about how often such a warrior never returned because he had died on the field of battle.

BERN QUICKLY REGRETTED LEAVING THE JEEP FOR ANNE. If he'd been driving his own vehicle, he would have slapped the portable flasher on top and barreled down to Scottsdale in a hurry. Not Will. He poked along at the speed limit.

Maybe he thought the sedate pace was going to give Bern a chance to calm down. Instead, by the time they arrived at the Holiday Inn, Bern's anger had been refined to a white-hot kernel of rage.

He was out of the car before it came to a full stop in a red zone right outside the hotel entrance. Will hurriedly slapped a placard that read *Police* on the dash and followed him into the lobby, where Bern flashed his badge and asked if the Graleys were still there.

There were two young women behind the front desk. One regarded Bern warily while the other, more than a little rattled, punched up a computer screen and verified the registration.

"Room numbers?" Bern asked. Better to double-check than to give some poor old snowbird a heart attack.

"I'm sorry," the flustered clerk said, "I don't think I'm allowed to—"

Bern grabbed the monitor and turned it so he could see the information, then turned it back toward the bug-eyed woman.

"Thank you, ma'am," Bern said with cold politeness. "And please don't call either of the Graleys to tell them I'm coming."

"Uh—sir?" the other clerk said timidly. "The Graleys? I think they're in the café."

With Will trailing behind, Bern went through the lobby into the crowded restaurant looking for Randy and Sharon. He found them outside on a patio where red and pink geraniums spilled from clay pots, and a dozen small brown birds hopped around among the diners, pecking at crumbs and twittering loudly.

Randy and Sharon sat at a table on the edge of the patio under the dappled shade of an acacia tree. Sharon had a plate of fruit and toast in front of her, but her son seemed to be on a liquid diet that consisted of a large stemmed glass of orange juice and a mug of coffee.

Both appeared to be out of mourning and dressed for a relaxing day off. Randy wore his brick-red sport shirt loose over off-white Dockers. Sharon's outfit was ice blue, a fine cotton knit, the pants almost tight enough to be leggings, the top hip-length with a V-neck and three-quarter-length sleeves.

Well, hell, Rachel's ashes were on their way to California. People can't wear sackcloth forever.

Sharon was facing in Bern's direction and saw him first. She froze in the act of spreading raspberry jam on a piece of dry rye toast and said something to Randy, who slouched in a cushioned chair, massaging his left temple with his fingertips.

He turned, and Bern heard him say, *"Shit."* Bern could tell Randy was glaring at him behind his aviator sunglasses. Bern would also bet that behind the shades his eyes were bloodshot and that he'd been hitting the Scotch after Mom went off to bed.

Getting his courage up before he came to set fire to Anne's house or winding down afterward? Or could it be that his mama, attuned to his habits, waited until her sonny boy drank himself into a stupor, then drove out to do the job herself?

Bern grabbed an extra chair from the next table over, leaving Will to mumble an explanation or maybe an apology to the startled couple, dropped it with a thump between Randy and Sharon, and sat down.

"Enjoying your breakfast?" Bern asked, putting a hard edge on the innocuous question.

"We *were*." Sharon carefully put her toast and knife on her plate and dabbed her fingers on a napkin. "I'm sorry, Lieutenant, but our attorney has told us not to speak to the police unless he's present."

"Yeah," Randy growled. "So get the fuck away from us."

"Common misunderstanding, isn't it, Will?" Bern said. "All that stuff about lawyers."

"It's TV," Will said. "Puts the wrong ideas in people's heads."

Will didn't sit. He stood right behind Bern. Will didn't look at all like a cop. Actually he looked like a cross between Huckleberry Hound and Columbo. Funny thing, though, there wasn't a person on that patio who saw Will standing there in that casually alert slouch with that droopy-eyed face who didn't immediately know what he did for a living. You could almost see the other patrons withdrawing, distancing themselves.

"Technically," Bern said, "Miranda rights only apply when I arrest you and start asking questions. But, see, I'm here to tell you something, not to ask anything."

"And what is that?" Sharon asked warily.

"Somebody set fire to my house early this morning."

"Oh, yes," Sharon said. "I *thought* the two of you—

well—'' She turned to her son. "Remember that bit on the radio this morning, Randy? It *was* Dr. Menlo's name I heard. The report said nobody was hurt, Lieutenant, and the house didn't burn completely. So you're a lot luckier than we were.''

"Yeah,'' Bern said, "lucky, but when I catch whoever did it, that person sure as hell won't be.''

"Well, since you're not arresting us, I guess you don't have any evidence, do you?''

There were things detectives were barred from doing. They could not threaten or beat up a suspect; deny the suspect food, water, use of a bathroom, or sleep; or question the suspect without reading the Miranda rights once an arrest had been made. There were no rules against stretching the truth or downright lying.

Bern grinned at Sharon, a smile that was just a baring of his teeth. "Just because we don't make an arrest doesn't mean there's no evidence.''

"Ah, he's bluffing,'' Randy said. "Making threats.''

"Threats? No, I'm just telling it like it is, Randy.'' Knowing he was edging close to violation of those rules of conduct and not really giving a damn, Bern added, "And one more thing—anybody comes near my place again, I'm going to know it, and I'll fucking put them in the ground.''

Neither of the Graleys said anything as Bern got up, replaced the chair at the next table, and walked away with Will. Bern noted that Randy looked a little white around the gills; however, Sharon had only regarded him with veiled malice and no fear whatsoever.

BECAUSE OF ALL THE PEOPLE WHO WERE IN AND OUT OF the house, Anne had put her purse in a bedroom drawer for safekeeping. Her pager was in the purse. So she missed being beeped and also missed the first two phone calls from Cynthia Lynde. Since the answering machine was on the kitchen counter, it had been unplugged and removed.

So it was lunchtime before she happened to be inside near a phone when Cynthia called for the third time.

"My God," Cynthia said. "I've been trying to reach you all morning."

From the agitation in Cynthia's voice, Anne assumed she must have heard about the fire. She said, "Oh, Cyn, it's been a real mess, but we're okay, thank goodness."

"What?" Cynthia said, bewildered. "What are you talking about?"

"The fire," Anne said. "Isn't that why you're calling?"

"Fire? Wait. Hold it. You had a fire?"

"Yes. Last night. What else has happened?"

"Somebody broke into the office again," Cynthia said. There had been another break-in two years before. "None of us had any patients scheduled, so we didn't know about it until I got a call from the security patrol about nine this morning. I got hold of Andy, and we both came over. You'd think these idiots looking for drugs would learn the difference between psychologists and psychiatrists."

"How big a mess is it?" Anne asked. Coping with one disaster was quite enough; she wasn't sure she could handle two at a time.

"Listen," Cynthia said. "It's not really that bad, just pisses me off more than anything. I called Peggy, and she's here, helping sort things out. You said you and Bern were okay. What about the house?"

Anne gave her a rundown on the damages. "As soon as the crew finishes up on the temporary repairs, I'll come help."

"You'll do no such thing. I'm sure the three of us can manage. If something comes up that we can't handle, we'll call you."

After she hung up, Anne sat on the side of the bed, feeling sick and overwhelmed, and gave in to a few tears. She felt a cold nose touch her elbow and found Duke gazing up at her with a worried look in his yellow eyes.

"Bad day, doggy," Anne said, rubbing his head and

following the line of the drooping ear, wishing she felt more comforted by the gesture.

Instead, she was thinking that she'd better check her pager to see what else had gone wrong. A cold knot of premonition was already forming in her stomach when the readout told her the service had been trying to reach her.

Several of the messages were expected: those left by Cynthia and Andy in their ongoing attempt to find her. The others were from Rena Trent.

Chrissie had not been reassured by Anne's strategy with the posters after all. Shortly after breakfast that morning, the little girl had disappeared.

twenty-four

ANNE HAD NOT BEEN CERTAIN THAT CHRISSIE WOULDN'T
run away again, but she'd had a strong feeling that the
child was willing to stay put. Chrissie had even begun to
accept the possibility that her mother was dead. Given that
fact, why would she go looking for her? Was the very act
a form of denial?

"Maybe I was wrong to want to keep her with me,"
Rena said. "Maybe somebody else could have taken better
care of her."

Anne gripped the phone more tightly and pinched the
bridge of her nose. The bones in her forehead were beginning to ache, a combination of sinus irritation from the
smoke and pressure from stress.

She tried to shift the focus from herself to Rena, whose
misery was all too apparent in her voice.

"Rena, I'm sure you've done the best job possible with
Christina," Anne said. "I don't understand this either. Tell
me exactly what happened."

"She slept straight through the night," Rena said, "and
she ate a good breakfast. My husband and I were cleaning
up the kitchen. Brian took Chrissie outside to play on the
swing set. Brian's my youngest. He's nine."

Brian had come back inside to use the bathroom. He

had been teaching Christina how to pump herself on the swing. She wanted to stay and play, so he left her there.

"He shouldn't have done that," Rena said. "But it was only for a minute, and he feels just terrible. It's my fault, Anne. I should've made sure the kids knew that Chrissie was never to be left alone."

"Rena, you must stop blaming yourself," Anne said firmly. "It's impossible to be on guard every single second. You called the police?"

"Of course. Right away."

"There's something I don't understand. Did you go looking for her yourself?"

"Yes. The kids and I went on foot. My husband took the van and drove up and down. Some of the neighbors joined in, too."

"How long had Chrissie been gone at that point?"

"Not long. Five minutes, maybe."

"It just seems so odd," Anne said. "How could she vanish so quickly?"

"I don't know," Rena said. "I've been wondering the same thing. Those posters, Anne—do you think Chrissie's mother might have seen them and somehow discovered Chrissie was staying here?"

"CPS would not have told Ms. Bowes where her daughter was, and I certainly wouldn't have. Anyway, nobody contacted my office." She had put her office number on the posters along with the one for CPS.

"Well, I hoped—I mean, I just hate to consider the terrible alternatives."

"Me, too," Anne said.

After Rena promised to keep her informed, Anne hung up, then sat with one hand on the receiver, trying to think of anybody she could call, anything she could do to help find Chrissie. Bern had enough on his plate. Besides, he'd already intervened on Anne's behalf once before with the investigator who was looking for Sue Lynn Bowes.

Duke had sat down on the floor right next to Anne. She

could feel just a ripple of resistance in his body when she put her hand on his neck; then he relaxed against her as she leaned down and gave him a hug.

"Too bad you weren't there for Chrissie," Anne told the dog—and realized she was already expecting the worst.

WHEN THEY GOT CLOSE TO THE JACKRABBIT TRAIL turn-off, Bern called county sheriff dispatch and asked them to have a patrol car meet him and Will at the Vaughns' trailer.

"Oh, good," Will said. "Now we'll have a witness for the IA hearing. Be real sure we get our badges lifted."

"Better than getting shot," Bern said.

To tell the truth, he was coming down off the adrenaline, but he was sick of hearing Will tell him to chill out and stop acting like a damn fool. That kind of advice just made Bern more determined to go ahead with his original plan of action.

He figured if they were lucky, maybe either Stuart or Darrel would do something stupid enough to give them probable cause for a warrantless search of the trailer and the vehicles.

But Darrel's pickup was missing, and Stuart came out empty-handed to stand in the shadowy cave of the covered porch and watch their arrival.

Bern steeled himself as they exited the car. He wasn't sure if his vigilance could prevent the memory from blind-siding him today. In any case, he looked at the porch and saw only some rough-cut timbers shaded by a thicket of overgrown sunflowers, castor beans, and weeds, and he approached it without a shred of uneasiness.

"Whaddaya want?" Stuart Vaughn demanded.

"Few things we need to discuss," Bern said. "I don't think you've met my partner, Will Hanson."

"Mr. Vaughn," Will said.

Stuart gave him a curt nod.

The passage of time was reducing the older man to bone and gristle. A raggedy-ass pair of jeans hung so low on his hips that they showed the loose elastic of his BVDs. A flannel shirt, washed to a vague blue plaid, swallowed him like an oversized sack.

His jaw bristled with gray stubble. That lazy left eye wandered crazily, as though he were watching Bern and Will with one eyeball while keeping the other on the uniformed patrolman who stood beside his unit.

"You can come inside," Stuart said.

He led the way through the dark porch area past an assortment of white resin chairs and one old TV table with an overflowing ashtray. A large cement block served as a step up to the door of the trailer. Bern and Will waited politely, letting Stuart go first.

Rufina Vaughn had spent her days tending to other people's houses. It was understandable if she had no energy left for this cramped, dingy place.

Except for limited space for walking, every surface appeared to be covered with either furniture or clutter. An odor of years of meals, heavy on the chili pepper, underlay the current smells of dust and cigarette smoke.

The front section of the trailer held a small kitchenette and a living area that contained a couple of upholstered armchairs, a portable TV on a rickety table, and a narrow, built-in sofa with storage drawers underneath. A shelf ran along the wall near the top, perpendicular to the sofa, displaying knickknacks, mostly ceramic figurines. Heavy thermal drapes covered the windows, making the interior of the trailer almost as dark as the porch.

A door was ajar off to Bern's right. He went over and pushed it open to reveal a bedroom section, two twin beds with just enough space between them to walk straight ahead into a bath.

"Nobody here but me," Stuart said. "You can sit if you want."

"I'm fine right here," Will said, slouching back against the door frame.

Rather than opening the curtains, Stuart switched on a floor lamp, then perched on the edge of one of the rump-sprung chairs. Bern took the other.

"I keep seein' you out there," Stuart said. "So I knew you'd be comin' back. Just didn't know when."

"You thought you saw us here earlier?" Bern asked.

"Well, I'm not blind, you know," Stuart said irritably. "I know when people are around watchin' me."

Will shot Bern a look that told Bern they were thinking the same thing: The old man probably thought every jack-rabbit that hopped by was a government agent in a bunny suit. Still, Bern knew he ought to eliminate the possibility that somebody did have the old guy under surveillance—as far-fetched as the idea seemed.

"Stuart, why do you think you're being watched?"

"Because that's what happens," Stuart said. "People get it in for you, they never let you alone."

"Well, I can assure you neither one of us has been out here, not since my visit the other day."

Stuart snorted in derision and disbelief and muttered, "Yeah, sure."

"Tell us what you saw," Bern said. "Can you give us descriptions of the people, license numbers of vehicles?"

The questions forced a temporary reality check, and un-certainty followed. "Well—I guess not." He hunched his shoulders and added stubbornly, "But I know what I know."

Will gave his head an almost imperceptible shake that signaled Bern of his conviction that what the man knew was based on paranoid delusions.

"Were these people watching you last night, Stuart?" Bern asked.

"Maybe. I don't keep track all the time."

"Where were you?"

"Here. Where else would I be?"

"You didn't go out?" Will asked. "Get something to eat? Go to a movie?"

"My wife just died," Stuart said, as though he couldn't believe their insensitivity. "I don't go out anyway. Too dangerous."

"So you were here all night?"

Stuart nodded.

"What about Darrel?" Bern asked. "Was he here with you?"

"For a while, but we—well, we had words."

"You argued?"

"He's on edge," Stuart said defensively. "My son's takin' his mother's death real hard, what with you people botherin' us, and we can't even have a decent funeral 'cause there's something about medical records. I keep tellin' 'em I don't know about records, that Rufina wouldn't go to regular doctors around here, that she'd always go over the border to them *Mexican* quacks even when we had good medical insurance—"

"When did Darrel leave?" Bern cut in impatiently, unwilling to sit through a lot of prejudiced ranting.

Stuart blinked, shifting gears. "Seven, maybe. Eight o'clock."

"Did he say where he was going?"

Stuart shook his head. "I figured he was gonna hang out with his friends. Thought it was a good thing, maybe get his mind off all this bad stuff."

"He didn't come back, did he?" Bern asked.

Stuart hunched his head even deeper into his bony shoulders and sagged back in the chair. "Yeah, he did, real early this mornin'. He changed his clothes and left again. I didn't want to start up another argument, so I didn't say nothin'. He probably went off to look for snakes. He does that."

"Rattlesnakes are hibernating this time of year," Will said.

"I didn't say for sure. I just said maybe. What's goin'

on here? Why are you askin' so many questions about Darrel?''

"Because somebody torched my house last night, Stuart," Bern said grimly. "I think it was the same person who set fire to the Graley house and killed your wife and little Rachel Graley."

"That's crazy," Stuart said.

If the shoe fits, Bern thought.

He said softly, "Did he do it, Stuart? I know you're worried about your son. I know you want to protect him. Maybe the fire at the Graleys' was an accident. Maybe he didn't mean it to happen. But this one last night—trying to kill a policeman—is serious business. Cops don't take a thing like that lightly. If you really want to protect your kid, you need to help us stop him right now."

Stuart shook his head, mumbling, "Darrel loved his mama. He was with his friends last night."

"Then let us look around," Bern said. "If we find nothing to tie your son to the fires, we'll have to agree you're probably right. Will you let us do that?"

Bern knew immediately the old man wouldn't go for it. He bristled with hostility as he said, "Oh, you'd find something all right. I'll just bet you'd find *something*." He levered himself up, his hands trembling on the arms of the chair. "I don't want to talk to you no more. Go away and leave me alone."

Bern sighed. Well, he knew it had been a long shot.

"We'll do that," he said. "For now. Soon as you tell us where we can find Darrel."

"I told you I don't know."

"You know his friends. We need some names, Stuart."

It was an effort, but he came up with three people, including Oscar Yoder, Darrel's friend who was supposed to be in Las Vegas looking for work. He gave them the names while standing at the door, growing more and more agitated as he waited for them to leave and slamming the door shut as soon as they had cleared the threshold.

"A fucking cuckoo bird," was Will's opinion.

Bern knew he was probably right, but he had the same uneasiness he'd had when he had listened to Stuart Vaughn's disjointed babble at the station two nights ago. He couldn't help feeling that in the midst of all that paranoid rambling, Stuart saw something he didn't want to accept, something that scared him worse than any imagined demons.

twenty-five

BERN WAS BACK BY THE TIME THE WORKERS HAD FIN-
ished their temporary repairs. Will dropped him off, then
went on home. When he admitted they hadn't stopped for
lunch, Anne scrounged up a meal of canned soup and
crackers. She and Bern ate in the living room, where Duke
watched every mouthful with intense concentration.

She held off telling Bern the rest of her bad news while
he gave her a brief accounting of his meetings with the
Graleys and Stuart Vaughn.

"So did you pick up on anything?" Anne asked, feeding Duke a cracker.

"You're going to spoil that dog," Bern observed.

"I certainly hope so. You didn't answer my question."

"Ah, Annie, I don't know. Sharon and Randy—I tend
to lose my objectivity real fast around those two. And old
Stuart—I think he's scared of something. I just wish I
knew if what he's afraid of is real or something he
dreamed up."

Bern looked incredibly weary. After spooning up the
last of his soup, he put the bowl on a lamp table, leaned
back against the sofa, and closed his eyes.

Bad news could wait.

Duke tagged along as she took the dishes out to the

kitchen. It was quiet in the house, now that the emergency crew was gone. The debris had been swept up and removed, and she could no longer see sky through the hole in the roof. A wet vac had removed much of the water, although now the carpet added a moldy, mushroomy smell to the stench of smoke.

Back in the living room, Bern had slipped down to sprawl on the sofa, sound asleep. It was cool with all the windows still wide open, so Anne covered him with a blanket. Then she and Duke went into the bedroom and closed the door.

First she called Rena and learned that the police had still not found Chrissie. Then she called her office.

Peggy answered, demanding more details about the fire and reassuring Anne that the office was almost shipshape again.

Anne had been thinking about it all day and had come to a decision. She needed time to devote to the house, and she wanted to finish her interviews on the Graley case and do as much as she could to help Bern find the arsonist.

"Peggy, I'm going to have to take a few days off," Anne said. "Can you rearrange my schedule?"

"Of course. Anything else?"

Anne explained the situation with Christina. "There wasn't any response yesterday to the posters, was there?"

"No. I would've told you."

"That's what I thought," Anne said. "Well, if anybody should call, be sure to let me know."

"Will do. Anne? You keep saying you don't need anything, but Cynthia and I are going to pick up some food when we finish here and bring it by. Don't say no. We've already decided."

Anne knew she'd better make a start on rewashing all their clothes. On the way from the bedroom to the laundry room with an armful, she heard Bern call her name. The sound was infused with such terror that she dropped the clothes and hurried to the living room.

Duke got there first but hung back, whining softly in alarm.

Bern was still asleep but in the throes of a nightmare, his body bowed with tension, his hands balled into fists, and his face oily with sweat. When she touched him, he jerked awake, peering blindly at her for a second before he struggled up. Before he shrugged off her hand, she felt him trembling.

"Anne—what? What is it?"

"Nothing," she said. "I guess you were having a bad dream about the fire. I'm sorry I woke you."

"Fire?" He stared at her as though he had no idea what she was talking about, then blinked. "Oh—yeah. Must have been a doozy. Looks like I even scared the dog. It's okay, boy," he said, holding out his hand.

Duke darted over to give Bern's fingers a quick lick, then retreated to sit and watch them anxiously.

Bern picked up some paper napkins, left on the lamp table from their late lunch, and blotted his face. "How long was I asleep?"

"Not long enough," Anne said, eyeing him with concern. "Why don't you lie back down for a while?"

He shook his head. "No, thanks. I'd just as soon be awake. Anyway, I've got too much to do. I think I'm going to have to have my afternoon ration of caffeine, though. You want some?"

While he went off to brew the coffee and make some phone calls, she started the washing machine, then began, regretfully, to close the windows. As the sun rapidly sank westward, a breeze sprang up, stirring a cloud of ash and sending the fine particulate drifting in through the screens.

Bern brought the coffee back into the living room and handed her a mug, asking, "Have you given any thought to dinner?"

Since Peggy and Cynthia would be arriving soon, she explained about the break-in at her office.

"Jesus Christ, Anne," he said incredulously. "Why did you wait so long to tell me about this?"

"Because I thought you had enough on your mind." She was taken aback by his reaction. "It's happened before, Bern. I didn't think it mattered."

"No?" he said. "Then ask yourself: How did the arsonist find us? There are lots of ways if he's smart and has some time. What if he's in a hurry? Well, he can locate your office easily enough."

"And there are papers in the office with my home address," Anne finished, feeling both dismayed and stupid for not having thought of this logical conclusion.

Bern put down his mug, looking as though the taste of the coffee was making him ill. "Please tell me somebody called the PD and that the office got printed."

Anne really had no idea, but Bern had the chance to ask Cynthia firsthand because she and Peggy arrived just then, bearing two bags of Chinese take-out and setting off loud barking from Duke.

At some point the two may have been dressed for the office. If so, they had changed their clothes. Slender, blond Cynthia looked elegant even in old navy sweats, with her hair pulled back in a careless ponytail. Peggy wore her white shirt tucked into the elastic waistband of her denim slacks and had a gray cardigan draped around her shoulders.

Cynthia stayed by the door until Anne got Duke calmed down, but Peggy marched right in. Nothing much fazed her after years of dealing with unruly young patients.

Growing darkness rendered the blackened hillside invisible, but Cynthia and Peggy had gotten a look at the carport, and that was enough to horrify them. They barely got to say a few words of sympathy, however, before Bern launched into questions about the break-in.

Cynthia explained that, yes, she had called the police, but the patrolman who came by to take the report had not suggested taking fingerprints. Of course, she hadn't known about the fire out here, not until she spoke to Anne. And even if she had known about the fire, she doubted any of them would have connected the two events.

"Do you really think it's likely?" Peggy asked.

"Oh, yeah," Bern said. "I sure do."

"Then I've got more bad news. We put everything away and cleaned up the place. I wiped off everything with window cleaner and furniture polish. Won't that make it impossible to find any fingerprints?"

"Harder," Bern said. "But not impossible."

AFTER BERN CALLED AND ASKED FOR A FORENSIC TEAM to meet them, Anne rode with him in the Jeep to the office. Cynthia and Peggy followed, bringing the dinner that was uneaten and growing cold. Bern had said there was no reason for the women to come, but from the dismay on their faces, Anne knew Cynthia and Peggy were envisioning another round of chaos as bad as the one they just cleaned up. Thinking they were probably right, Anne agreed they should all tag along.

At the office the only sign left of the burglary was the splintered frame on a back door.

"He used something to pry it open," Bern said. "Maybe a jack handle."

Andy Braemer had nailed some boards across the door as a temporary measure; somebody was coming in the morning to make repairs. After the boards were carefully removed, the print tech went to work. When he finished, a mold would be made of the toolmarks left on the wood. Meanwhile, another technician was checking the area out back for footprints and tire impressions, although he was skeptical about how useful such evidence would be. Who knew how many people and how many vehicles had been in the vicinity throughout the day?

Back in the reception area, Bern asked Cynthia to describe how she'd found the office.

"A mess," Cynthia said.

More specifically, the storage room had been trashed; locked desks and file cabinets had been broken open, file folders pulled out, their contents spilled.

"Just like that time a couple of years ago," Peggy said. "Kids looking for drugs. We thought it was the same kind of thing."

Restricted to the sofa and chairs in the reception area, the women decided they might as well eat while they observed Bern and the technicians at work. Anne was too starved to care if the kung pao chicken was cold.

In spite of their misgivings, the forensic team carried out its work quickly, targeting certain locations with a minimum of disruption. The place was cleaned every night; however, as Anne had pointed out, dozens of patients were in and out of the office. So the techs concentrated on the storage room, file cabinets, and desks. To Anne's relief, they did not insist on taking apart case folders.

The last thing they did was take comparison prints from the women—and Andy, summoned from home. Finally they all went their separate ways—just as the cleaning people arrived.

Peggy had placed the leftover food in the refrigerator in the storeroom. Anne took it home. No prodding was necessary to get Bern to eat. Ravenous, he wolfed down everything, leaving only a little rice for Duke.

Bern had hunched over the wheel on the drive back to Cave Creek, silent and gray with exhaustion. Anne held off asking any questions until he had finished eating and they were in the living room sipping decaffeinated tea.

She said, "How soon before you know something?"

"A day or two, depending on how busy the lab is."

"You don't sound hopeful. You found prints, didn't you?"

"Oh, yeah. We also found lots of smudges." He stared down into his steaming cup.

"What does that mean?"

"It means," he said heavily, "that printing your office was probably a waste of time because the bastard who broke in was most likely wearing gloves."

twenty-six

DETERMINED TO SALVAGE SOME REMNANT OF HER NOR-
mal routine, Anne went out first thing the next morning
to unlock the storage unit in the half-burned carport to
check on her bicycle. Seeing the ruins of the Camaro gave
her a fresh jolt of anger and frustration. Cars are such
personal possessions; still, it was amazing how deeply she
felt the loss.

These emotions were quickly followed by a cold tightening in her stomach as it hit her again just how close she
and Bern had come to being trapped in a burning house.
She realized her own experience linked her even more
firmly to Rachel and Rufina because she had shared a
small portion of their panic and fear.

The difference was that life would go on for Anne. The
insurance people would have the Camaro towed away tomorrow, and she would buy a replacement. Her house
would be repaired, the yard cleared. Eventually the bad
dreams that had haunted her sleep the night before would
go away.

As for those two victims in the Graley house, she would
do what she could for the living, to help Kathleen come
to terms with her little girl's death. And Bern, with what-

ever help she could give him, would exact retribution for the dead.

Meanwhile, she allowed herself a modicum of happiness at the discovery that the bike had some blistered paint but was otherwise in good shape. To Duke's great delight, she took him along, going even farther than their last ride, both of them needing the exercise.

Back at the house, she found Bern sitting on the sofa in his pajama bottoms, hunched over his first and only cup of coffee, haggard, glum, and as untalkative as usual. Showered and dressed in tan slacks and a purple knit top, both fresh from the dryer, she went foraging for breakfast. In the freezer she discovered a partial package of bagels. Grocery shopping was definitely on her list of things to do.

She toasted a bagel, took it and coffee into the living room, and sat beside Bern to eat, directing any conversation toward the dog. Fortified by the coffee, Bern was finally ready to discuss his plans for the day.

The fire at Anne's house and the break-in at her office would generate a ton of paperwork for him; he needed to go to work.

"The sheriff's patrols will be keeping an eye on the place," Bern said. "But I still don't like leaving you here."

"I don't need a babysitter," Anne said. "Really, I'll be all right."

At any rate, she didn't intend to remain stranded. Her insurance covered a rental car. On a Sunday, the best place to pick one up would be at the airport. She called and made the arrangements while Bern showered and dressed.

On the drive south to Sky Harbor International, Bern made his worry very clear. "Somebody went out of his way to find us, Anne. I really want you to keep your head down until I can figure out who this asshole is."

"I don't plan on taking any chances," she assured him.

As the poet Robert Burns could have told her, and as

Anne was soon to find out, even the best-laid plans often go terribly, irrevocably wrong.

ANNE PARKED THE RENTAL CAR, A RED FORD TEMPO, across the street from the charred ruins of the house where Rachel had died. She'd come here on impulse, unwilling to just go home as Bern wanted. She really didn't think she could contribute much to his quest for the person responsible for the fires. But she could do her job for Kathleen, and this was as good a place as any to start.

She went over to ring the bell at the house next door, the one where Darrel Vaughn had stood talking to an older woman that first day Anne had come here to meet Kathleen.

When the door opened, a safety chain allowed only a small space for the woman to peer through. She was short, about Anne's height. Otherwise, all Anne could make out was a halo of white hair and eyes that were bright with suspicion behind round wire-rimmed glasses.

"Yes?" The woman had to raise her voice to be heard over the noise of a television set that played loudly in the room beyond. "What do you want?"

"I'm sorry to disturb you. I'm Dr. Anne Menlo." Anne hesitated. How could she explain that she was putting together a profile on a dead child? She chose instead to say, "I'm working with the police, investigating the deaths in the fire next door."

"The police have already been here," the woman said. "They still haven't found out who did it?"

"I'm afraid not."

"Don't know why I should be surprised," she muttered. "How come they're sending a doctor to ask questions?"

"I'm a psychologist," Anne said. "I'm just filling in some additional details."

"Well—you got some identification?"

Fortunately, Anne had an official card identifying her connection with the police. The woman studied it for a long moment, then took off the safety chain and let Anne in.

A small entry led right into a dark, fussy room, lit by the glow of a good-sized TV. A gallery of framed photos sat on top of the TV as well as on the end tables. On the screen in black and white a half-dozen men with machine guns robbed a bank, blasting a guard who offered resistance. Rather than turning off the set, the woman simply muted the sound.

"I'm sorry," Anne said, "I don't think I have your name in my notes—"

"Gladys Niles."

Anne recognized her as the woman she had seen with Darrel. In her late seventies, Mrs. Niles had papery skin, finely etched with wrinkles. She wore a royal blue velour top, matching pants, and white Reeboks with the laces untied.

She shooed two big, fluffy gray cats from a small sofa and gestured for Anne to sit down. There was so much cat hair on the cushions that the fabric appeared to have grown fur. A faint odor of urine suggested a litter box somewhere nearby. On the whole, Anne decided she preferred Duke.

Mrs. Niles lowered herself stiffly into a platform rocker and said, "I told the other fellow about seeing Darrel drive off that day, a good hour before the explosion, maybe more. Don't know what else I can add."

"How well do you know Darrel?"

"Not well at all. I just saw him coming and going, heard Rufina talk about him."

This much was said grudgingly, but Anne leaned forward and waited, focusing her full attention on the elderly woman. Most people *wanted* to talk. Given an audience, they usually opened up. It was the basis of therapy and, once again, it worked its magic on Mrs. Niles.

She said, "Rufina was always going on about that son of hers. She had a birthday a couple of weeks before she died. Darrel surprised her by bringing somebody out to her place to clean for her. He really loved his mother.''

''How long had you known Rufina?''

''A couple of years. She worked for the Swales one day a week until they moved out to Sun City. I can't afford help on a regular basis, but I'd ask her to come over once in a while. Tell you the truth, though—and not to speak ill of the dead—but she wasn't much at cleaning.''

Judging from the state of her house, neither was Mrs. Niles, although age and infirmity might have been the reasons. Dust lay like furry mold along the bottom shelves of the lamp and coffee tables. Anne could see the cat hair clinging to her pants.

''I was surprised that Rufina went to work full-time for the new people,'' Mrs. Niles went on. ''I think they talked her into it. Then they started leaving the child, too. She didn't like it much.''

This corroborated what Darrel had told Anne and Bern. It also told Anne that Mrs. Niles had seen more of Rufina than she was letting on. Maybe there was a little snobbishness at work here. She wouldn't want it to be thought that she was hobnobbing with a maid.

''Did she have problems with Rachel?'' Anne asked.

Mrs. Niles nodded. ''Rufina said the child was always whining and crying and throwing tantrums. I can vouch for the crying. I'd hear her over there—ten or eleven o'clock at night. My bedroom was across from hers, and I like to sleep with the window open. Course, I'm not doing that anymore. Not taking chances.''

Mrs. Niles shifted in her chair, and the old black-and-white movie on the television reflected in her glasses, rendering them opaque.

''I can still hear that little girl. She'd cry and cry and call for her mommy.'' Mrs. Niles took off her glasses and pressed the back of her hand against her eyes. ''The thought of that child—the fire—well, the whole thing has been very upsetting.''

"I'm sure it has," Anne said soothingly, "especially when it happened right next door." She took some tissues from her purse and handed them to the woman. "Mrs. Niles, this is very important. Did Rufina tell you how Rachel was treated by her father and her grandmother?"

Mrs. Niles wiped her eyes and replaced her glasses, keeping the wadded tissue in her hand. "Well, she said the girl was spoiled rotten, I remember that. Had a ton of toys, but instead of playing with them, she'd follow Rufina around and pester her. I don't think much of parking kids in day care, but seems to me it might've been the best for her. At least she'd've had other kids to play with."

"I agree," Anne said. "It certainly would have been better for Rachel."

Maybe somebody would have listened to her and figured out that she had been taken from her mother—which was no doubt exactly why the Graleys wanted her at home. In addition, surely a professional caregiver would have spotted signs of abuse if there had been any and made a report.

"Did Rufina tell you whether she ever saw the child being spanked?"

"No, but I raised two kids of my own." Mrs. Niles gestured to the pictures that crowded the top of the television set and the tables, adding with pride, "Two sons and six grandchildren. If you ask me, a good swat on the behind can work wonders. But Rufina had her orders not to touch that little girl. The only thing she could do was put her in her room."

"There was an outside lock on Rachel's door," Anne said. "Did Rufina tell you that?"

"No, but it doesn't surprise me. People these days, I swear they've forgotten how to raise children. Never give 'em a whit of discipline and then wonder why they act the way they do. And all these broken families—I heard there was a mother, but God knows where she was."

Trying desperately to find her child, Anne thought.

On the TV screen a cordon of square-jawed policemen silently mowed down the bad guys. Clear-cut crimes and swift, sure justice. So neat and tidy. Nothing like the messy complexities of real life.

Mrs. Niles stared off at the television, although Anne wasn't sure whether she really registered what she was seeing.

She said, "My kids have been after me to sell this place and move to a senior apartment. I might do it, too. I can't sleep for worrying. What's to keep that firebug from coming over here next?"

"I don't think he's going to do that, Mrs. Niles."

"But you don't *know*, do you? You're a psychologist, but can you say for sure why he killed two innocent people?"

"No," Anne had to admit. "I can't say for sure."

But there was one thing for certain. She was going to do her best to find out.

twenty-seven

ANY DETECTIVE WHO MADE IT INTO HOMICIDE KNEW THE hours would be long, irregular, and unpredictable. The paperwork alone was backbreaking, with a typical case generating a hundred-page report. And, as Will often said, when did they ever get a typical case?

So Bern wasn't at all surprised to find a couple of other people in the office. One of them was Frank Trusey, who was talking on the phone. When he saw Bern, he pointed to Jane's office, signaling that the boss was also here, working on a Sunday morning.

Jane Clawson's door was open. No way around it. Bern would have to say hello sooner or later. He was hoping for later, but she called out, "Bern?"

"Yo," he said, and crossed the room to stand in the doorway.

Jane had abandoned her usual crisp business suits. Today she wore jeans and an old, worn, Western-style denim shirt with pearly snaps instead of buttons and a yoke embroidered with cowboys twirling lariats. Her earrings were Navajo—silver dreamcatchers, each with a single silver feather.

"Morning, Lieutenant," Bern said. "Surprised to see you here."

"The problem is I'm not here enough." She gestured to a stack of files on her desk next to a mug of coffee. Apparently on Sundays she abandoned her bottled water to indulge in caffeine like the rest of them. "Too many meetings with the brass and not enough time to keep up with my work. Sit down, Bern. I heard about the fire at your place. Will called me."

Bern took the chair across the desk from her, wondering what else Will had told her. Was there a memo somewhere in that pile of stuff on her desk recommending a psych review? And, now that he thought of it, would such a memo be justified? For three days now he'd been limiting his caffeine intake, and all he had to show for it was a constant dull headache. He still had the dreams, the edginess, and the anxiety.

"Are you really convinced the two fires were set by the same person?" Jane asked.

"Oh, yeah," Bern said.

He told her about the break-in at Anne's office and how he thought the burglar was trying to find him through Anne.

"But why would he risk going after a cop?" she asked.

Years ago, when he was a rookie patrolman, Jane Clawson had been his partner. Not for long—she was about to move up to detective. But he'd learned a lot from her during those few months, and any notion of superiority based on the fact that he was male was once and forever banished.

He said, "A good cop once told me to figure out the why and then I'd know the who. That's the problem here. I can't find a motive for anybody to burn down that house and kill a little girl and a housekeeper. As for coming after me, hell, I don't know. Maybe I'm getting too close but just don't have sense enough to see it."

"Wise words from that cop." She gave him a wry smile. "Nice to know you were actually listening. Let's think about this."

She put her elbows on the desk, laced her fingers together, and propped her chin on her thumbs.

"There are two ways to go here. First: The fire's the primary crime that just happened to kill two people. Second: The murders are primary with the fire as a cover-up or the weapon of choice. So—how about the insurance? House? Life? Or an inheritance? Does anybody stand to gain anything?"

He shook his head slowly as she ticked off the questions, disposing of the money angle.

"Are there any major debts that would be canceled out by the fire?"

"If the Graleys owned the house, I'd be considering the possibility," Bern said. "Nothing solid yet, but there's something not quite kosher about those two. But the old couple, the Swales—they own the house outright, and it's been producing income for them. No reason I can see for them to burn it down."

"Revenge?" Jane asked. "A pyro?"

"Possible," Bern agreed, "but remote."

"Well, then," Jane said. "That leaves murder. But which one of the victims was the target?"

She picked up her coffee and took a sip. This was the old Jane he used to know, before the upper-echelon meetings and the battles with the Maricopa County Attorney's office. This was the Jane who was always willing to listen to the newest detective in the squad and liked nothing better than to brainstorm a difficult case.

"Do you think Kathleen Graley was right?" she asked. "Was the father abusing that child and suddenly became afraid somebody would find out?"

"Could be, although so far there's no proof of it. And what about the timing? What could've pushed his buttons?" Bern shook his head. "I don't see it. Anyway, my impression is the guy's gutless. Sharon? Maybe. But not Randy."

"What about Sharon?"

"I think she's a real piece of work," Bern said. "Could she kill her own granddaughter? Yeah, I think she could, but I keep coming back to why."

"So maybe the little girl isn't the main victim. That leaves the housekeeper—"

"Rufina Vaughn," Bern supplied.

"If I remember right, her husband thinks somebody's out to do him harm. What if he thought that person was his wife and he decided to get her before she could get him?"

"Could be, I guess."

"How long had they been married? Thirty years? Believe me, that many years with the right person could drive you to paranoia, not to mention murder."

Jane had just ended a twenty-three-year marriage, and her words rang with the conviction of experience.

"Still," Bern said, "if Stuart was going to do it, I'd expect he'd blast her with his shotgun. This took some planning."

"The son, then," Jane suggested.

"From all I can find out, he loved his mother. Why would he kill her?"

"Even people who love each other argue. Sometimes those arguments turn into fights. And—"

"Shit happens," Bern finished. "Darrel's dropped out of sight. His dad doesn't know where he is. Gave us some names of friends, but so far none of them has seen Darrel, and an APB hasn't turned him up."

"I'm sure you'll have some questions for him when you find him."

"You'd better believe it. Meantime, maybe we'll get lucky and identify a print from Anne's office."

No need to spell out that a print—whoever that print belonged to—would justify a search warrant, which could lead to some solid physical proof.

"I hope so," Jane said, only now it was Lieutenant Clawson doing the talking, with the twin demons of worry and responsibility perched on her shoulders. "Just be careful how you handle this, Bern. Get me some hard evidence and make sure you protect our butts. You know how it is with our esteemed county attorney these days."

He did indeed. Bern could name his own run-ins with Gerald Ellis, the overzealous county attorney who only seemed interested in trying cases that were a dead-bang lock.

Back at his desk, Bern looked at his notes to see if there was anything he could clear up before he started the paperwork. He reached two of the people Stuart had named yesterday. No, they hadn't seen Darrel. The third was Oscar Yoder, Darrel's old high-school buddy and part of the happy trio whose hobby was going out in the desert to harass rattlesnakes.

Bern didn't have much hope of reaching Yoder, which was why he'd left him for last. According to his mother, Yoder was out of touch up in Las Vegas, looking for work. But now, covering all the bases and, yes, stalling—might as well admit it—Bern dialed Yoder's number.

Not only was Oscar Yoder back from Las Vegas, but he answered the phone.

AFTER ANNE LEFT GLADYS NILES, SHE TRIED OTHER neighbors. All of them refused to talk to her, except for one man who said he knew nothing about "those new rental people" except that they were an unfriendly lot.

Back in her car, Anne sat for a moment, gripping the wheel and staring at the blackened rubble of the burned house. Mrs. Niles had told her enough to make her heart ache for that poor little girl, locked in her room at night, crying and calling for her mommy.

The terrible story told of Rachel's feelings of desolation and abandonment. Was there more? Anne knew from her tragic experience back in college and from the cases she worked with now at the clinic that it was possible.

Sickened by the thought, she leaned back against the

headrest and closed her eyes. The window was down; she could smell the stench of the fire, subtly different from the one at her own house: older, more complex, full of dark secrets.

Maybe those secrets had died here with Rachel and would be scattered at sea with her ashes. Maybe there would never be an answer to Kathleen's desperate questions: *What was I not seeing? What didn't I hear?*

Anne started the car and drove away. She ought to go home. Tend to her own needs. Worry about herself and Bern. Tomorrow would be soon enough to make decisions about this case.

She wouldn't give up, she couldn't. Not yet. There were still people to interview in California, especially Rachel's doctor and her teacher. But here in Phoenix—what else could she do? Could she get anything from Randy and Sharon? She honestly didn't think so.

But it struck her suddenly that there was one person she had never really spoken to about Rachel, somebody who might very well be able to tell her something.

She'd seen him twice, once at the police station and again out in his trailer near Buckeye, but she had never talked directly to Stuart Vaughn.

twenty-eight

AS SOON AS SHE THOUGHT OF STUART VAUGHN, ANNE knew she had to talk to him. The question was, of course, whether she would do the interview with or without Bern.

She knew Bern wouldn't like it if she went alone. No, not quite right. Bern would be furious. Both Stuart and his son were suspects, and Bern didn't want her within a mile of them.

Not that Bern didn't have good reasons for his fears. She certainly hadn't forgotten that day when Stuart had held them at gunpoint in front of his trailer. From her limited observation then and later at the police station, she would not attempt a conclusive diagnosis; however, she doubted he was schizophrenic. More likely his was a milder form of paranoid personality disorder. If she was careful and nonthreatening, she should be able to talk to the man. Wasn't this what she'd been trained for?

As for Bern, he couldn't have it both ways. He couldn't expect her to work with him on the case and yet restrict her every movement.

Later, she would remind herself that a person can rationalize almost any decision. Sitting there in the rental car, looking at the ashes of the house where Rachel had died, the choice seemed inescapable. Rufina Vaughn had spent a great deal of time with Rachel during those last weeks. And Stuart had been with his wife most of her off-hours. If she'd confided in anyone, surely it would have been him.

AS SOON AS BERN IDENTIFIED HIMSELF TO OSCAR YODER, Oscar muttered, "Well, fuck," then added, "I figured one of you cops would be on my tail."

"Your mother told you about my partner calling?"

"Oh, yeah, as soon as I walked in the door. She read something in the paper about Darrel's mom, and she's all weirded out—"

Oscar broke off as a woman began talking in the background. The sound became muffled, as though he'd put his hand over the mouthpiece, but Bern could hear the tenor of the voices: the woman's—Mrs. Yoder, Bern was sure—sharp and insistent, Oscar's truculent.

He finally said into the phone, "Listen, man, I don't rat out my friends, but my old lady's having a fit, saying I'm gonna get like implicated, some shit like that. Hell, I been up in Vegas. I don't know anything about this except I'm telling you straight—there's no way Darrel would've done anything to hurt his mom."

"Your mother's right, Oscar. We're talking about a double homicide. You could find yourself in deep shit here if you withhold information. If you know something about Darrel, you'd better tell me right now."

"Yeah, well," Oscar hedged, "it's about when Darrel went to Sacramento."

Bern could hear him taking a deep breath.

"Go on," Bern said.

"Darrel was going to school out there," Oscar said. "He was in the fire academy."

ANNE MADE A QUICK STOP AT A MCDONALD'S DRIVE-through window for fries and a strawberry shake. Then she pulled over in the parking lot, eating a couple of the hot, salty fries and smudging her cell phone with her greasy fingers as she dialed her service.

No calls, so at least Bern wasn't looking for her, but neither was Rena or Joyce. That meant there was no news about Chrissie.

She wiped off the phone with a paper napkin, sighed, and sent up a silent prayer. So many terrible things happening to so many children. Was it too much to ask for one small girl to be safe?

Driving west on Interstate 10, Anne polished off her lunch and decided she ought to try to phone Stuart and let him know she was coming rather than drop in on him—and his shotgun—unannounced. Considering the man's paranoia, she had little hope of learning Stuart Vaughn's number. But, to her amazement, when she called information, he was listed.

The phone rang only once before it was picked up. "Hello? Darrel?" Stuart said anxiously.

"No, Mr. Vaughn, it's Anne Menlo."

"Who?" Disappointment and suspicion mingled in his voice. "Oh, I remember. The other cop."

"I'm working with the police," Anne said. "But I'm not a member of the force."

"What's the difference?" Stuart said bitterly. "You're all lookin' to pin the fire on somebody. You're after my son now, just like you been after me."

"*I'm* not after anybody, Mr. Vaughn. I work with children, and my interest is the little girl who died in that fire with your wife. Her mother is in so much pain over Rachel's death. I know you can understand that—you of all people. Please, could I just come and talk to you about it?"

"Why? I don't see what good that would do," he said, but there was considerably less hostility in his voice.

"Your wife spent a lot of time with Rachel those last few weeks. Maybe something Rufina told you could help comfort the child's mother."

"Well—"

His words were interrupted by a static hiss that indicated Anne was moving out of cell phone range. ". . . can come if you like, but you're gonna have a long drive for nothing. I don't remember her sayin' much about the kid."

More static. She was losing the connection.

"That's all right," Anne assured him quickly. "I'll be there soon."

She passed the state prison and the old abandoned stadium. Heading off the freeway at Jackrabbit Trail, Anne was reassured by one thing. Darrel wasn't at the trailer. If he should show up before she got there, she would be able to see his truck, probably from the road. At that point she would drive on by and call Bern or the Maricopa County sheriff—from her cell phone if there was service. If not, she'd go on into Buckeye and find a pay phone.

Stuart Vaughn was waiting for her, standing in the entrance to the corrugated sheet metal canopy that fronted the trailer. When she had been here before, the enormous castor bean plants had been a dark, healthy green. A few frosty nights had left them limp and blackened, drooping against the wooden framework of the porch.

There was no shotgun in Stuart's hands, she noted with relief, only a cigarette. He looked strangely shrunken and subdued. Sunlight, slanting down from overhead since it was almost noon, emphasized his bony brow and the beak of nose. As she got out of the car and approached him, she could see that left eye canting off wildly as though his paranoia controlled the muscles, sending it off to constantly scan the landscape.

He returned her greeting with a stiff nod, then went through the covered area to open the trailer door for her. She was inside with him, the door closing behind them, when it occurred to her that just because Darrel wasn't here now didn't mean he wouldn't be coming.

• • •

OSCAR YODER LOOKED SCRUFFY, HUNG OVER, AND NOT at all happy to be sitting in the interrogation room across the table from Bern. Turns out he'd been home from Las Vegas for about fifteen minutes when Bern called, and he'd been looking forward to a shower, a nap, and a cold beer—not necessarily in that order—not a trip to police headquarters.

"Man, this is a drag," he grumbled.

Oscar was squat and lumpy with lank black hair in a bowl cut even with the top of his ears, the remainder shaved to a dark stubble that matched his unshaven jaw. He wore jeans and a gray T-shirt with a collar so frayed it looked as though it had been worked on with a file, and he exuded an odor of sour perspiration that didn't sit well on Bern's empty stomach.

About the only good thing was that he hadn't asked for a cigarette. Offered a choice between coffee and a Coke, he'd opted for the cold drink and sat down, rolling the can between his hands, where black hair sprouted on the tops of his fingers.

"I told you everything on the phone," Oscar said. "Whadja have to drag me down here for?"

"Just to make things official," Bern said.

And to look in your shifty eyes while I'm doing it.

When Bern explained he was going to tape the interview, Oscar said, "Do you have to? I don't know if I like that."

"It's for your own protection. So I'm not tempted to get out the rubber hoses."

Oscar gave him an uneasy look, as though he wasn't quite sure Bern was joking. "Hey, I mean it, man. Maybe I oughta have a lawyer."

Bern shrugged. "I haven't charged you with anything, but, hey, that could change. Obstruction of justice? Aiding and abetting? That could work. We can get you a public defender. They're always real happy to work on a Sunday.

Or maybe you should call your mom, ask her to find you somebody.''

"No, wait," Oscar said hastily, "I'm just sayin' like maybe. I mean, I guess it's okay."

"If you're sure."

"Yeah, all right. Let's just get it over with."

While Bern went over the routine of setting up the taping, he sneaked a glance at his watch. As soon as Bern had gotten off the phone with Oscar, he'd called Will at home and told him what was happening. Then Bern typed up an affidavit to obtain three search warrants, one for the Vaughn residence and one each for the vehicles. When Will arrived, he immediately took the affidavit and went in search of a judge to issue the warrants—not the easiest thing to accomplish on a Sunday—leaving Bern to question Oscar. Bern hoped by the time he finished here Will would be back, and they'd be ready to roll.

Having established all the particulars, Bern said, "So how did it go in Vegas, Oscar? Did you find a job?"

Oscar shot him a guilty look, ducked his head, and said, "Nah. I didn't find nothing."

With the economy booming in Las Vegas right now, Bern figured even Oscar should be able to find work—if he was looking, that is. Maybe the job hunting was just an excuse he'd given his mother while he went up to play craps and get in on a little lap dancing at some of the sleazier night spots.

"Too bad," Bern said dryly. "When's the last time you saw Darrel Vaughn?"

Oscar sipped some cola, considered, then shook his head. "I dunno. Few days before I left."

"You didn't talk to him today?"

"Today? No. I just got home and you called. When would I talk to him?"

Bern ignored the question. "Okay, that last time you saw him, was it after the fire?"

"After, yeah. The poor guy. I told you, him and his mom, they were real close."

"So you said. They never argued?"

"Yeah, well, sometimes—sure. Like everybody."

"He moved out once," Bern said. "How were they getting along back then?"

"Fine," Oscar said. "It was just, see, we decided to get our own place."

"You and Darrel."

"Yeah, me and him and this other guy, Bo."

"Ralph Waldo Beaumont," Bern said. "I've met Bo."

"Oh." Oscar shot him a startled look, considering the ramifications of that remark while he drank some more of his cola.

"I take it the living arrangements didn't work out," Bern said.

"Yeah, well, you know—rent and food and like that. It just cost too much."

The philosophy didn't surprise Bern. There was a whole section of this generation that considered their income disposable, meant to be spent strictly on toys and entertainment. Rent was too high a price to pay for independence.

"Tell me about Darrel going off to California," Bern said.

"Oh, yeah. Well, see, Darrel always wanted to be a fireman," Oscar said. "Last thing in the world *I'd* wanna do. I mean, go figure. But he was all hung up on it ever since he was a little kid. His mom—boy, she hated the idea. He was gonna enroll in the fire academy here, but she gave him so much shit, cried and carried on—you'd have to know his mom. So he went off to California. He had some relatives in Sacramento, a cousin or something on his mom's side. Darrel stayed with them, signed up at school like he was a resident, so it didn't cost him much. He called once in a while. Said he was doing great, he loved it."

"He finished the course?"

Oscar shook his head. "You've seen Darrel. Good shape, right? Well, he flunked the physical. I mean, like, does that make any sense? He said you gotta run up ladders and shit, carry all this heavy stuff. He couldn't hack it."

"He never tried again?"

"Nah, he was too bummed. Said fuck it and got on with his life. Listen, man, I gotta bitch of a headache. I told you what I know, so if I could just split now—"

"Soon," Bern said. "Darrel hasn't been home in a while. Where does he usually go when he takes off like this?"

"I don't know. With me. Or Bo. Out in the desert, shit like that. But I haven't seen him," Oscar added hastily. "I told you, I just got home."

"And when he's not hanging out with the homeboys, then what?"

"Well, then, he usually heads south, to Mexico."

"Where in Mexico?"

"Ah, man, I don't know. Somewhere in Nogales. Listen, can I go now?"

"Yeah." Bern switched off the tape. "Just be sure you call me if you hear from Darrel."

Oscar ducked his head in what Bern supposed passed for a promise. At the door he paused in his headlong rush to freedom. "I got to say, man, I think you're spinning your wheels here. Darrel loved his old lady. He wouldn't do this. It don't make sense."

Alone in the dismal room, Bern had to admit that Oscar Yoder was right. The situation didn't make sense. But then, things never did—until, as Jane always said, you knew the *why*.

twenty-nine

COMING OUT OF THE BRIGHT NOON SUNLIGHT INTO THE dark trailer, Anne had an impression of low, rounded walls and a clutter of furniture crowding the small space. This section encompassed both living room and kitchenette, about as long as Anne's living room and half as wide. Not a place for claustrophobics, she decided.

The few windows were placed high and shrouded with thick curtains, so she couldn't see out. Could she hear the sound of an approaching vehicle? There was so little outside noise here in this isolated place, how could she judge? All she could do was stay alert.

"Have a seat." Stuart gestured to the sofa, as though he were directing traffic rather than playing host. He sat in an upholstered armchair, one of two, with a TV tray between them that served as a table, and stubbed out his cigarette in an overflowing ashtray.

Eyes adjusting to the gloom, Anne perched on the cushion that topped some built-in drawers, her feet barely touching the floor. She was beginning to make out details when Stuart switched on a floor lamp beside his chair. She blinked in the sudden bloom of light.

Anne thought Rufina had tried hard to brighten up the place. A Mexican blanket, with orange and blue stripes against a gray background, covered the sofa. A couple of pink pillows rested in the corners. Anne also glimpsed a shelf crowded with knickknacks off to one side. From where she sat she could see that the collection included a vase with some red and yellow paper flowers. Somehow, though, in the poor lighting even these touches of color seemed dull and dreary.

A photograph stood on the rickety TV table, a five-by-seven in a plain silver frame. In the candid shot, Darrel posed with his arm around an older woman. Thick, dark hair framed her angular, unsmiling face dominated by large, intense brown eyes.

Anne leaned forward to study the photo and asked, "Your wife?"

"It's not very good," Stuart said as he picked it up and handed it to Anne. "She didn't much like to have her picture taken."

Photos record far more than just an instant of time. Looking at Rufina Vaughn's face, Anne thought she was not a very happy woman. But Anne could also read connection and affection between mother and son, confirming what she and Bern had been told about the relationship.

Giving back the photo, Anne said, "I haven't had a chance to say it before, but I'm very sorry for your loss."

Stuart ducked his head; the nod seemed to mean he accepted her condolences. Then belligerence stiffened his spine, pulling him erect in the chair. His good eye fixed on her, full of suspicion.

"You say you're not a cop," he said. "Well, I don't understand this business of your comin' out here with that detective and bein' there at the police station when he talked to me and Darrel."

"The police often call me in when a case involves a child." A half-truth, but she wasn't going to tell him about her personal relationship with Bern. "In this case, I'm also working for Rachel's mother—I told you about that."

"Rufina figured the woman musta run off and left the little girl," Stuart said.

"She didn't," Anne said. "As a matter of fact, it was the other way around. Kathleen—that's Rachel's mother—had no idea where her daughter was."

"You mean that Mr. Graley just up and took off with the kid?"

Anne nodded.

"Don't surprise me. 'Fina didn't much like either one of them people, him or his mother. They took advantage of her and didn't pay her near enough. Course, nobody did."

If Rachel had been molested sexually, Anne knew it was very unlikely that she would talk about it. The experience would be something too painful and frightening, too secretive, to tell. All Anne could hope for was something Rufina had observed that would be a clue.

"Mr. Vaughn," Anne said, "Rufina saw Rachel more than any other outsider during those last few weeks. Did she ever mention seeing bruises on the child or hear Rachel talk about being afraid of her father?"

"No, she never said nothing like that to me."

"Was she there for Rachel's bath or her bedtime?"

"Well, she stayed late a couple of times. They called her at the last minute, makin' excuses why they couldn't get home. But I don't know about puttin' the girl to bed. If 'Fina did, she never mentioned it."

"She didn't suspect Rachel was mistreated in any way?"

Stuart shook his head. "It was the other way around. They didn't get after her at all, far as 'Fina could tell. And she had strict orders not to lay a hand on the girl. I can tell you that child provoked 'Fina something awful, too. All she was supposed to do when the girl acted up was put her in her room."

"There was a lock on Rachel's door," Anne said.

"Yeah, that really tells you something, don't it? Those

people had no control over her at all, so they thought it was all right just to lock her up.''

''If your wife disliked the job so much, why didn't she quit?'' Anne asked.

''She did,'' Stuart said. ''Handed in her notice; told 'em she was leavin'. Ask me, she shoulda just not showed up and left 'em flat. They talked her into stayin' a few more days 'til they could find somebody. If she'd done what *she* wanted—but she didn't. They had it in for her, that's what I think,'' he added darkly.

No sense asking him to elaborate. People with Stuart's mental problems cast everything in the worst possible light, and the conclusions drawn from these suspicions did not have to be logical. In Stuart's mind, he could conceive of his wife's employers burning down the house to get back at her; never mind that their child had died in the bargain.

Anne reminded herself that Bern still hadn't ruled out the Graleys as suspects. Was it possible that Rufina had discovered that Rachel was being abused and threatened to report it? Somehow Anne found this difficult to believe. Even if such a thing had happened, Anne could imagine Sharon offering the housekeeper money or, more likely, taking her son and granddaughter and making a quick exit out of town. She could not picture Sharon using a fire to cover everything up. Would Randy act alone without telling his mother? Anne found that even harder to believe.

''No tellin' what people will do,'' Stuart went on, his words strangely contradicting Anne's thoughts. ''I could tell you all kinds of things. Yes, ma'am, I could.''

Hoping to derail the old man's paranoia by changing the subject, Anne said, ''I'm sure his mother's death must have been hard for your son. Everybody says how much he loved her.''

''Who says?'' Stuart demanded. ''Who's talkin' about Darrel?''

''Somebody in the neighborhood where she worked

who knew your wife. I heard that he even hired somebody to come here and clean the trailer," Anne said. "A surprise for his mother's birthday."

"That's right, he did. He was always doin' stuff for her."

"Well, it was a nice, thoughtful thing to do." Anne aimed for a calm and soothing tone because she could hear agitation growing in Stuart's voice.

"And that's why it's crazy for that Detective Pagett to be thinkin' Darrel would ever hurt her, 'specially in a fire. Not if you knew—" He broke off and jumped to his feet. "Lots of other people who would do something like that, out there just looking for the chance."

Stuart wasn't a big man, but he loomed over Anne. She had a sudden mental image of him with the shotgun and wondered where he kept it. Easing to her feet and picking up her purse, she decided she ought to get out of here before she found out.

"I really appreciate your taking the time to see me, Stuart," she said, and began edging toward the door. "I know it can't be easy, talking about your wife. Thank you very much for the time."

She had slipped around him, and her hand was on the doorknob. A few more seconds and she would have been gone. But in that moment before she turned the knob, she glanced up at the knickknack shelf.

Funny how the mind assimilates things. Consciously, she had not registered any of the porcelain figurines up on the shelf. This was understandable because Anne's height was only a petite five feet. The shelf was certainly not at eye level for her when she was standing. Sitting, she would see mostly the bottom of the shelf, if she had looked at all.

Subconsciously her brain must have recorded some degree of recognition. Otherwise this second casual glimpse would not have raised such clamoring alarm. She froze, staring up at the collection of figurines.

It was as though she had knocked a jumble of jigsaw pieces off a table and they had fallen together perfectly on the floor. The picture they revealed was as unbelievable as the likelihood of such a thing happening in the first place, but so clear that it could not be ignored.

"What is it?" Stuart demanded. "What're you lookin' at?" He turned to follow the direction of her gaze.

"I just noticed." Anne's voice was as unsteady as her legs. "Your wife collected angels."

BERN STILL HADN'T HEARD FROM WILL ABOUT THE WARrants. Meanwhile, the interview with Oscar Yoder had provided even more grist for the paperwork mill.

At his desk, Bern found it impossible to sit and doggedly describe the details of the investigation. He called Anne at home but got the machine, which was working again. So damn much to do there; he felt guilty for leaving it all on her, but the important thing was nailing Darrel. He left a message, explaining why he wouldn't be home for a while.

Frank had finally completed his calls. He started a fresh pot of coffee brewing, the aroma filling the squad room. Bern thought, *Fuck it*. He needed his head clear and operating without the ever-present headache, so he went to pour himself a mug.

Then he stopped by Frank's desk to ask if he was free to go along to serve a warrant. Bern and Will would ask the county sheriff for backup, but they could always use another body.

"Free as a bird," Frank said. "Mimi's in Florida visiting her mom. I heard about the fire. Is Anne okay? You guys need anything?"

Bern sat on the edge of Frank's desk to sip the coffee and give him a rundown. He brought Frank fully up-to-date, including his conversation with Oscar about Darrel Vaughn's likely whereabouts.

"Let's hope somebody picks him up," Frank said. "If he's in Mexico, we got a problem."

Frank was right, but Bern hated to consider the possibility. Back at his desk, he waited for Will and thought again about his conversation with Jane about motive. *Figure out the why and you'll know the who.* This time he had found out the *who* first—well, jumping the gun a little, some might say—but Bern knew in his gut that it was true, and never mind that it didn't make sense.

As for the *why,* he still had no idea what Darrel's motive was to commit such a terrible crime. But the old taboos held little force in this violent new world. People killed parents with as little compunction as when they killed total strangers. They killed for revenge, for money, or for no reason at all.

Yet still—and always—the rational mind posed the eternal question: Why?

ANNE'S BREATH SEEMED TO BE TRAPPED IN HER CHEST.

Angels. . . .

She exhaled shakily and told herself she must not jump to conclusions.

Lots of women had collections similar to Rufina's. Anne's own mother did. Doris Menlo had once remarked wryly that the problem with telling your kids you liked something was that they kept giving you the stuff forever. She had a small glass-doored cabinet full of owls that proved her point. Glass owls, wooden owls, pewter owls. Owls of every size and variety of artists' renderings. A whole cabinet full of Mother's Day, birthday, and Christmas presents that she couldn't possibly ever chuck or give away.

"I been meanin' to pack up that stuff," Stuart said. "It's just sittin' there, collectin' dust."

And if a person had been here to clean the trailer, the figurines would have been dusted, picked up, and looked at, perhaps polished with a soft cloth.

"That one on the end, next to the vase," Anne said. "Could I see it? It seems very—interesting."

Stuart hesitated, already suspicious, but then he always was or seemed to be with that crazily roaming eye. Still, he went over, took the figurine down from the shelf, and handed it to her.

Holding the china sculpture, seeing the detail of wings, halo and face, Anne's remaining doubts vanished.

"Stuart, the woman Darrel brought here to clean the trailer—do you remember her name?"

"What?" No doubt what he was thinking now; he thought Anne was crazy.

"Her name," Anne persisted. "What was her name?"

"Seems to me it was Sue," he said.

thirty

THE CHINA ANGEL WAS PERHAPS FIVE INCHES HIGH.
Feathery blue wings, a white robe. Dark eyes, a sweet
smile, and a tumble of dark curls beneath a gold halo.

Sue Lynn Bowes had added a yellow glow around the
figure in her sketch. Artistic license. Certainly she had
seen no such celestial light in this dark, grubby place. The
colors in that drawing on the inside of the cardboard carton
where she and Chrissie lived had been brighter than the
others, unstained by rainwater seeping in, because it had
been done only weeks ago, maybe even the same day Sue
Lynn came here to clean the trailer.

Anne could picture her recreating what she had seen for
her daughter, talking about the other angels that lined Rufina's shelf. Just the sort of story a child would want to
hear.

"Mama went to the angel lady," Chrissie had said.

And, even though she knew better, Anne had put her
own interpretation on the child's words. It had seemed a
logical inference, but she had been totally wrong. Sue
Lynn had indeed gone to the angel lady, only not to
heaven—or even here to the trailer. She'd gone instead to
that house on Carolton Street, and she had never left.

"What's goin' on?" Stuart demanded, snatching the angel from Anne's hand. "What're you askin' about that woman for?"

So many things she needed to know, so many ways to go wrong. How could she tell him the truth, that his wife was alive and his son was a murderer? She had to get out of here, call Bern, let him help her sort it out. Her mind was screaming for her to hurry, to think about the fire at her place, the break-in at her office, and Chrissie.

But in the meantime Stuart was staring at her, waiting for an answer.

"The strangest coincidence," Anne said, hearing how lame the explanation—the lie—was, even as she gave it. "This woman—Sue—who cleaned for me. She told me about another job she had—about these angels. It was just so odd, that's all." She tried a smile but found it strangely difficult, as though her lips had forgotten how. "Probably not the same person—who cleaned for you, I mean. I'm running late. I really do have to go."

She stepped back toward the door, but Stuart went around her, moving swiftly for a man in his sixties. He slammed the door shut and stood in front of it, barring her escape.

"You ain't real good at lyin', lady," he said. "You ain't goin' nowhere. Not until you tell me what the hell is goin' on here."

WITH NO BREAKFAST AND NO LUNCH, BERN WAS ON A full-blown caffeine high by the time Will finally got back to the station, carrying a pizza box. On anybody else's face, Will's expression would barely qualify as a smile; for Will it was a beaming grin of triumph. Bern knew he had the warrants even before he put down the pizza and withdrew the papers from the inside pocket of his jacket.

"Judge Fuller?" Bern asked.

"Yep. Had to track him to hell and gone, but he signed 'em. Lunch," he added, opening up the extra-large cardboard box to fill the squad room with the odor of tomato sauce, melted cheese, and what looked like every extra topping Pizza Hut had to offer. "Figured you didn't eat yet either, and we wouldn't have time to stop."

The accuracy of his guess was proven by the way Bern ripped off a piece of the pie and began scarfing it down. Frank came to join them, drawn by the appetizing smells.

What the hell, Bern thought.

They could surely afford the time to take a lunch break.

"STUART, REALLY," ANNE SAID, "I TOLD YOU—"

"You think I don't know when people are lyin'?"

He grabbed her, clamping his fingers tightly around her upper arm and shoved her back toward the sofa. She felt the wooden base of built-in drawers against the backs of her legs and sat down abruptly. He let go but planted himself right in front of her and shoved the figurine under her nose.

"I want some answers," Stuart said. "What are you really doin' here? How come you took a look at this thing and almost passed out?"

Hurry, she had to hurry. More puzzle pieces were falling together, telling her what must have happened to Chrissie.

Could she get past him and out of the trailer? She didn't think so. He might be twice her age, but he was far from decrepit, and she had felt his strength when he gripped her arm. Even if she made it out, there was the shotgun to worry about.

Striving for calmness, Anne said, "It's complicated, Stuart. The woman, Sue—Sue Lynn Bowes—she wasn't the one who told me about the angels. Her daughter did. Sue Lynn has disappeared. I got a shock, that's all, thinking that perhaps Sue Lynn had been here, that maybe this could be—I don't know—a *clue*, somehow, to help find her."

The explanation sounded weak to her own ears. No surprise that he didn't believe her.

"I ain't buyin' it," Stuart said. "When you looked at

that statue, you weren't thinkin' about anything good. You were thinkin' about something awful.''

Only one option left. So much time had already passed, more than twenty-four hours, since Chrissie had vanished.

"You're right, Stuart," she said. "I'm sorry. But the truth can be a very painful thing. Are you sure you really want to hear it?"

There was terrible dread on his face as he jerked his head in a nod. Perhaps his paranoia also kept him prepared to hear the worst. Or maybe he had had doubts and inklings of the truth all along.

"Please," Anne said, touching the sofa beside her. "I think you ought to sit down."

No argument. He sank onto the sofa as suddenly as Anne had. "Tell me," he said hoarsely.

"I think it was Sue Lynn Bowes who died in that fire, not Rufina," Anne said. "I believe your wife is alive, Stuart, and you must take me to her. A little girl's life may depend on it."

BERN, WILL, AND FRANK WENT TOGETHER IN BERN'S Cherokee. They rendezvoused with a county patrol car about a mile from the Vaughn trailer, put on Kevlar vests and raid jackets stenciled with *Police*, and drove on in together.

Coming in off the asphalt onto the narrow dirt track, Bern could see the old dark-blue Bronco parked out front, so Stuart must be home. Unfortunately Darrel's Nissan truck was missing.

They parked on the dirt circle in front of the trailer and got out slowly. Bern steeled himself, but today the porch was just a porch, the corrugated sheet metal nailed atop the wooden post shimmering a little in the sunlight. Surrounded by dried sunflowers and dying castor beans, it looked unkempt but completely nonthreatening.

The place also looked deserted. Bern had learned long ago, however, not to rely entirely on gut instinct, especially when it came to dealing with guys who greet visitors with shotguns.

"Stuart Vaughn," he called. "This is the police. We have a warrant to search your premises. Please come outside with your hands in plain view."

A minute ticked past.

"Think he's in there?" Will asked.

"I hope this is not going to turn into a barricaded situation," Frank said gloomily. "I fucking *hate* that kind of shit."

"Guess we'd better find out," Bern said.

The three detectives and the patrolman moved swiftly up to the trailer, went through the dark porch area, and took positions on either side of the door. Bern knocked loudly and announced their presence again.

Still no answer.

"Now what?" the patrolman asked.

"We go in," Bern said.

"NO COPS," STUART HAD SAID. "YOU WANT ME TO TAKE you on this wild-goose chase to look for Rufina, we go by ourselves."

So now Anne was driving south on Interstate 10 with Stuart sitting tensely beside her, contaminating the air with a Camel. His jacket lay on the floor at his feet, covering his shotgun. He'd made no overt threat, but just the fact that the gun was there told Anne that this trip would be played by his rules.

She was already tired from tension and driving an unfamiliar car in the heavy Sunday afternoon traffic, and her head ached from the smoke. All kinds of vehicles crowded the highway, everything from semis highballing it cross-country to shoppers bound for the factory outlet malls in Casa Grande.

Anne's panic increased with every mile. How much longer to get to the border? A couple of hours, perhaps. Enough time to talk some sense into Stuart, to call Bern.

So far her words had fallen on deaf ears. Stuart just sat, staring straight ahead—or at least his good eye did. The left eye wandered crazily in her direction as though it were constantly scanning her, and a vein throbbed in his temple.

"You really must be sensible about this, Stuart," Anne said. "Let me call Detective Pagett. He's a good man. He really is—"

"*Sensible?*" Stuart burst out. "There ain't no sense to any of it. Darrel might be down there in Nogales. He's got reason to be scared, reason to run off. But all them other terrible things—it can't be true. It can't be."

"Stuart, your wife was identified only by her jewelry. You said yourself she only went to the doctor and the dentist in Mexico—"

"No," he said, shaking his head stubbornly.

"The medical examiner's office doesn't have those records for comparison, so—"

"Shut up," he said savagely. "Just shut up. My head hurts. I need to think."

No point in provoking him. She concentrated on driving and considered whether she should slow down to try to buy time.

But every instinct urged her to get to Mexico as soon as possible. Find Rufina and Darrel. And Christina—was she really there in Nogales? Or was she already dead, either buried out here in these wild tracts between cities, or her body just left for the scavengers and the carrion birds?

She'd give Stuart a little time, and then she'd try again. He was in shock, of course. Anybody would be, after hearing what Anne had said back at the trailer.

"I think everybody was right when they said that Darrel loved his mother too much to kill her. As a matter of fact, I think he loved her enough to help her when she decided to fake her death. I don't know why your wife would want to do that, Stuart, but she did, and I believe Darrel brought Sue Lynn there to die in her place."

Anne tried to put the whole thing in sequence. Darrel

worked all over the Phoenix area. She remembered the man standing along Broadway with his *Will work for food* sign. Had Sue Lynn done that, trying to feed her child? It made sense. Darrel could have seen her, gotten the idea about surprising his mother, and brought Sue Lynn out to the trailer. Then he remembered the homeless woman later and brought her to substitute for Rufina in the fire.

Anne also assumed that Darrel must have known about Chrissie and feared she might be able to link him to her mother. What she didn't understand was why he hadn't gone after her earlier. But then again, maybe he had.

Maybe he'd gone to the homeless camp as soon as he was able. That couldn't have been immediately because he had too many things to do. First and foremost he had to go to Nogales to establish an alibi, and at the same time get Rufina away and out of the country. By the time he returned to look for Chrissie, Child Protective Services had taken Sue Lynn's daughter away.

How had Darrel reacted to this turn of events? Anne thought back to the two times when she had seen him. He had been nervous, certainly, especially during the interview at the police station. But she did not remember that he seemed to be repressing panic.

Perhaps he'd just taken the whole thing in stride. A little homeless kid is abandoned by her mother. So what? Nobody would ever make a connection with a woman who died in a fire, a woman whose identity had not been verified, but was not strongly questioned.

Go a step further, however, and assume he had not quite given up on his quest for Chrissie. He goes by the homeless camp once in a while, asks around.

"Some people ain't so damn pushy. Some people don't expect things for free." That's what the homeless woman Audrey had said, the one who had taken over the cardboard box where Sue Lynn and Chrissie had slept. So maybe Darrel came around, paying for information. He got nothing, until. . .

Suddenly Anne remembered standing in that dismal place, talking to Audrey before she and Rena went on to put up the posters. She remembered the whole conversation, the belligerent woman defending her pitiful belongings, Anne offering reassurance, and Rena telling her that their only purpose was to find Chrissie's mother.

What had Rena said?

"Dr. Menlo and I are just trying to help get them back together."

And Audrey's reply? *"Well, she ain't* here. *So you and Doctor* Menlo *just get the hell away. . . ."*

The next time Darrel returned, Audrey had something to sell. Anne's name. A name that must have pushed all of Darrel's panic buttons.

Inadvertently, despite all of the best intentions, Anne herself had led him to Chrissie.

thirty-one

CLAIMING SHE NEEDED TO MAKE A BATHROOM STOP, Anne pulled into a rest area south of Picacho Peak and shut off the engine. She did need the stop, but she also hoped she'd have a chance to get away from Stuart for a minute to use her cell phone and call Bern.

"Keys," Stuart barked and held out his hand.

Reluctantly she surrendered them and reached for her purse.

Stuart, long schooled by paranoia, snatched it from her hands, opened it, took out the phone, and handed the purse back. "Don't take too long."

In the bathroom, a young mother was helping a little boy wash his hands and talking to another child in a stall. Anne hesitated, debating, heart hammering.

Should she run back outside, try to get to a pay phone while Stuart was using the toilet? *If* he was using the toilet. Maybe he was waiting, anticipating her move.

The woman looked up into the mirror at Anne. Anne could see the wary question in her eyes. Then she moved in back of the boy and called to the other child, "Melissa, honey, hurry up. We have to go."

Tell her. Ask for help.

"Melissa, come on out of there," the woman called

sharply, and now there was fear in her eyes as she pulled the boy with her over to stand guard at the stall.

How could Anne blame her for being afraid? So many crazies out there; Anne of all people knew that. And the frantic look on her own face—how different was it from Stuart's expression?

Suppose she convinced the woman. What then? There were so many people in this rest area, so many children. Like the little boy and the girl, maybe eight years old, coming out of the stall and being hustled from the rest-room with her brother. And Stuart with the shotgun in the car—no, Anne couldn't take the chance.

She assumed he'd used the men's room. If so, he was out in a hurry, smoking and waiting for her. In the car driving away, she saw the woman and the two children getting into a blue van. Had she done the right thing back in the restroom? Stress and fatigue were taking their toll, so maybe she wasn't thinking straight.

A glance at Stuart convinced her she had been right. He was on the edge and unpredictable. Bern would understand the situation, but how could she explain it quickly and succinctly to a total stranger? Even given that she could convince somebody of her sanity and explain her situation, a sensible person would simply call 911. And then what?

A confrontation. A standoff. With paranoia feeding Stuart's panic, all she could foresee was disaster involving innocent people.

Even if she was wrong, even in the best-case scenario, involvement with state police would take time. And so much time had passed already. More than twenty-four hours since Chrissie had vanished. Anne couldn't risk any more delays. Finding Chrissie had to be her first priority.

Bern . . . if she could only get to Bern.

Stuart had kept the phone. It was small enough to stick in his shirt pocket. She could see the top of it as he hunched on the passenger seat and stared out the window.

Think, she told herself.

She shifted, trying to get comfortable on the unfamiliar seat, and rubbed her neck. They'd be in Tucson soon; another hour or so after that and they'd be at the border. She'd been to Nogales a few times—the Nogales in Mexico, there was a town by the same name in Arizona—but that was back in college. The crossing was similar to the one at Tijuana, south of San Diego. Cars were just waved on through with little scrutiny. It was the entrance back into the United States that was different, and probably more so these days with the swell of illegal immigration. Vehicles would be stopped and sometimes searched, the drivers and passengers questioned.

"Stuart, please, we have to talk." She tried to keep the desperation out of her voice and knew she was not succeeding.

"How'd you do it?" he demanded, turning to glower at her.

"Do what?"

"I ain't blind. I see 'em back there, followin' us."

The seat belt stopped him as he reached down. Impatiently he undid the belt and grabbed up the shotgun from the floor.

"For God's sake," Anne cried. "Put that down. You have my phone. You were with me most of the time at the rest stop. How could I contact anyone?"

"Maybe you got one of them trackin' thingamajigs on your car. I don't know. But somebody's back there."

Logic did not work, she knew that. She would not be able to reason him out of his delusion.

"Which car?" she asked.

"Green Camry," he said. "Behind the Chevy pickup."

Anne began slowing down. The pickup rode her bumper until he could pull out in the passing lane. Anne slowed even more. Now the Camry was coming up, closing the gap.

"What are you doin'?" Stuart demanded.

"You'll see."

The Camry darted out and passed them, the driver giving them an irritated look. Anne maintained her speed, and soon the Camry was gone.

"Maybe it's somebody else," Stuart said sullenly.

"Nobody's following us, Stuart," Anne said, speeding up to a normal rate.

Slowly he put the gun back on the floor. Then he sat, hunched forward, his neck drawn down into his bony shoulders. This close, she could see the brown age spots on his scalp under the fine white hair.

"I'm sorry if what I'm saying hurts you," Anne said. "I really am. But there are things we have to consider. If we find Rufina—"

"We won't find her. She's dead."

Back there in the trailer, she knew he had faced the truth. Now his denial seemed to grow with every mile that brought him closer to facing that terrible reality.

"Your wife's alive," Anne said. "I just hope and pray that Chrissie is, too. She's all I'm concerned about now. I want to find her safe and bring her back. Let the police sort out the rest of it. But that won't be simple or easy. Your son broke into my office to find out where Chrissie was."

Stuart began shaking his head, no.

"He set fire to my house. He's not going to just hand Chrissie over to me, Stuart."

"*No*, it's too much. Darrel—my boy—he's done some things. He's not perfect. But this—settin' a fire and leavin' that woman and that little Graley girl to die, and now takin' another little girl and—and—" He turned a grief-ravaged face to Anne. "Dear God, doin' things like that, he'd have to be—"

He broke off, unable to put such a name to his child. But Anne knew what he couldn't say: *He'd have to be a monster.*

● ● ●

SEARCH WARRANTS ARE NOT A LICENSE TO GO ON A FISH-
ing expedition. They spell out specific items that may be
looked for and seized. So Bern and Will took dirty clothes
from a corner of the tiny bathroom, noting the cami pants
with a dried leaf stuck to the cuff, and a pair of old Nikes
from a closet.

Meanwhile, Frank found some paint-splashed boots that
smelled of benzene out in the shed, along with a can of
the stuff. They also took the jack handle from the Bronco,
although Bern was fairly sure that the one that had been
used to pry open Anne's office was in Darrel's white Nissan pickup.

The whole time they were in the trailer, Bern had an
uneasy feeling. He knew what his father would say: *Things
always go from bad to worse.* The problem was that Bern
could no longer trust his instincts. He'd been living for
months now with this kind of hyperactive dread that made
him jump at shadows.

It just seemed damned odd that Stuart wasn't home. He
had not given any indication of having a social life. Bern
felt sure he was isolated from people by both his choice
of residence and his fears.

"You suppose Darrel came back and picked up his
dad?" Will asked as they stowed the evidence in the Cherokee.

"Probably."

The APB had not brought Darrel in, but that wasn't
altogether surprising. White Nissan pickups were as plen-
tiful as cactus, and license plates can be stolen and
switched.

"Ten to one," Will said, "they're sipping margaritas
south of the border by now."

"Darrel, maybe. But Stuart? He hates Mexico."

Anyway, the house hadn't looked as though they'd left
it for good. Why hadn't they taken their clothes? Tooth-
brushes and razors? Pictures? The one thing Bern knew

was missing was Stuart's shotgun. No sign of that in either the house or his vehicle.

He stood looking at the trailer, the Bronco, the acres of desert beyond, and felt his uneasiness deepen to a sick dread. He already suspected Darrel of killing his mother. What if Stuart had confronted his son with that question?

"What are you thinking?" Will asked.

"That maybe Stuart didn't go with his son. Maybe he's still here someplace."

ANNE KEPT TRYING TO TALK TO STUART, BUT HE HAD retreated into a stony silence. They stopped for gasoline about halfway between Tucson and the border. Anne used her credit card at the pump, hoping to leave some kind of trail for Bern. Grasping at straws, she supposed, but it was all she could think of.

Stuart went inside with her into the Mobil minimart. There was a pay phone right outside the restrooms, but he was over by the cashier with a cigarette in his mouth when she came out of the ladies' room. He was holding a paper bag, handing the young man some money, and he saw her right away.

Back in the car, he put the lighted cigarette in the center ashtray, took out two hot dogs and two small coffees in foam containers from the bag, and handed her half the food. After a bite of the greasy, spicy frank, Anne rolled down the window and waved away the smoke.

"Bother you?" he asked.

"Yes, it does."

He tossed the cigarette out onto the pavement.

He finished before she did and sat silently, sipping the coffee for a minute before he said abruptly, "I met Rufina when I was stationed down at Fort Huachuca. I didn't care much for Mexicans, but she was so pretty and always laughin', and to tell you the truth, she acted like she didn't really want to be one anymore. I mean, she wouldn't even eat a taco. I figured pretty soon she'd be just a regular American.''

He took another swallow of coffee. ''But then we were transferred outta Arizona, and right away she started writin' to some of her family. And after we come back to Phoenix, she started goin' to see 'em once in a while. It got to be more and more often. She was always runnin' down there. She knew I didn't like it, but she didn't care. She took Darrel with her, and pretty soon the two of them were talkin' Spanish half the time.

''She had a little money she saved up from her jobs. I never minded she had her own nest egg. Then one day she tells me she don't have it anymore. She took it and bought this little house outside Nogales. She and Darrel were fixin' it up. She wanted me to move down there. I wouldn't go, of course. Some broke-down old shack in the slums—no, thanks.''

He began wadding up napkins and hot dog wrappers and putting them in the bag. Then he sat, staring into the sack. When he looked at Anne, his eyes shone with unshed tears.

''She did this to get away from me, didn't she?''

''Oh, I don't think so,'' Anne said. ''If she'd wanted to do that, why not just leave? Would you have tried to stop her?''

''Mighta tried to talk her out of it.''

''But she was still free to go.''

''Yeah. Still, if I'da just gone down there with her, none of this woulda happened.'' He folded the top of the trash bag down with quick, firm turns. ''No matter what he did, I can't hand Darrel over to the cops. You understand that?''

She nodded. It was emotional and wrongheaded, but she understood.

''You may not think so, but I'm a good man, Dr. Menlo. If we get down there and find out you're right, I promise you one thing. I'll do my best to help you bring that little girl back.''

She knew how difficult the decision had been for him, and she believed he meant what he said. But if she was right about Darrel, he'd already committed two murders and a kidnapping. Why would he flinch from killing two more?

thirty-two

FIVE MILES TO THE BORDER. THIS TIME OF YEAR, SUNSET came swiftly. Anne estimated they had only another hour of daylight left.

"You do remember the way to Rufina's house?" Anne asked.

"Never been there," Stuart said. "But she told me where it is. Don't worry. I can find it."

"What about the gun, Stuart?" She was sure they'd be in a lot of trouble if they were stopped and the weapon was found in the car.

She hated guns. Sometimes she thought the whole country was as paranoid as Stuart, insisting on being armed to the teeth for protection. Only how much protection was there when every drug dealer, gang member, and borderline sociopath was also packing heat?

Still, she was relieved when he said, "We might need it," wrapped it in his jacket, and put it under the seat.

She wasn't sure he could use the shotgun on his own flesh and blood. Could she use it? She hoped she didn't have to find out.

AFTER TRAMPING AROUND IN THE DESERT ADJOINING STU-art Vaughn's trailer for over an hour, Bern and the other three men had nothing to show for their effort except for burs, stickers from dried plants, and some nasty cholla barbs that were razor-sharp and damn near impossible to shed.

"Well," Will said as they climbed into the Cherokee, "if he aced his old man, he planted him someplace else."

The sun was at their back as they headed into town. It rode the western horizon, half hidden by clouds that were tinged a bright blood red. Will leaned back against the headrest and closed his eyes. In the backseat, Frank was snoring by the time they reached the interstate.

Bern felt the weariness in the small of his back spreading up the muscles to his shoulders. His uneasiness grew as well. How long before he could go home? Two hours, at least. Three was more realistic.

Anne was all right, he told himself. Duke was there to sound a warning if anybody came near the house. A patrol car was going by at regular intervals. Still, the worry persisted. Giving in, he tried her on the cell phone.

No answer.

Will opened his eyes and studied Bern's face. "Anne?"

"Probably out with the dog," Bern said.

Or maybe she'd put off going to the supermarket since she knew he would be late. Maybe she was sick of staying around the smelly house alone and went out with Cynthia.

He called her service and asked to have her paged.

She never called back.

At headquarters, the evidence had to be booked in, all the i's dotted, the t's crossed. When everything was unloaded, Bern said, "I hate to stick you with this, Will, but—"

"Don't worry about it," Will said. "Go."

STUART HAD CONFIDENTLY DIRECTED ANNE THROUGH Nogales. Now he wasn't so sure of himself anymore. He leaned forward, frowning as the street they were traveling on turned into a patchy asphalt road and wandered off into a rapidly descending darkness.

The streetlights on the outskirts of town had been inadequate at best; now there was more light in the sky than on the ground—stars coming out as though controlled by a rheostat that was gradually turning up the brightness. Here and there, a few windows glowed in houses only dimly seen in folds of rough, rocky hills.

"She said just a little ways outta town," Stuart muttered. "A cantina—I remember that. Up there."

He pointed to a spot of light ahead with a lone spark of red in the weaker electric haze that resolved into a neon sign promising *Cervezas*.

"Go slow," Stuart ordered as they passed the cantina. "Should be a driveway. Here. Stop."

A narrow graveled strip led off the asphalt. No telltale lights marked a house. But then, perhaps Stuart had been right all along. The house wasn't visible because it was dark and deserted, its owner a charred husk on a morgue slab back in Phoenix.

Anne turned and drove slowly up the road. After a quarter of a mile, Stuart said, "Don't seem right. Must be the wrong way—"

He broke off as they rounded a knob of hill and saw the house hidden there, surrounded by mesquite and acacia trees. The road really was a driveway that dead-ended in a wide gravel turnaround.

Although the house was not palatial, it was by no means the shanty Anne knew Stuart had envisioned. The modest adobe structure, roofed with hand-thrown tiles, sat behind a stuccoed wall that supported drifts of scarlet bougainvillea. Gates in the wall stood open. Lit by both the windows and Anne's headlight beams, this courtyard looked lushly planted with fan palms, oleander, and huge bird of paradise with gigantic blue flowers. Stone pavers formed a path to the front door.

"Can't be it," Stuart said.

Anne thought he was probably right. There was just one vehicle parked off to the side, an old gray Ford Escort. No white Nissan pickup with Arizona plates. She took her foot off the brake pedal, ready to wheel around and go back to the main road.

Just then the front door of the house opened. A woman stood there, looking out, lifting a hand against the glare. Anne might not have recognized her. She'd seen only the one picture, and the lighting now was not the best. But Stuart knew her instantly. Anne heard his strangled gasp and saw him go rigid and staring.

He fumbled for the door handle and stumbled from the car. Anne braked, shut off the engine and the lights, plunging the graveled area outside the gate into shadow, and hurried after him.

Rufina Vaughn still peered vainly, trying to make out who the visitors were. "Darrel?" she called. Then more sharply, *"Quién es?"*

Stuart strode up the stone pathway. When his wife realized his identity, she froze for a second, then backed inside and tried to slam the door. But Stuart grabbed it and threw his weight against the heavy wood slab, forcing it open. Anne was right behind him.

Rufina retreated as he pushed his way inside. A small entry, paved with painted Mexican tile, opened into a living area. She backed into the middle of this room. With its whitewashed walls and heavy, new furniture, it was a far cry from the trailer where she had lived with Stuart. American dollars translate into a lot of pesos, Anne supposed, and maybe Rufina had put away a lot more dollars than Stuart ever knew.

Rufina was short with a heavy bosom, but she was not fat. Hard work had given her knots of muscles in bare skinny arms, along with the permanent lines of discontent carved in her face. She wore green knit pants and a matching top with a scooped neck that was decorated with a design of painted cactus and silver-colored metal conchos.

"What are you doing here?" she demanded. "Who is this stranger?"

"Real nice to see you, too," Stuart said, his voice rising to thunder. "For sweet Christ's sake, woman, how could you do something like this?"

"I had to," she said. "I would call you, soon now, Stuart, and tell you—this awful thing that happened, that it was a mistake." Her gaze shifted back and forth from Stuart to Anne. "Is she *policía*? Why do you do this to me?"

Ignoring her question, Stuart said, "You let me believe you died. And you say it was a *mistake*?"

"*Sí*," she cried. "Yes, it was. The people I work for, they hire a new person. She came and I left. Then boom— I saw the fire. I thought I would be blamed. This happens, Stuart. You know there are people out there who watch and wait and do terrible things. You always say this. I was afraid and I ran away. This is the truth. I swear it."

Of course Stuart wanted to believe her. And she was clever, Anne had to admit that, using Stuart's own paranoia in her effort to convince him.

Seeing his anger and resolve weaken, Anne said, "She's lying, Stuart. The Graleys hired no one else. It was Sue Lynn Bowes who died in the fire."

Rufina registered shock at hearing the name but tried to cover it with bluster. "Who is this person who calls me a liar in my own house, Stuart? I tell you the truth."

"I'm Anne Menlo, and I'm here to find Sue Lynn's daughter. Is she here? What have you done with her?"

"*Loco*," Rufina spat. "*Madre de Dios*, Stuart, you bring a crazy woman. How can you believe these lies?"

Stuart's left eye rolled wildly in its socket. He looked as though he was being torn in half between the two of them, the woman he had been married to for more than thirty years and the one he had just met with her story that would shatter his life forever.

My God, Anne thought, horrified. *He really might believe her.*

UNABLE TO ABIDE THE TRAFFIC, BERN SLAPPED THE flasher atop the Cherokee and drove hell-for-leather, reaching Cave Creek in record time. Dread was a cold, hard knot in the back of his throat as he came down the street and turned into the driveway. The house was dark. There was no rental car, no vehicles at all except the burned-out Camaro waiting to be towed.

He heard Duke's barking as soon as he shut off the engine. That vicious, snarling, powerful bark would have deterred anybody who had tried to force his way inside. The dog damn near didn't let Bern in the door, he was so upset. When he finally accepted who Bern was, he ran outside, made a beeline for a bush, and lifted his leg.

A long time since he'd been out to urinate, Bern realized. Probably not since they had left him this morning. Had Anne come home at all?

Nothing inside the house gave any clue. Duke followed his every step, whining, returning again and again to look out the front window.

In their bedroom, Bern sank down on the bed, picked up Anne's pillow, and held it, breathing in her scent.

It's happening again, he thought.

Last summer she had been abducted by a suspect in the case they worked on. He'd sworn then he'd never let her get near danger again. He'd even insisted that she spend a few hours with him on the gun range learning how to use the spare .38 he kept in the bedroom and the shotgun that was on a shelf in the closet. All that, and here he was with that same feeling of black certainty that something had happened to her and he was at fault.

Duke nosed her shoes on the closet floor and came back to sit at Bern's feet and look at him. Even the dog knew something was wrong. He gave that strangled cross be-

tween a whine and a bark that plainly said, *Get off your
ass and fix it.*

Bern put Anne's pillow back in place and reached for
the phone.

ANNE, OF ALL PEOPLE, KNEW HOW IMPORTANT, HOW
binding, the ties of blood and family can be. She saw it
every day in her practice and especially at the abuse clinic.
For the love of a parent, a child would endure almost
anything. And that pull, that obligation, went well beyond
childhood, binding women to batterers, men and women
to alcoholic spouses, parents to children who were set on
destroying themselves and everyone around them. Both
curse and blessing, these ties, and very, very powerful.

She thought of something else, too. Darrel's truck might
not be here, but his mother must be expecting him back.
Rufina had thought at first it was him when they arrived.
Anne had to do something—and fast.

She left Stuart and his wife, walked quickly into a hallway leading toward the back of the house, and shouted,
"Chrissie! Chrissie!"

Rufina lapsed into shrill, rapid Spanish, flew after her,
and grabbed her arm with fingers hard as bone.

Anne tried to push her away and yelled again, "*Christina Louise,* where are you?"

Anne thought she heard something, but Rufina was
shrieking now, drowning out everything else, until Stuart
bellowed, "Shut up!"

This silenced her for a second, but that second was
enough. From the back of the house, both he and Anne
could hear a child's muffled cry.

"Mommy? *Mommy?* Come get me, Mommy, please
come get me."

thirty-three

BERN'S FIRST CALLS WERE TO CYNTHIA AND TO THE BEI-
dermans. None of them had spoken to Anne all day. He
thought of the homeless child Anne had been so concerned
about but found no notes giving information about the foster parents, and the clinic was closed now.

Next he phoned the rental agency at the airport. After
only a minimum of bureaucratic resistance, he was given
the make and license of the car Anne had rented. Then he
called in an APB.

After that he began the grim task he had done for so
many other people. He contacted every hospital in the
Phoenix metropolitan area and then the morgue.

That done, thank God with no results, he sent a city
patrol car to the Holiday Inn to check on the Graleys and
a county car to the Vaughn trailer. County reported there
was still nobody home. As for the Graleys, they were just
returning to the hotel from dinner and threatening suits for
harassment.

Will checked in as soon as he finished booking in the
seized evidence. After he heard Bern out, he wasted no
breath on reassurances. Instead, he said heavily, "Shit."

"I'm missing something," Bern said. "What the hell
am I missing?"

"Could she have been working on this case?" Will asked. "Working on the profile of the little Graley girl, I mean."

"She wasn't supposed to be," Bern said. "She *promised* me—"

He broke off, remembering her exact words: *I don't plan on taking any chances.* What the fuck did that mean, exactly?

"Say she was." Bern fought to separate himself from his sickening fear, to move off and look at the situation coldly and logically. "The question is, who would she have interviewed?"

"Neighbors," Will offered. "The father and the grandmother."

He hesitated, and Bern supplied, "Stuart Vaughn. If she was out there, and Darrel showed up—"

"No," Will said, "think about it. Where's her car? You ask me, even though it was Darrel who went to fire school, maybe we've been focusing on the wrong nut case in that family."

"The old man," Bern said. "He and Anne are in her car."

"Yeah. If Darrel had Anne, I'd say he was headed for Mexico, but with Stuart, I don't think that's likely, do you?"

"No," Bern said. "I think it's the last place he would go."

RUFINA'S FINGERS LOOSENED ON ANNE'S ARM. ANNE GOT a look at Stuart's face as she pulled free. His hope had died completely at the sound of Chrissie's voice. Now she saw only terrible desolation.

"Watch your wife," Anne told him and hurried down the dimly lighted hallway, calling Chrissie's name and listening for the child's answering cry.

Behind her she heard Rufina beginning a litany of excuses and explanations, a wounded, wordless roar from

Stuart, and the sound of flesh striking flesh.

A part of Anne's heart ached for Stuart. He might be crotchety, prejudiced, and paranoid, but she also believed he would do the right thing. She'd do what she could to help him deal with this tragedy later—and pray to God there was a later. For now she had to think only of Chrissie.

Chrissie's voice led Anne to a room with a door that had a shiny new brass-colored sliding bolt. Anne slid it open. Rufina's savings must have been spent on the living room. The only furniture in here was a twin bed, a simple table, and a lamp. A low-wattage bulb provided very little illumination; the room was steeped in gloom.

Chrissie had backed away from the opening door. She stood, her face full of puzzlement and crushed expectations.

"It's Anne, honey," Anne said. "It's Dr. Anne."

"Is my mommy here? Did you bring her?"

"No, honey, I'm sorry." Anne went to kneel beside her. "Are you all right? You're not hurt?"

"Unh-uh," Chrissie said. "But where's my mommy? The man said he would take me to her. He said we couldn't tell Rena 'cause she wouldn't let me go. We drove a long way, but Mommy wasn't here. Is she coming, Anne? Did you find her?"

"Yes, baby, but we'll have to talk about it later." Anne hugged her, then stood up and took Chrissie's hand. "We have to go now, sweetheart. We have to hurry."

Anne could hear Stuart and Rufina arguing, their voices growing louder as she led Chrissie down the hallway. The couple was in the living room. Rufina sat in a straight-backed chair of heavy, dark wood with woven leather strips for the seat, glaring defiantly up at Stuart, who stood over her.

"You tell me now," Stuart was saying. "You tell me the truth."

"All right, I tell you. How about you, *metiche*?" Rufina called out to Anne.

Anne didn't know what name the woman had used, only that the word was infused with contempt.

"Don't you wish to hear me, also?" Rufina said.

Anne knew she shouldn't stop, that she should get Chrissie away, but she had made a promise to Kathleen to find out what had happened to her daughter. How could she not listen to the one person who really knew?

"Let's go, Anne," Chrissie urged. "I don't like her. She's not a nice lady."

"You'd best take that child and get movin'," Stuart said.

"I'd like to, but I can't," Anne said. "I'll be right back."

WILL SAID HE WOULD HANDLE THINGS FROM THE OFFICE, that Bern might as well stay home. But Bern couldn't stand the thought of being in the house with the grim reminders of the fire and the dog anxiously pacing the rooms.

"No, I'm coming in," he said. "Call me in the car if you hear anything."

Duke tried to muscle his way out the door as Bern was leaving. Given the chance, the dog could probably do a better job at finding Anne than the humans.

At least better than I'm doing, Bern thought.

In the Jeep he exerted every effort to reestablish that objective distance that would allow him to look at the facts. Were they right about Stuart or were they missing something? He couldn't pinpoint the reason; he only knew he couldn't quite believe that the old man was crazy enough to set the fires and kill his wife.

About fifteen minutes from headquarters, Frank called him on the cellular phone.

"Bern, listen, this is weird. Remember that wino you had me looking for?"

"The guy who witnessed the knifing," Bern said.

"No, not him. The other one Anne wanted to find named Harlan. Well, I was leaving the station, just about out the door, when somebody over in the detox unit called. I'd asked them to give me a jingle if they happened to see either this guy or the other one, Bunny. Turns out old Harlan's been there all along. No ID, just now able to tell them his name."

"That's good, Frank. Do me a favor and pass it along to the investigator looking for the mother tomorrow. I've got other things on my mind right now."

"No, wait," Frank said. "That's not the weird part. Okay—see, I figured I had nothing better to do, so I might as well come over here to the jail and talk to this Harlan. Who knows? He might take off. Well, he's rambling, but he's coherent. And pretty upset about the mother. He said her name is Sue Lynn Bowes, by the way. Said he saw her drive off with some guy—get this, Bern—some guy in a white Nissan pickup."

Bern felt as though he'd had a cold bucket of water dumped on his head. "Description?"

"Better," Frank said. "He got a partial plate number."

LEAVING RUFINA'S HOUSE, ANNE WALKED CHRISSIE through the courtyard to the rental car. Opening the door, she said, "I want you to wait here, sweetie. In the back. Lie down on the seat, okay? And don't get up until I come and say it's okay. Can you do that?"

Another child might have asked questions, but Chrissie and her mother must have constantly been subjected to dire and unpredictable situations; Chrissie did what she was told. Anne locked the doors and hurried back inside.

Rufina greeted her with sullen contempt, and said, "All this for a *nadie,* a nobody." The imprint of Stuart's hand was red on her dark skin.

"You just start explainin' what happened," Stuart ordered, his voice heavy with menace.

Rufina waited just long enough to show that she still had some control of the the situation. Then she said, "That *niña*, that Rachel, she was making me crazy. Bad as this one you came for—crying for her mama. I could not help myself. I gave her a slap. But she wouldn't stop crying. So I took a big spoon from a drawer and hit her for a long time."

"Dear Lord, you killed that child," Stuart said.

"No, of course not." There was a touch of indignity in Rufina's voice. "But there were marks, and the way she looked at me—I put her in the room and locked the door so I don't have to see her. I told the *abuela,* the grandma, I don't want to stay there. I said this, and now I know I would be in jail even though it was not my fault. It was *una pesadilla,* a nightmare."

"You should have called me," Stuart said, sounding as sick as Anne felt. "Why didn't you call me?"

"And what would you have done?" Rufina said scornfully. "What you do now? Bring somebody like her? Or *policía? Gracias de Dios*, my Darrel came. He said not to worry, he would fix it. And he did."

"He went and got Sue Lynn," Anne said.

Rufina nodded indifferently. "He thinks about such things as teeth and that we are about the same size. You never thought so," she said to Stuart, "but he is a smart boy. He says no one will miss her. It was later I remember that the woman talked about her *hija* that day in the trailer when she came for my birthday present. Darrel went to where the woman was living and tried to find the *niña*, but she was gone. He said it didn't matter. Then he discovered that you were asking questions about this Sue Lynn." She gave Anne a sly, venomous look. "He will get here soon. When he does—"

"When he does, *I'll* be here, too," Stuart declared.

"So you will," Rufina said softly.

"You get outta here," Stuart told Anne.

"Stuart, come with us. You don't have to stay here."

"Yes, I do," Stuart said.

Anne couldn't waste any more time arguing. She gave him a quick hug, said, "Thank you, Stuart," and headed for the door.

Outside, she thought she saw a flicker of headlights. *Don't panic,* she told herself. The lights could very well be on the main road. Running through the courtyard, however, she saw them again, and she knew she had made a terrible mistake. One little girl was dead already. In staying to hear Rufina's story, she may have doomed the second child because now there was no doubt about it.

The headlights were rounding the knob of hill and coming fast.

thirty-four

THE HEADLIGHTS OF THE PICKUP WERE ALREADY STROBING across her as Anne jammed the key into the Tempo's lock. The simple act of turning the key and opening the door seemed to take forever.

The pickup slid to a stop behind her, spraying gravel as she jumped into the car and slammed the door. Fine rock peppered the car like hail. Darrel was out of the truck and running toward her, yelling something.

He'd left the lights on in the pickup. They blazed like spotlights, showing him exactly who was in the car as he ran up beside her.

"Anne," Chrissie wailed.

"Get down, Chrissie. On the floor. Now."

Anne tried frantically to insert the key into the unfamiliar ignition as Darrel pounded on her window with his fists. She could hear him now.

He shouted, "Wait, stop. Bitch—"

His voice was momentarily lost in the roar of the engine as she found the slot and turned the switch. He danced back and ran for the pickup. Anne dropped the gearshift lever into reverse. If she backed up just a little, she could swing around, hopefully without hitting the other car, the

Escort that was parked there. But could she get past the pickup?

The next moments were a jumble of frantic motion. She saw Stuart coming out of the house with Rufina trying to hold him back, dragging at him like an anchor, and caught a glimpse of the terrible wrath on his face. But it was Darrel she had to be concerned with, and he, crazily, was moving the pickup out of the way, so she could back up and wheel around.

She thought for a moment he was simply letting her go. Then she saw she was terribly wrong. Behind her, he slammed on the brakes and skewed the truck sideways, blocking the narrow drive.

Could she get around him? Too many trees on one side. On the other, there was an opening, but there were also some low, thick shrubs and no way to tell what lay beneath them. Nothing else to do. She had to take the chance.

She aimed for the opening, going as slowly as she dared, heard the scrape of the plants hitting the underside of the car, and then a horrible, jolting thud of something big and solid—a stump or a rock—that brought the car to a lurching halt.

In the rearview mirror she saw Darrel racing toward the car with something in his hands. He was raising the thing as he approached the driver's side—a metal rod, no, a jack handle.

She threw herself across to the passenger's side, screaming to Chrissie, "Stay down! Hide your face!" as the jack handle smashed into the window.

Glass pellets stung her head and arms as she ducked, slid down on the floor, and covered her head with her arms. His first blow had punched a jagged hole in the window. Through it she saw him swing his weapon back for another whack.

She fumbled for the door, realized it was locked, and had to waste precious time pulling up the pin. When it finally opened, she stumbled out, backward, from the car,

an awkward, turtlelike retreat made more ungainly because
she caught her heel on the edge of—what?

Stuart's jacket . . .

The jack handle exploded against the car window again,
showering her with more glass. Chrissie's screams rever-
berated in the car.

Blessing the stubborn, irascible, hardheaded old man
who had brought her here, Anne quickly pulled the jacket
from beneath the seat and took out what was wrapped
inside.

"LET ME GET THIS STRAIGHT," WILL SAID INCREDU-
lously as Bern pawed through the files for the autopsy
report. "*Darrel Vaughn* picked up this woman Anne's
been looking for? When was this?"

"Near as Frank can figure, the same day of the fire at
the Graley house." Bern came up with the report and
scanned it quickly. "No positive ID on Rufina Vaughn,
Will. Stuart was still complaining yesterday when we were
out there about the fact that the medical examiner hadn't
released the body. Remember?"

"Yeah," Will said grimly. "You thinking the same
thing I am?"

Bern nodded. "It wasn't Rufina who died in the fire. It
was Anne's homeless woman, Sue Lynn Bowes."

"Christ," Will groaned. "If Rufina Vaughn's alive, that
means we got the whole wacko family to worry about."

They were sitting at Bern's desk in the squad room.
Three guys from the skeleton night squad were over in the
corner, shooting the bull, but otherwise Bern and Will had
the place to themselves.

Bern felt as though he'd been hit squarely in the center
of the forehead with a baseball—right out of left field.
Think, he told himself. Take the fact that Darrel had substituted the Bowes woman for his mother—and forget the
*why*s for now. Where did he go that day after the fire? To

Mexico. By all accounts, just where Rufina would want to be.

Okay so far, but what about the rest of it? The fire at Anne's place, the break-in at her office? Bern's assumption had been that the arsonist was after him. But now he knew he was wrong.

"What?" Will demanded.

"When Darrel torched our house," Bern said, "Anne was the target, not me."

"Because of the Bowes kid?"

"Had to be."

"But why?"

"I have no idea," Bern said. "Listen, do me a favor. Call CPS. Get the name of the foster family. The child's name is Christy, I think. No, Chrissie—Christina."

While Will went to work on the phone, Bern sorted through everything he could remember about the episode. The little girl had run away. Was that before or after Anne asked him to intercede in the search for the child's mother? In any case, she had been found, he remembered that.

His head was pounding, a drumbeat of pain in his temples that seemed to echo inside his skull. While Will patiently worked his way through an uncooperative chain of command at CPS, Bern washed Advil down with coffee— and fuck the doctor's advice. Didn't know what he was talking about anyway.

Back at his desk, Will passed him a name and number scribbled on a message pad.

A man answered at the Trent residence, and Bern asked for Rena. When Rena came on the line, he said, "Mrs. Trent, this is Detective Pagett from the Phoenix PD. I don't think you know me, but—"

"Yes, I do," she said. "Anne's mentioned you. Did you find Chrissie?"

"Find her?" Had the goddamn headache totally short-circuited his brain? "I'm sorry. I'm confused here. I was sure Anne said the girl had been found."

"The first time," Rena said. "Oh, I was really hoping you had good news."

"She disappeared again?" Bern asked sounding concerned. "When?"

"Yesterday. Saturday morning. She just vanished. Didn't Anne tell you?"

He saw it then, not everything, but enough to see some pattern in the chaotic design.

"Detective Pagett? What's wrong? I don't understand—"

"Sorry, I'll have to get back to you." He stabbed at the disconnect button, whispering, "Son of a bitch."

"You gonna make me guess?" Will asked.

"That's got to be where she is," Bern said.

"Where?"

"Just where we figured she wasn't," Bern said. "In Mexico."

EVEN THOUGH ANNE DETESTED GUNS, SHE HAD GIVEN IN last fall and gone to the police gun range with Bern for a brief lesson in their usage. Something he'd said when demonstrating the shotgun he kept in a closet at home had stayed with her, and she remembered it now.

"Nothing chills the blood as much as this sound," he'd said, demonstrating by chambering a round with the slide action.

She could attest to the scary feeling, having experienced it out at the Vaughn trailer when Stuart greeted them with the shotgun. She only hoped Darrel would have the same reaction.

He had seen that she was out of the car. He came loping around the back with the jack handle in his hand. She stood up to face him. Chrissie was still crying in the car. Stuart was halfway from the house to Anne's wrecked Tempo, Rufina still determined to hold him back, chattering away in a mixture of hysterical Spanish and English.

And in the background, the pickup's engine rumbled away.

Still, that distinctive sound as Anne cocked the gun worked as advertised. Darrel, rounding the back of the car, stopped in his tracks and stared at her in disbelief.

"Stay back," Anne ordered.

The big gun felt impossibly heavy in her hands. Could she really pull the trigger and shoot another human being?

A dozen places on her arms and face stung as though she had been set upon by Africanized bees. She felt blood trickle down her cheek. Her heart was hammering wildly, and her mouth was dry from a massive charge of adrenaline. The Anne who abhorred violence because she saw daily its awful effects on children could never fire this gun and tear apart human flesh. But this man had already killed one little girl and would kill another one as well as herself if she didn't stop him.

"You wouldn't do it," Darrel said, but he didn't sound so sure.

"Don't try me," Anne snapped, then called, "Chrissie, honey, come out now."

Chrissie emerged from the car slowly. From the corner of her eye Anne caught a glimpse of blood on the child's face. Light glistened off beads of glass in her dark hair.

"Stay behind me," Anne said.

Chrissie complied, clinging to Anne. Anne could feel the tremors of fear that shook her little body.

"Fucking bitch," Darrel said bitterly. "Just when I had somebody lined up to take the kid off my hands. Shoulda took some more time and made sure you fried. How'd you do it? How'd you talk the old man around?"

"She told me the truth," Stuart said.

Darrel turned to face his father. Rufina let go of Stuart and ran over to stand beside her son. In the poor illumination from the two sets of headlights, much was hidden, lost in shadow. Anne wondered what Stuart saw as he stood there, staring at his wife and son.

Was he seeing something far more terrible than any of his imagined demons? Or was he remembering that this was, for better or worse, his family?

"Dad?" Darrel said. "Dad, you got to help us now. I was only doing what I had to do to protect Mama. This woman can't shoot both of us. If you help me, we can get out of this. Dad?"

Stuart didn't reply. He took a step or two, circling, toward Anne. Each step seemed to be an enormous effort as though he had weights tied to his feet.

"Stuart?" Anne heard the uncertainty in her voice.

"Stuart, *mi esposo*, we are *familia*," Rufina cried.

Stuart came closer to Anne and held out his hand. "I'll take the gun. Get in the truck and go."

Anne stared into the older man's face. Obscured by shadow, it showed just a hint of eye socket, a thrust of bony jaw; it was impossible to read. Common sense told her not to trust him. His paranoia might already have refashioned the situation here, casting her as the enemy.

And remember blood, her mind cried out. *Thicker than water. The telling factor.*

How could she possibly put her fate and Chrissie's into his hands?

He took another step toward them. She felt Chrissie press closer against the backs of her legs.

His words came back to her then, the things he'd told her in the car when they'd stopped for gasoline. He had said, *"You may not think so, but I am a good man."*

In the end, she knew, all any of us can do is trust our hearts. She handed him the gun.

thirty-five

HEADING SOUTH ON I-10, BERN RODE IN THE PASSENGER seat of a Phoenix PD patrol car. Will was in back. By chance, the patrolman at the wheel was Toby Jessup, the same man who had met Bern at the Holiday Inn the night he and Anne had gone there looking for Kathleen Graley.

Jessup drove expertly and fast, lightbar flashing, passing out of the metropolitan area south of Chandler and into the darkness of the Gila Indian Reservation. Just to make sure the semis stayed the hell in the left lane, a state patrol car was out in front, leading the way. The truckers were notorious for their tailgating speed runs on this stretch of road, but the sight of two sets of flashers and a reminding blast of sirens ought to keep them in line.

Bern would have preferred a copter or a plane, but, ever mindful of budget, Jane Clawson, reached at home, had nixed his request, saying, "It's Sunday night, Bern. I know some people in Nogales, and I'm sure I can get them to cooperate, but I seriously doubt that much will be done before morning."

Since then, he had been on the radio and the phone, talking to people in Santa Cruz County and the sister city of Nogales, Arizona. He'd spoken with Immigration at the border. If he'd forgotten something, Will would have jumped in to remind him. No, he'd done everything he could, and he still had the feeling it wouldn't be enough.

With every mile that passed, that feeling grew stronger, turning into a terror that ran like flame into every corner of his mind. Five months had passed, and yet he knew finally that he had never really left Florence Mosk's yard. He was still there, exposed and defenseless, his fate in the hands of a brutal woman with limited intelligence who was busy dulling what lucidity she had with wine so she could finish him off.

This was the scene he'd been living over and over again. There was a difference this time, however. He was lying on the ground and standing apart, all at the same time, Bern the man and Bern the cop, both living and observing the experience in the same instant.

Seen with a little objectivity, he understood that although the pain and the fear of dying had been bad, the helplessness had been the real pisser that night.

Whatever other disappointments had happened in his life, he had always felt he had maintained at least some measure of control. In his relationship with Anne, he could choose to either persist or call it quits. If he didn't love his job he could damn well leave it. He could hearken back to his father's sour homilies or refuse to let them rule his life. But just then, at that time and place, there had not been a damn thing he could do except lie on the hard ground and wait for a crazy woman to make up her wine-soaked mind.

All men have a breaking point. No doubt about it, he knew exactly when he'd reached his. Something important had broken inside him that night in addition to the rib that punctured his lung. And while that rib bone had mended, the other thing had not.

He'd heard for a while now that women really were the stronger of the sexes. Well, judging by experience, he knew Anne was a damn sight more capable of handling captivity. After her ordeal last summer, she had managed to work through any lingering fears, to exorcise the demons that haunted her sleep. Truth be told, she was far tougher and more resourceful than he had ever imagined.

In admitting this, he let go, just a little, of his fear for her. Love would not relinquish its terror entirely, not even to the calmest examination and logical conclusion. And it didn't hurt to send up a prayer, asking God to be there and help her survive the night.

To Anne the moment seemed frozen in time, eerily silent as the shotgun passed from her hand to Stuart's.

Then she sensed movement from Darrel. *Now,* she thought. *I'll know.* And pay the price if she had guessed wrongly.

"You just stay where you are," Stuart barked at his son. To Anne he said, "Go on. Git."

"God bless you, Stuart," Anne said gratefully.

She grabbed Chrissie's hand and ran across the graveled yard to the pickup. Stuart went along, his back to her, the gun trained on his wife and his son, guarding her retreat.

"Dad!" Darrel cried. "Goddammit, Dad—"

Later, Anne would try to assemble what happened next into some coherent whole. But then she was busy picking up Chrissie and lifting her into the truck, getting in herself, doing all the steps necessary for the two of them to escape, so she saw the scene in the yard in bits and flashes.

Darrel rushing his father.

A crazy dance between father and son.

Rufina jigging around the two of them.

When the roar of the gun shattered the night, Anne was already driving away. She dared a glance in the rearview mirror, but she had removed much of the light when she left. So it was impossible to see what had happened. Still, she heard Rufina's scream, ululating through the darkness, and knew that something terrible had taken place.

She thought from the tone of keening that it was Darrel who had been shot, but she couldn't count on it. So she drove pell-mell down the narrow, bumpy road, not even taking the time to fasten their seat belts. Chrissie was scrunched down beside Anne, her face buried just beneath Anne's arm. There was blood on both of them, but not enough to raise major concerns. Certainly not enough to consider stopping.

When she reached the asphalt, Anne turned right and headed into town. There might have been a phone in the cantina, but she did not dare stop that close to Rufina's house. Ironically, her phone was still in Stuart's shirt pocket. She hadn't thought to ask him for it. Well, she'd had a few other things on her mind.

She did observe a street sign as soon as there was light enough to read it and tried to commit the name to memory. After that she had to find her way to the border through poorly lighted, disorganized, hilly streets that began to seem more like a maze than something designed for reasonable human beings.

The muscles in her shoulders and down her arms burned with fatigue. She felt light-headed and disoriented. There were no landmarks, nothing to use as a guidepost, no bread crumbs leading the way home.

She had her darkest moments then. It seemed entirely possible that it was Stuart who had been shot, that at any moment Darrel would appear in his mother's car to block the way and stop them, to force them to return to the house or simply use the shotgun then and there.

She forced herself to keep going. A few cantinas and _restaurantes_ were open and doing business. Sometimes she heard laughter and the sound of mariachi trumpets spilling out. Mostly, however, the streets were empty except for roving packs of lean dogs who ran and barked alongside the truck. They reminded her of Duke, and she suddenly felt a bolt of longing for the ugly mutt. And for Bern. She'd barely spared a thought for him. By now he would certainly know she was missing. He must be desperate with worry.

"Anne?" Chrissie said, the faintest little peep. "Anne, are we safe from the bad people yet?"

"I think so, honey," Anne said.

"Where are we going?"

"Home," Anne said, with growing conviction. "We're going home."

Ten minutes later she saw the lights of the border crossing.

JUST MILES BEFORE BERN WAS TO CROSS INTO MEXICO, a call was patched through from Immigration on the American side. The information was sketchy. Darrel Vaughn's white Nissan pickup was at the border station, identified by the APB, but Darrel was not driving. A woman was. She had a child with her.

"Anne?" Will asked, incredulous.

Bern didn't believe it until he was inside the station with Anne in his arms.

There was blood on her clothes, small cuts on her arms and in her scalp, but she brushed his concern aside and urged him to send somebody to Rufina Vaughn's house in Nogales.

"I tried to get the people here to listen, but they just looked at me like I was crazy," she said. "You've got to help Stuart, Bern. He's probably hurt, maybe dying."

There was no time to sort out how Stuart Vaughn had suddenly become a good guy, but Bern was willing to take it on faith. An urgent message to the Mexican authorities brought Jane's contact himself. After Ramon Suarez listened intently to Anne's description of the location and the name of streets as best she could remember, he dispatched patrol units.

Then he took Bern and Will with him into Nogales while Anne waited at American Immigration. One of Suarez's patrols found the Vaughn house fairly quickly. The news was not good.

Forensics would sort out the details later. What Bern

saw when he arrived with Suarez and Will was two bodies: Stuart and Darrel, father and son, lying in the circular dirt area in front of the house. Darrel was shot in the chest, Stuart in the head.

Anne had not been sure of what she saw; she'd had only an impression of what had happened. But Bern thought she was right. The gun had gone off in the struggle, killing Darrel. And then Stuart had shot himself.

As for Rufina, both she and the gray Ford Escort were gone.

thirty-six

RUFINA VAUGHN SURFACED EVENTUALLY. AFTER WITnessing her son's shooting, she had left her husband sitting there, crazed with grief, and fled to a cousin's in Hermosillo. There she recovered her strength and hired herself a lawyer to fight extradition.

Jane fully expected Rufina would win this battle and stay in Mexico, given the record of their chickenhearted asshole of a county attorney. As Jane told Bern, "Damn good thing Darrel's dead. Gerald Ellis would probably have let him walk."

Back in California, the Orange County Sheriff's Department and various other agencies took a long look at the Graleys' activities. Some of their convoluted deals came close to being criminal—close, but no cigar, as one investigator wryly said. He added that he was real happy the pair were no longer doing business in Southern California.

This all happened down the road, however; by then, there had been some changes in Bern's life, and he got the reports secondhand from Will.

THE FIRST DAY AFTER HIS RETURN FROM NOGALES started out on that wave of euphoria only survivors of

near-catastrophes know. Bern figured there was only one
other creature on earth happier than he was that Anne was
home safe and sound. *No thanks to me*, he reminded himself. Whatever animosity Duke had for the human race, he
had now put it aside for Anne. As soon as she walked
through the door, he stuck closely to her, making sure, or
as sure as a dog could, that she was protected from harm.

The happiness, at least for Bern, was not to last. Almost
immediately it was undercut by moments of sheer terror
when somehow the helplessness he'd felt when Anne vanished became mixed with what he'd experienced that night
lying in Florence Mosk's yard.

The only difference was that he understood a little better
what caused the cold sweats and heart palpitations, the
vivid dreams that drove him from sleep. The department
shrink had given it a name: post-traumatic stress. At the
time Bern had discounted the idea because he associated
the syndrome with POWs, hostages, Vietnam vets. He was
a *cop*, for God's sake. He got paid to confront people like
Florence, to sometimes get the shit kicked out of him and
spend time in the hospital.

But now he remembered the way the shrink described
what brought on the condition: a situation of absolute
helplessness, a total loss of control, and training and personality that leaves a person unprepared to cope.

So the shoe fits, Bern thought. *Now what?*

He was up long before dawn, pacing the house, watching clouds roll in from the west. A cold gray rain was
falling as he drove to work. There he slogged through
paperwork until Jane returned from a meeting. She was
taking off her jacket and putting it on a hanger when Bern
rapped on the open door of her office and asked, "Got a
minute?"

"Sorry, but I—" She broke off to study him for a second, then said, "Sure. Come on in."

He closed the door behind him as she circled the desk
and dropped wearily into her chair. Then, slowly, he took

out his badge and his gun and put them on the desk.

"I want to tell you what's going on with me," he said, "what's *been* going on—and then you can decide what I should do with these."

She nodded, saying nothing, as he sat down and told her he didn't think he'd ever fully recovered from the episode with Florence Mosk, that he didn't feel he could do his job without risk to himself and others. If she thought he meant just the physical part, he didn't correct her. Even knowing that what he was going through was more than just physical, he couldn't bring himself to admit it to Jane.

"Can't you handle desk duty?" she asked.

"Maybe I could, but I don't want to. I need to be away from this for a while. To get my strength back and just not think about people killing each other. After that, well—" He shrugged.

"What are you planning to do for now?"

"Take it one day at a time." For all his dad's sour disposition, he'd been a pretty good weekend carpenter and had passed along some of his skills. "I want to work on rebuilding the house. Spend some time with Anne. Get well."

"All right," Jane said, "then do it. But take these with you." She handed him the badge and the gun. "Bern? I hope you don't stay away too long. We need you here."

ANNE SPENT A WEEK IN CALIFORNIA, FINISHING UP HER work on the profile of Rachel Graley. She interviewed neighbors, Rachel's kindergarten teacher, and her doctor. She even found some time to spend with her family in San Diego.

Amazingly enough, Bern did not insist on going along. The storm system had finally cleared, and he said he wanted to get started on the back deck. Anyway, he thought he ought to stay home with the dog because, come to think of it, experience in the K-9 unit probably really hadn't prepared his friend for a week of caring for Duke.

With her schedule back to normal and Bern around much more, she had a chance for observation and found herself remembering what Rosemary had asked. Had Bern really dealt with his experience last summer?

Anne was sure he hadn't, but she also knew it would be just about impossible to get past his stubborness and prickly pride until he was ready to allow her in. All she could do was be patient and wait and let him deal with it on his own.

He did fly over the last day she was in L.A., arriving early on Saturday morning, to be with Anne when she gave Kathleen her final report.

In a coffee shop in Marina del Rey, Kathleen thanked Bern for finding the man who had killed her daughter.

"Don't thank me," Bern said. "Anne figured it out first."

"Just dumb luck," Anne said. "Bern was right behind me."

"Well, I thank you both. I'm glad he's dead. Maybe that's a terrible thing to say, but I am. Rufina—she won't be brought back and prosecuted, will she?"

"Probably not," Bern said.

"Well, she has her punishment anyway. She lost her son. What could be worse than that?"

The waitress came then, bringing coffee; tea for Kathleen. She hunched over her cup, still looking fragile and haunted. After today, however, Anne hoped at least one small ghost would be laid to rest.

"Tell me about Rachel," Kathleen said.

Anne knew she wanted every detail, so she gave them all. Summed up, Randy Graley was an indifferent and self-centered father—just as Kathleen had described him, a total shit. But Anne could find no evidence that he had abused Rachel.

"Why do you think she was so upset that last time after Christmas?" Kathleen asked.

"I believe children see things and feel things on levels

we have learned to suppress,'' Anne said. ''She lived with Randy and Sharon, too, you know. It's likely she knew the signs that a move was coming. Maybe she sensed they were taking her away from you.''

''She was trying to tell me, wasn't she? If I'd listened. . . . You have to explain to them, Anne—the mothers and dads—make them understand how important it is to listen before it's too late.''

She jumped up from the booth and ran toward the door. Anne thought it was just too much for Kathleen to handle, but she wasn't bolting from the room. She had gone to meet a man entering the coffee shop and bring him back to meet Anne and Bern.

Daniel Dees was younger than Anne expected. He must have been a student of Rosemary's at ASU, Anne decided, not a colleague. Maybe forty, he was lanky and fit with sea-green eyes and a sailor's tan.

After introductions, he said the boat was checked out and ready to go. ''Are you okay with this?'' he asked Kathleen.

She nodded and said simply, ''It's time.''

THERE WAS JUST ENOUGH WIND TO FILL THE SAILS ON Daniel's sixteen-foot boat and ruffle the waters with white-caps as they left the channel, cleared the breakwater, and headed a few miles out to sea.

It was Bern who stood at the rail, gripping Kathleen's shoulders as she tipped the container and spilled the contents. If Anne felt any envy for the bond between them, it was balanced by thankfulness that the man she loved was capable of giving such support.

With sunlight shattered on the water like a million tiny mirrors, Rachel's ashes floated out on a gentle breeze and barely disturbed the bright surface. Only the single pink rose Kathleen dropped in the boat's wake marked her daughter's passing.

•   •   •

THREE WEEKS LATER, ANNE WAS FINISHING HER SESSION at the abuse clinic when Rena arrived with Chrissie. The little girl had come to say goodbye before she went to Kentucky with her grandmother.

"Just when you stop believing in miracles," as Rena had said that day when she called Anne to tell her that CPS had heard from Ellen Bowes.

There had been a lull in the news from celebrity trials, politics, and brushfire wars, enough so the media gave some play to a homeless little girl whose mother had been murdered. Ellen Bowes had told Anne she rarely watched TV anymore. A neighbor saw the news report, caught the name, and called.

Ellen had come to Phoenix right away, staying at a motel for a few nights, then sleeping on Rena's couch while she got acquainted with her granddaughter.

Now Chrissie came swooping into the clinic's reception area, her dark eyes crackling with excitement.

"We're going to Granny's house, Anne. I'm gonna stay in Mama's old room. There's great big trees and chickens and kitty cats, and we're gonna fly on a *airplane*."

"All that energy, darlin'," Ellen said. "You just flap your arms, you're gonna fly on your own."

At the suggestion, Chrissie began to do just that, flapping her arms and making engine sounds, zooming over to say hello—and goodbye—to Joyce with Rena right behind her, leaving Anne alone with Ellen.

Not more than fifty, hard work and heartache had pared Ellen Bowes down to a spare, hard body on the outside and a flinty fortitude on the inside that Anne was sure shielded the softest of hearts—especially where Chrissie was concerned.

Ellen had told Anne about a husband dying of cancer, leaving her with a rebellious teenage daughter and a small farm to run. Sue Lynn had problems with drugs, boys, and a pregnancy that Sue Lynn aborted without telling her mother. Rifts became chasms. Sue Lynn vanished, came back pregnant with Chrissie, and stayed with her mother for a while until their arguments over lifestyle once again escalated into battles. This time Sue Lynn had taken Chrissie and disappeared for good.

Now, staring at her granddaughter, Ellen said, "I wasn't more than a baby myself when I had Sue. I made so many mistakes with her. It just scares me to death, Dr. Menlo, thinkin' about how many ways I could go wrong with Chrissie."

"You know more," Anne said. "You'll try harder." And then remembering Kathleen's plea, she added, "Just talk to her, Ellen, and be sure you listen when she talks to you. And love her, of course."

"No problem with that one," Ellen said as Rena brought Chrissie back, and reminded them they had to get going to the airport or they would miss the plane.

Anne walked outside with them where Chrissie gave her a final hug and said, "Bye, Anne. Thank you for coming to get me from the angel lady."

"You're welcome, sweetheart."

Standing there in the bright sunlight, waving goodbye, Anne wanted to wrap herself in Chrissie's happiness. Instead, she found herself thinking of Rachel and all the others it was too late to save.

Later that afternoon, a detective from the Phoenix PD drug unit called her office. She had a little girl, picked up at a raid, seven years old. Her mother routinely locked the child in a closet to protect her, where she was often forgotten and left there for days at a time. Was Anne available?

"I'll be right there," Anne said.

MAXINE O'CALLAGHAN

ONLY IN THE ASHES

A child psychologist explores the mysteries of a little
girl's life...and death.

0-515-12077-4/$5.99

SHADOW OF THE CHILD

A three-year old boy may have witnessed a murder.
Now a child psychologist must break through his
silence. And share his worst fear...

0-515-11822-2/$5.99

Payable in U.S. funds. No cash accepted. Postage & handling: $1.75 for one book, 75¢ for each
additional. Maximum postage $5.50. Prices, postage and handling charges may change without
notice. Visa, Amex, MasterCard call 1-800-788-6262, ext. 1, or fax 1-201-933-2316; refer to ad #727

Or, check above books   **Bill my:** ☐ Visa ☐ MasterCard ☐ Amex _____ (expires)
and send this order form to:
The Berkley Publishing Group   Card#_____

P.O. Box 12289, Dept. B   Daytime Phone #_____ **($10 minimum)**
Newark, NJ 07101-5289   Signature_____
Please allow 4-6 weeks for delivery.   **Or enclosed is my:** ☐ check ☐ money order
Foreign and Canadian delivery 8-12 weeks.
Ship to:

Name_____ Book Total $_____
Address_____ Applicable Sales Tax $_____
       (NY, NJ, PA, CA, GST Can.)
City_____ Postage & Handling $_____
State/ZIP_____ Total Amount Due $_____
Bill to: Name_____
Address_____ City_____
State/ZIP_____

ROBERT W. WALKER

BY THE ACCLAIMED AUTHOR OF THE *INSTINCT* NOVELS FEATURING FBI PATHOLOGIST JESSICA CORAN

Introducing ex-cop Lucas Stonecoat and police psychiatrist Meredyth Sanger, *Cutting Edge* is packed with the same razor-edged suspense that defined Walker's Jessica Coran *Instinct* series.

Cutting Edge

__0–515–12012–X/$6.99

VISIT THE PUTNAM BERKLEY BOOKSTORE CAFÉ ON THE INTERNET:
http://www.berkley.com

Payable in U.S. funds. No cash accepted. Postage & handling: $1.75 for one book, 75¢ for each additional. Maximum postage $5.50. Prices, postage and handling charges may change without notice. Visa, Amex, MasterCard call 1-800-788-6262, ext. 1, or fax 1-201-933-2316; refer to ad #698

Or, check above books and send this order form to:
The Berkley Publishing Group

P.O. Box 12289, Dept. B
Newark, NJ 07101-5289

Please allow 4-6 weeks for delivery.
Foreign and Canadian delivery 8-12 weeks.

Bill my: ☐ Visa ☐ MasterCard ☐ Amex _____(expires)

Card#_____

Daytime Phone #_____ ($10 minimum)

Signature_____

Or enclosed is my: ☐ check ☐ money order

Ship to:

Name_____ Book Total $_____

Address_____ Applicable Sales Tax $_____ (NY, NJ, PA, CA, GST Can.)

City_____ Postage & Handling $_____

State/ZIP_____ Total Amount Due $_____

Bill to: Name_____

Address_____ City_____

State/ZIP_____

"MULTI-LAYERED PLOTS THAT TAKE SURPRISING AND SATISFYING TWISTS."
—*The Miami Herald*

Steve Martini

THE NATIONWIDE BESTSELLERS

THE JUDGE
"A TENSE AND GRITTY COURTROOM DRAMA."
—*San Francisco Chronicle*

__0-515-11964-4/$6.99

UNDUE INFLUENCE
"TERRIFIC...A MULTIPLE-LAYERED PLOT THAT TAKES
SURPRISING AND SATISFYING TWISTS."
—*The Miami Herald*

__0-515-12072-3/$6.99

PRIME WITNESS
"RIVETING...INGENIOUS...FIRST-RATE!"— *Publishers Weekly*

__0-515-11264-x/$6.99

COMPELLING EVIDENCE
"RICH, CUNNINGLY PLOTTED... REMARKABLE."—*Los Angeles Times*

__0-515-11039-6/$6.99

THE SIMEON CHAMBER
"A FINE FOOT-TO-THE-FLOOR THRILLER!"— *New York Daily News*

__0-515-11371-9/$6.99

Payable in U.S. funds. No cash accepted. Postage & handling: $1.75 for one book, 75¢ for each additional.
Maximum postage $5.50. Prices, postage and handling charges may change without notice. Visa,
Amex, MasterCard call 1-800-788-6262, ext. 1, or fax 1-201-933-2316; refer to ad # 432b

Or, check above books and send this order form to:	Bill my: ☐ Visa ☐ MasterCard ☐ Amex _____ (expires)
The Berkley Publishing Group	Card# _____
P.O. Box 12289, Dept. B	Daytime Phone # _____ ($10 minimum)
Newark, NJ 07101-5289	Signature _____
Please allow 4-6 weeks for delivery.	Or enclosed is my: ☐ check ☐ money order
Foreign and Canadian delivery 8-12 weeks.	

Ship to:

Name_____	Book Total	$_____
Address_____	Applicable Sales Tax (NY, NJ, PA, CA, GST Can.)	$_____
City_____	Postage & Handling	$_____
State/ZIP_____	Total Amount Due	$_____

Bill to: Name_____

Address_____ City_____

State/ZIP_____